BLOOD RETRIBUTION

A LUCAS KNOX NOVEL #1

BLAKE HUDSON

Blood Retribution
A Lucas Knox Novel #1
Copyright © 2017 Blake Hudson
Published by Hudson Indie Ink
www.hudsonindieink.com
This book is licensed for your personal enjoyment only.
This book may not be re-sold or given away to other people. If you would like to share this book with another person, please purchase an additional copy for each recipient. If you're reading this book and did not purchase it, or it wasn't purchased for your use only, then please return to your favourite book retailer and purchase your own copy. Thank you for respecting the hard work of this author.
All rights reserved.
This is a work of fiction. Names, characters, places, brands, media, and incidents are either the product of the authors imagination or are used fictitiously. The author acknowledges the trademark status and trademark owners of various products referred to in this work of fiction, which have been used without permission. The publication/use of these trademarks is not authorised, associated with, or sponsored by the trademark owners.

Blood Retribution/Blake Hudson
ISBN-13 - 978-1-915118-41-7

CONTENTS

Warning	v
1. The Voyeur	1
2. Southern Shindig	13
3. Thoughts	37
4. The Nest	47
5. Diablo & Son	59
6. Deposit & Brief	77
7. Tech Wizardry & Naked Misery	93
8. Lunch with a Bang	109
9. Knock Backs	121
10. Dani	135
11. Drive Two	149
12. Juggernaut	163
13. Old Friends	177
14. Chase and Scrape	189
15. Stitched	199
16. Fishtail & Tux	209
17. Fine Dining	223
18. Splash & Grab	241
19. Truth or Bull Crap	255
20. Isabella Raid	273
21. Corpse	285
22. Hurt	299
23. Blood Retribution	313
24. Burnt NEST	325
Words from the Author	337
Acknowledgments	339
Also by Blake Hudson	341
About the Author	343
Other Authors at Hudson Indie Ink	345

WARNING

This book is a work of fiction. Names, characters, places and incidents are either a product of the author's imagination or are used fictitiously. Any resemblance to actual people living or dead, events or locales is entirely coincidental. British English spelling and slang is the dominant language in this publication, unless inappropriate to a character.

For all the latest news, competitions and interaction with fans and the author join us at the Lucas Knox Series Facebook Group.
Or feel free to email or send a message via the website.
<u>Facebook Page</u>
Lucas Knox Series
blake@authorblakehudson.com
<u>http://www.authorblakehudson.com</u>

Lucas Knox: Blood Retribution is dedicated to my beautiful wife Stephanie. Her unique humour, warm-hearted kindness and humility not to mention love, has brought happiness, joy, laughter and blessings to my life. A life that started when I was lucky enough to have her accept me into hers.

1

THE VOYEUR

Sunset on the Mediterranean. It was August and it seemed the heat of summer would never end. The mile-long empty beach, with jagged cliff faces at each end towering like giant bookends. The N-340 coast road ran alongside with a gravel pull in the length of the pebble and sand beach. Small waves rolled ashore from the calm rich red and orange stained sea. The whole sky looked as if the God's themselves had set it alight.

A darkly dressed figure of a man was leaning back against his Bonneville 1200HT Bobber motorcycle. Black frame, wire wheels, burgundy fuel tank with that classic name adorning it, Triumph.

He stood watching over the beach, his gaze only interrupted as he looked down to shield a cigarette from the warm breeze. Cupping his hand as he lights, taking a long drag, he steps forward lifting his face into the radiant setting sun. There was something poignant yet transient about it all. It reminded him almost too vividly of a moment etched on his soul.

Coarse, hot, dry powder sand, the painful grit of it wet between his toes in his boots. A sand that turned rags to sandpaper as they wiped endless sweat from dirty tan lined skin. How he'd dreamt of what he saw before him now, swimming or just falling into the rolling waves.

The scent of hot metal, oil and petrol fumes rising from the engine completed the memory of that hell hole on earth. It may have been a long time ago now, but that memory was like having a bounty on your head. And no matter how long you've been running, it's still right over your shoulder. Catching up with you with just the slightest of triggers.

How far he had come since then and the regiment he was destined to join. Impatiently he took a step as he flicked the cigarette, pulled his shoulders out of their slouch and slammed the memories back where they belonged. In the dark abyss locked away with all the other memories of that time.

A man with years of flaunting with danger and death. Earning the right to fight another day with blood, sweat and pain. He was not stood here by luck, well that's what he told himself. No, he was here because men gave their lives. A debt that could never be repaid. And the daily cost of that was living with the guilt.

Buzzing in the pocket of his cargos signalled an end to the thoughts.

"Knox," he fired out after opening the cheap black flip phone.

"Well that's a lovely phone manner Mr Knox, do you talk to all the ladies like that?" replied a sweet playful feminine voice.

"Dani…" He said her name with a warm familiarity reserved only for her.

"… only to the ones, I treat mean," Knox smirked and waited for what he knew would be a sassy response.

"Mr Knox, you tease, you are never mean to me. You wouldn't dare, you value your manhood too much, but I may start to think I am missing out…" she replied with a put-on sigh and you could almost hear the back of her hand hitting her forehead.

"Come on Dani, less of the Mr, I have told you, you can call me..." Knox was interrupted before he could finish.

"Sweetheart? I reserve that name for my lovers only. You know that Lucas." Dani tried to sound serious.

"Cold... that's cold." Knox took in a deep inhale of breath through closed teeth like a mechanic when asked for a price.

"Lucas, you know if you want to be my lover you have to wine and dine me, and well I haven't so much as seen a box of chocolates let alone three courses and a bottle of fizz." Dani knew the reaction she would get.

"It's lovely chatting as ever Dani, but is there a reason for the call?" And there it was, the reaction Dani knew was coming, Knox, ignoring anything to do with dating.

"Lucas, you are impossible. I won't be single for ever you know... As it happens, yes, I am calling to see if you are working." Dani's playful tone was replaced with a more controlled one.

"I have a few irons in the fire, nothing concrete. Why, are you looking to hire?" Knox replied trying not to sound too interested.

"I have heard a few things on the cyber grapevine, and some of it made me think of you, so if..." Knox cut her mid flow as he heard a pop and a crackle in the distance followed by the building revs of a powerful engine reaching its redline before dropping down and starting the symphonic crescendo once more.

"Dani, I need to go, can you give me twenty-four hours? I'll be in touch" Knox said annoyed to be ending the call so soon.

At that moment, a beautiful deep metallic green convertible supercar pulled off the coast road at speed onto the gravel, skidding as it came to a stop just in front of a small low stone wall. The throttle blipped and burbled as the engine cut, announcing its arrival.

"For you handsome I will give you forty-eight, now run along and try not to blow anything up." And with that, the line cut dead.

The sun was almost kissing the sea on the horizon. Already he could smell the jasmine that had all day lain hidden, suppressed beneath the heat. Knox hated jasmine as it reminded him of an ex. Flocks of birds were in quick retreat, pitching their camps on power cables, trees and the terracotta rooftops of the nearby town. Lights were coming on littering the coastline like stars in the night sky.

Stepping out of the sleek machine onto the gravel was a sight just as stunning as the car. Long bare modelesque legs of a woman, bronzed and sun kissed satin skin, thick wavy dark hair falling just past her shoulders. Dressed only in a perfect bright white swimsuit, so tightly fitting you could be forgiven for thinking it was painted on. She wore it in a way that made it worth every penny of it's sure to be obscene price tag. The gentle curve of her backbone was deeply indented, suggesting more powerful muscles than is usual for a woman of her size. Her behind was almost as firm, rounded but beautiful heart shaped. She was not an ethnic girl, but she had invested a lot of time in her tan. Around her neck, a thick flat designer gold necklace that would scream tacky on anyone else but this siren.

The whole scene, empty beach, sun setting, alluring girl with her hair dancing in the wind and the abundance of diamonds and gold. It reminded Knox of something.

Yes, that's it, she was like a young Monica Bellucci, at home on the big Hollywood screen just as much as modelling the perverse ideas of the high-end fashion houses.

In a matter of moments, the woman had dropped down from the low stone wall, crossed the expanse of sand and stopped before the water's edge to tie her hair up. She kicked off her fine strappy sandals and dropped her oversized jewel encrusted sunglasses on top of them.

She paused, basking in those last-minute beams of orange sunlight before it descended once more into the sea, casting the deserted beach under the cover of dusk. She ran the last few yards into the waves, her momentum carrying her through the shallows before gracefully diving into the cool ocean.

She held her breath for what seemed like an age. Knox began to feel uneasy, his eyes darting as they surveyed over the calm still waters. He felt his heart rate rise and the adrenaline begin to flow. And just as Knox was about to run, the sleek effortless swimmer surfaced fifty or so metres out. A smile crossed his face acknowledging the woman's athleticism.

Knox slowly made his way down the uneven rough weathered pathway, his eyes flickering from the woman to his footing. Two golden blonde girls out together for their evening run in bikini tops and brief shorts made their way up the pathway, playfully racing each other up towards him. They flaunted their bodies at him as they passed saying 'Hola' followed with giggles and smiles. They looked back over their shoulders to see if he would look and respond, when he didn't, they muttered something in German then picked up the pace and sauntered on up towards the town's high road where Knox's motorcycle was parked.

All the girls did, was leave Knox wondering why it was that they had more prominent pouty lips than most. Was it injections or some other godawful form of self-mutilation?

Knox shook off the thoughts and turned his focus back to the swimmer. She was still there but now maybe a hundred or so metres further out to sea, treading water for a few moments before she turned to begin heading back to shore. She wasn't showing any signs of fatigue if anything she raced back faster than she swam out.

Knox thought to himself that maybe she swam for her school team or at club level. He slowed down his pace when he reached the coastal road, looking up and down the beach's great expanse of sand, checking it was still deserted.

No, not quite! Two hundred metres down the road was a black van with two men getting out. Knox had failed to see the van or hear it pull up from his view point above the pathway, as it was secluded by the rock face. Both men were stocky, well-built with short crew cuts, dressed in running gear. Brand new running gear in fact, seemingly innocent at first glance to most people, but not to Knox.

Years of training and deployment told him this didn't feel right, a feeling he'd learned to trust a long time ago. That trust had got him out of more scrapes than he cared to remember.

He walked slowly over to what he could now see was a brand-new Lamborghini Huracan Spyder, quite a vehicle for the woman to handle. Running his hand over the glass like painted body work, Knox felt that it was still warm to the touch. That unmistakable smell of hot rubber, accompanied by the exhaust ticking as it cooled. Not only could the woman handle the beast of a car, she drove it hard.

Ducking down the side of the Lambo out of sight of the men, Knox watched as the woman emerged from the waves, her white swimsuit catching all the available light as the salt water glistened over her body.

Knox went on watching, his eyes locked on a vision he had enjoyed watching many times before from afar. But this time, as the darkness drew closer to the rhythm of waves breaking, Knox was the closest he had ever been before. With the tension building in the air he was waiting for her to do something, or for something to happen. Knox didn't know what, just something different from all the other times this same scene had played out.

Knox had an instinct that she would end up in some sort of danger. Or was it that the smell of danger in the air was down to his suspicious nature? A stench he could never rid from his nostrils, he always saw danger in every situation and ninety-nine percent of the time there never was any. But for Knox that one percent is what drove him and was now his vocation.

Knox only knew that he mustn't leave her, particularly now that she wasn't alone. The woman stopped walking when her feet met the dry sand, clear of the water rolling majestically ashore. Running her fingers through her hair after she had released it from its binding, she paused, savouring every drop of cold refreshing salty droplets cascading down her tightly toned skin.

Picking up her sandals and shades, she began to walk purposefully back towards the car with a swagger more suited to a Milan fashion week catwalk.

Knox checked on the 'all the gear and no idea' men at the van. They hadn't started running or doing anything. Both had half-empty bottles of energy drinks sat on the bonnet. They didn't talk, they just stood and watched intently. Knox couldn't blame them, it was something he had watched just as intently countless times before. But their stillness, their manner, would have made anyone watching put them in the category of 'bad news'.

Knox hoped they would soon be on their way and he was just being paranoid, even if every fibre in his body thought otherwise.

He left his shelter of the car and dropped down onto the sand from the small wall, stooping down into the shadow it cast. He knew that when the woman walked past she would not see him, let alone be aware of her voyeur watching her every move.

As the woman closed in on the wall, the two men made their move. One jumped into the van starting it up, the other began running at a light pace but soon stepped up his speed. His focus was like a big cat hunting on the African plains with an urgent deadly precision. This was it Knox thought, that one percent coming to fruition.

The woman had no awareness as the runner swung out in an arc so he would come at her from behind. She wouldn't stand a chance of hearing his approach on the sand. The pattern had a nasty and all too familiar look to it. The beauty in white, the knucklehead thug pursuer, the van, it had all the hallmarks of a trafficking kidnapping about it.

The van revved hard and sped forward towards the car and stopped abruptly at the wall's edge, this drew the attention of the woman. She was startled at first and then puzzled.

"Get out of there! Run!" Knox bellowed from the shadows in a deep gritty Scottish accent.

The van's lights flicked on with full beam, the voyeur was too late. Blinding the woman, she put her hands up to block out the dazzling light. This was it, it was going down.

With rapid nimble reactions, Knox accelerated into a hot footed sprint. Just as the intercepting knucklehead reached out to grab the woman, he failed to see the two hundred and forty pound juggernaut flying at him. With a hard thud and a cracking of ribs, Knox's shoulder barged into the knucklehead, lifting the assailant three feet off the sand and landing down hard. Knox, on top of his target, reached out to a large, smooth, ocean weathered rock. And before the attacker knew what had happened a fast swing came across and knocked him clean out, a spray of blood splattering from the knucklehead's mouth onto the coarse sand.

"¡Bájate de mí! ¡el cabrón!" The woman shouted out in her native spoilt girl Spanish tongue. Knox knew that calling them assholes and telling them to get off would be as effective as asking a blind man if her butt looked big.

Knox turned to see the second kidnapper struggling with the feisty banshee, he seemed caught off guard with confronting the woman. Their plan was unravelling and he was having to improvise, slapping her across the face, the strike echoing in the air.

Knox slung the blood-stained rock that was in his hand. Smashing the windscreen of the van, both the woman and attacker froze mid tussle as they looked at the shattered glass.

The attacker's attention then turned to the culprit of the vandalism, and with this distraction, the woman saw her chance. She bit down hard on the wrist of her assailant, simultaneously kneeing with all her might into his groyne. The attacker fell backwards onto the van groaning, clutching his manhood.

Knox had no time to think, he was up and running at full pelt to the emasculated attacker. The woman, seeing a figure emerging towards her from down on the beach, had already started backing away to her car.

Knox jumped knee first into the struggling attacker's chest. This time the attacker was thrown back against the van, winded as he slid down to the floor. Knox came down with both elbows hard onto the top of fallen man's head.

The thunderous roar of the V10 Lamborghini fired into the heavy air as Knox pulled on the door handle of the van popping it open. Taking a two-handed grip of the frame before swinging it open. Knox pushed the attacker's head onto the open foot well with a boot to his shoulder. Knox brutally slammed the door in three rapid blows into the attacker now turned victim's head. The ruthless onslaught was made even more dramatic, now lit up by the beaming intense red glare of the

Lamborghini's lights as it reversed back up to them and stopped.

The woman hesitated in disbelief at the image in her side mirror. As she selected first gear Knox turned and their eyes met in the mirror. In that moment time stopped for a second.

Gravel hurtled at Knox, who sharply looked away as it showered him like hard hail as the spinning rear wheels of the five hundred and sixty-two horse power marque super car danced for traction before finally biting down, propelling the machine like a bullet from a gun.

Knox's attention turned to the men. He had no idea who these men were, who they worked for, what this was all about. On the theory that worry is a dividend paid to disaster before it is due, he consciously relaxed his muscles, slowed his breathing and emptied his mind of questions.

Dusting himself down, picking a few bits of gravel out of his hair he ran his fingers through it lifting it off his face. Knox knelt in front of his victim's bloodied face, pressed two fingers on his neck checking for vitals. A faint pulse was felt as Knox's other hand patted him down looking for anything that may give a clue to who he was, but found nothing.

He looked ex-military, eastern bloc maybe, but nothing more than a grunt with few years' service. Nothing too taxing judging by how he reacted to the woman and then Knox.

Moving around to the passenger side of the van, Knox opened the door checking the pockets and glove box. Nothing, just an airport vehicle rental form. Everything about this felt more and more off. Moving on to the back of the van, Knox found a Leroy Merlin plastic bag with duct tape, cable ties and some rope. Along with a receipt with a partial credit card number on it.

"Christ, amateurs!" Knox said under his breath at the fact it was all still in the packaging not ready to use, along with a potentially trackable credit card number.

Dropping the bag to the floor, Knox shut the door, knowing it wouldn't be long until someone would see all this mess. It was time to clean up and fast. Leaning over the driver's seat Knox started the van up, then dragged the blood-soaked man away from the vehicle and pushed him over the wall. Knox then checked and was happy the first attacker was still out cold.

Standing in the open doorway of the driver's side, Knox put his foot on the clutch engaging the failed abductors' van into first gear. Letting off the handbrake, Knox stepped away, letting the clutch out. He turned and walked away heading back to the hillside pathway.

With a loud crash of breaking glass, crumpling metal and plastic, the van had driven over the stone wall dropping onto the beach, nose planting into the sand.

Knox reached for his box of Marlboro reds, tapped one a third of the way out the box before he put it to his lips like he had a million times before. Rolling out his Zippo lighter from his pocket a click, tap and a flick, it lights…

Blasted forward, Knox hit the floor as if he was drop kicked square in the back. Shaking his head to clear a high-pitched ringing, like PA feedback crippling his ears. Knox's thoughts and hearing slowly came back as he rolled onto his back and looked over to the source of the explosion.

A blazing inferno of flames reached high into the dark sky illuminating all around him. No way did those knuckleheads have anything to do with this, Knox thought as he picked himself up. This wasn't a kidnapping, it was a hit, by someone who wanted no loose ends. The two dumb nuts were just expendable pawns.

"What now!" Knox fumbled into his cargo pocket pulling

out his vibrating phone, flipping it open as he lifted it to his ear, stretching out his shoulder pushing the pain away.

"Ten AM tomorrow, you know the drill," a calm emotionless male voice stated before hanging up.

Knox looked up to his Triumph to see a blacked out, black JLR Range Rover sat menacingly watching over him. Knox closed his phone and with that, the luxury power house of an SUV slowly pulled away.

"I'm getting too old for this shit…"

2

SOUTHERN SHINDIG

Knox walked passed the Cathedral de la Encarnacion on the paved stone streets, that was over looked by the imposing, Alcazaba fortress in old town Malaga. Knox weaved his way between the loud groups of guys and girls, obviously out for a fun time. One thing about the Spanish, you couldn't help but smile as the Malagueños knew how to party. They didn't need a nightclub or a DJ for singing or dancing, just the old 19th-century ornate street lantanas to light up the fun.

But unfortunately for Knox, that was exactly where he was heading and the idea of it filled him with abhorrence.

Sala Gold was the venue, away from the elitist cocktail bars and restaurants of the Marina, where the playboy billionaires moor their mega yachts and held lavish parties. Ones where every gold digger with a permatan, from up and down the Costa del Sol, hung out trying to get just a sniff of an invite.

. . .

Sala Gold nightclub was in the heart of the old town, less than a mile from the Marina but it may as well be in a different city altogether such was the contrast.

Knox approached the double fronted, pale stone building with its decorative masonry. On the left, the old stone was modernised with ~~the~~ sleek, black gloss panelling, adorned with gold inlays. A video screen displayed photos and clips of what awaited eager clubbers inside. To the right, matching panelling displayed the name of the club in gold embossed letters. The letter was fitted above plain black double doors with small portal windows.

At the foot of a ramp leading up to the entrance stood two doormen. Both as emblematic as they were tall and wide. You couldn't get any more cliché with long black coats and the street lights shined off their bald polished like heads. Knox knew the type well. Hell, it could have been him standing there if he had taken a few different paths early in his career as a soldier.

Knox was blocked by one of the doormen as he attempted to walk in. Then came the brief pause, before Knox was being clicked at for identification. Knox gave them a depicted look of are you serious. He then reached into his jacket pocket, pulling out a driving licence from a plain brown leather wallet, one he kept uncluttered.

Just one credit card, driving licence and a few hundred Euros in mixed notes and nothing more.

. . .

"Jack Noble?" Muttered the doorman before handing the card to his partner who declined to take it with a grunt. Opting instead, to look and sneer as he slowly shook his head in time with the low bass beat seeping from behind the thick stone walls.

"I know I have a handsome baby face *chicos*, but clearly I am over twenty-one." Knox jibed with a smile and a wink.

The two men unknowingly looked over his fake but perfect driving licence courtesy of Dani. He had bank accounts, passport and birth certificate to match, thanks to his cyber hacking tech guru, one that also happened to have a sweet arse.

"No..." Grunted the first doorman handing back the licence. Knox slipped the licence back into his wallet in a cool, calm and collected manner, at the same time pulling out a fifty Euro note. He then adjusted his jacket as he looked around making sure all was clear.

"No *problemo, mi amigo*." Knox rattled off in fluent Spanish slapping the crisp, fifty Euro note into the doorman's hand. He gave him a deadpan look in return.

"Thank you, English man, still no!" He scoffed, putting the note in his pocket just as his pissed off buddy stepped up, creating a wall of cheap, black polyester.

. . .

"Right, and the reason is?" Knox said through gritted teeth at being called an English man. Knox had no issue with the English. In fact, he served with a handful he classed closer to him than his own brother, but he was also a proud Scot and that would never change.

He stepped back to size up the situation.

"No Good, now go lose yourself, you get me, English man?" Asshole number two pointed at what Knox was wearing, before they both stepped in, closing the gap Knox had just made.

Knowing it was foolish to push anymore, Knox moved away holding his hands up at waist level. Okay so maybe black tactical boots, cargo trousers and a biker jacket weren't the gear to be seen in with the young and trendy, Knox thought to himself. He slipped silently into a doorway, out of sight of the doormen, as their attention was now drawn by three barely dressed girls. They tottered over expecting admittance without ID, which of course, they got.

Knox stayed hidden, biding his time as the one thing he knew about establishments like this, they were never free from trouble for long. Knox smirked the second his prediction started to play out, taking all of two minutes before he was proven right.

A third member of security burst through the double doors, man handling a cocky, skinny runt. One that looked to weigh no more than a bag of sugar, piss wet through. He didn't stand much of a chance as the bouncer was even bigger than each of the doormen. This could be it, the chance he was waiting for.

"Come on…just one more." Knox whispered to himself, eager to make a move and sure enough, it came in the form of two screaming tarts'. The disgruntled women started screeching out about unfair treatment. They lashed out like feral cats in an alley. First at the cheating runt, forcing the two doormen to intervene and then at each other. Soon all three were trying to control the situation as now they were receiving a verbal assault from the ballsy runt, no doubt fuelled by being three sheets to the wind.

Knox spied his chance and side stepped out of his cover to cross the narrow street. Eyes locked on the security men, Knox with his back to the wall, stealthily sneaked up to the doors and strolled into the club.

"*Abrigo señor?*" Knox turned to the hatch in the wall to his left as he reached for the next set of doors. There stood a striking redhead asking for his coat with a welcoming smile but a look in her eyes that said otherwise.

Knox never checked a jacket as the last thing you needed was a damn queue when you had to get out of somewhere fast, plus he liked his leather jacket. Hell, he's had it for that long, it probably has a piece of his soul stitched in the lining.

· · ·

"*Gracias pero no*," Knox said holding a hand up, giving her a slightly awkward smile. He carried on walking, pushing through the main doors as his body was met with a blast of sound waves. His eyes adjusted to the arrays of pinks, purples and blue lights.

Knox paused for a moment against a chrome mosaic pillar. Gone were the days of cigarette smoke filled rooms and taking that lingering odour home with you. His nostrils flared at the smell of the electric and vibrant crowd, now only taking in the scent of sweat and stale booze.

Walking slowly across to the main bar beside the entrance, he found it bustling with a group downing shots and a hen party so excited they looked ready to explode. Knox caught the eye of the bar maid, deep dark skin with an impressive afro. Her wrists were adorned with lots of silver, leather, and fabric bangles that all jangled as she poured drinks. Denim mini skirt, camo vest and Doc Martin boots finished off her sexy look.

It was like she knew his drink would be an easy one. She made a beeline for Knox, motioning drink with her hand. Her big brown eyes lit up as big as her smile. It was almost as if she was predicting what Knox was going to order and was expectantly waiting to be proven right.

Knox was shown the beer taps. He smiled and nodded to one, forgetting all about the bottle of water he was going to order. After all, it would have been rude not to have a beer when offered. The beauty's smile quickly turned into a smirk. She looked Knox straight in the eyes and ran one nail over Knox's hand as he took hold of the ice cool San Miguel. Knox reached for his wallet and the girl held up five fingers, ones he could see wrapped around something other than his beer. She winked but then dropped the sexy smile as soon as she took payment and had to move onto her next punter, interesting.

Knox took a seat at a table in the far corner, perfect for scanning the room. Checking his Breitling Chronomat 44 watch, and as always, admiring the black steel finish and its expensive efficiency, he saw it was 11:05 pm. Knox settled into his vantage point and waited.

The night club was dedicated to 70's and 80's pop classics. This was Knox's personal Hell, second only to the real Hell on earth being Iraq. The locals loved it and it was the place to be seen. Seen with very little on, judging from where Knox was sitting anyway, but shit, at least there was one reason to like the place.

Knox examined the sea of faces and read body language. It was a habit trained into him. One he couldn't shake, not that he'd wanted to. No, in truth people intrigued him. Something that aided him now as Knox's eyes were drawn to the man stood close to the DJ. You could be forgiven for thinking he was his body guard if you would have even noticed him.

Tall, focused, in shape and watching the room like a hawk. He was a professional, but what was he doing here?

. . .

Knox finished his drink and no sooner had he put the empty pint down it was swept up by the afro rocking barmaid. She looked over her shoulder at Knox giving him a cheeky wink. Knox thought of all the nights to be hit on. But then, what the heck, he rolled with it. Knox put a twenty Euro note down on the table, smiled back at the girl. Pointed to himself, then her, and mouthed the word *Drink?* To that she walked away with such a sassy walk Knox wondered if he could handle it. One thing was for sure, it would be fun finding out.

The guy stood by the DJ, now christened, Mr Pro, was joined by a friend or should we say twin. Christ, they could have been dressed by their mother for a family photo shoot. Loose suits, plain shirts and ties, comfy black shoes you could run in if you had to. Oh, and not forgetting the timeless classic, a curly wire ear piece that could be seen from a mile away, even if they were reaching for their ears to hear some twittering voice barking orders. Okay, so maybe he would have to change that to Mr Semi Pro.

They exchanged words, studying something on one of their smartphones. They looked like government agents but this wasn't the way they do their business. Knox tried to reason with himself, that maybe he was over reacting. Looking for trouble that wasn't there thanks to the events of earlier putting his senses on over load. Something Knox took reassurance in was they were not looking for him, as he'd not been registered on their radar…and nor would he, thanks to the company strutting his way. No, thanks to the barmaid with a seductive glint in her eyes walking his way, he just looked like some guy out on the hunt for a sexy piece of arse for the night. Oh, and that pout just screamed trouble, *his kind of trouble.*

Knox shunted over, making room for the barmaid's exquisitely lush arse, one she freely showed off as she bent over straight legged, placing the drinks down.

"Beer for you peaches, and bourbon on the rocks, for me." She said looking back at Knox over her shoulder. What he wasn't expecting was the evocative southern belle American accent, like sweet nectar to his ears.

"Thanks, Darlin', my names Lucas. So, tell me, South Carolina or Georgia?" Knox held out his hand which was graciously received as she used it to guide herself down.

"Well aren't you just a sweetie pie, I do like a well-mannered man. Susannah Mai be my name Sugar' but you can call me Susie. And come on now sir, all the best girls hail from Georgia." Her words dripped like syrup from a spoon.

"Well, I will toast to that," Knox said clinking his glass to hers and taking a swig of his thirst-quenching lager, taking the edge off the muggy aired club.

. . .

"Tell me, Susie, how did a pretty southern Cherokee rose find herself here in sunny *España?*" Knox said knowing a Cherokee rose was Georgia's state flower and trying hard not to let his eyes stray down over the glistening skin and ample curves of her low-cut vest...well, at least he *tried.*

"My, my you do have a silver tongue. I see I'm gonna have to keep my eyes on you. Not that, that's a hardship now." she said making a provocative noise like she wanted to see if he tasted as good as he looked.

"Daddy, well, he'd be stationed at the Moron air base. He's in high cotton up there. We moved out here when I was but a teen. I am all the family he has." Susie's smile dropped for a moment before taking a large sip of her bourbon. Knox knew when not to pry and promptly dropped the subject. Daddy issues didn't really make for enjoyable conversation when trying to chat up a lass.

"Well I'm here for the sun, sea and great food, oh and not forgetting the drink." He said shaking his glass before taking another swig.

"The weather here is good for my bones, not like back home." Knox scanned the room checking on Mr Semi Pro and his twin.

"And where might home be? I can't quite place that adorable accent of yours peaches." Susie's beaming smile returned bigger than ever.

. . .

"I grew up in West Scotland, a village not far from Fort William. In the shadow of Ben Nevis. It's a quiet place, very different to here. My father was born and raised there, my mother, well let's just say she wasn't." Knox laughed a little at the memory of his mother.

"Oh, do go on, you can't leave a girl half-cocked," Susie said biting down on her lip, one he wanted to see being bitten for a different reason.

"My mother was from Londonderry Northern Island. And well I think if I had half her temper I would be a force to be reckoned with." He smirked.

"Tell me Lucas darlin', are they your mother's eyes or your father's?" Susie wasn't shy in being forward putting her hand on his leg, and Knox found it fascinating.

"Maybe if you ever see my temper you could judge for yourself," Knox said as he leant in closer to Susie's ear.

"You are a feisty one, I just love it. Listen honey pot I am only on my break, give me your cell." Susie leant into his shoulder and looked up at him with her big brown eyes.

Knox thought for a moment and after not seeing an issue with it, he started to reel off his number.

. . .

"Hold your horse's sweetie pie, hand over your cell I will never remember your number, bless your heart." She slapped Knox's leg before holding her hand out.

Knox pulled out his elemental budget phone and Susie eyed it with a smirk before saying,

"Shut my mouth! You are just the cutest with that thing, but you do know they come with screens bigger than your thumb nail, these days, don't you?" She teased. Knox was about to respond with a cocky reply when she leant in, pressing her ample breasts into his arm, he enjoyed the feel of her heat.

"Lucky for you I like a man with big hands and you can call me anytime darlin, I would love to get to know you a *whole lot better.*" Susie laughed as she entered her number under the name 'Southern Belle xxx'.

And with that, she knocked back the last of her drink, blew a kiss good bye and headed off with a spring in her step back to the bar.

Knox thought of calling it a night whilst he was ahead, but just as he was about to stand, in she walked. With all the class and glamour Knox had become accustomed to seeing over the last few weeks, but tonight she was anything but.

· · ·

The woman from the beach was wearing the cliché little black dress but taking it to a whole new level… a lower level that was, thanks to the plunging neck line that was almost down to her navel. Ruched fabric covered each breast with impossibly thin straps holding them in place on her shoulders. In fact, how she wasn't flashing the club was beyond Knox's knowledge.

Sky-high heels, completed the outfit that had her towering over her entourage of friends. But unlike her friends, she walked in those heels with poise and grace, like she was born wearing them. She led her group in a formation, like an aerial display team, to a roped off VIP area. It was clear this woman had the management eating out of her hand. Bottles of champagne on ice with dedicated waiting staff waiting to do her bidding, as this woman no doubt liked to party like a celebrity. For all Knox knew some of her friends may well be but he had zero interest in trash magazine, celebrity bull shit.

Knox now had two things to stew over, one more pressing than the other. Would the woman spot and recognise him? Back on the beach, their eyes had only locked for a moment in the small mirror, so thankfully, the chances were low. But still, Knox slunk into the dark corner a little more. The more pressing issue was Mr Semi Pro and his twin now stood flanking the VIP area. They didn't escort the woman in when she arrived, or communicate with her in any way, so chances were, they weren't her personal body guards.

· · ·

Knox didn't think they worked for the club management either, as they hadn't interacted at all with the security staff who had patrolled the floor most of the night. Which begged the question, who the Hell were they? It just wasn't adding up to Knox.

What had changed, and what else was she involved in? Knox couldn't help but feel as though she was just a route to getting to someone else. But there was one thing he was sure on and that was that things were getting complicated fast.

Knox felt the call of nature and decided now was the perfect time to see if he was on their radar. Besides, the woman was surrounded by enough people that even Knox could be sure, now wouldn't be when they made a move on her. He made his way to the men's room subtly watching his back as he did.

Entering down a dark hallway, a colourfully dressed African man stood at the far end next to the door to the men's room. There he stood with the usual little table of knock off aftershaves and spray on deodorants. A friendly enough fellow, smiling and nodding his head.

"All right smiles..." Knox said as he nodded, slapping the attendant on the shoulder.

For all the millions pumped into Malaga over the past few years, compliments of their Mayor Francisco de la Torres, they had left out upgrading the shamelessly vile toilets. Even if he was trying to push for his vision of turning the city into a cultural hub. The bathroom attendant is missing a trick as disinfectant on the way out would generate him bigger tips.

Knox did his business and washed his hands at the only working sink. Whilst doing so he hears the abrupt and rude tone of somebody speaking to the attendant.

"Get the fuck out of my way..." Knox ears pricked up as he watched the reflection of the door in the greasy mirror in front of him.

Knox reined in a smirk, as right on cue and like he suspected he would, in walked Mr Semi Pro's twin. He scrutinised every inch of the room with a stern cold stare. Knox dropped his eyes a little and carried on washing his hands even though he *was do*ne.

The twin walked along the stalls checking no one was in them and Knox almost rolled his eyes...seriously, could this guy be any more obvious. What did he want Knox to think exactly, that the asshole was just looking for toilet roll?

The hairs on Knox's neck stood on end with an electric wave making his skin tingle. There was that gut feeling again. Knox turned off the tap, extended his left hand out to the side and pulled a sheet off the hand towel machine. Crunching the paper into a ball over and over, letting out a long breath…Knox simply waited for the first move, for his *first mistake*.

A flurry of movement triggered Knox's senses, dropping the paper as he spun and side stepped to his right. The guy's size twelve boot clattered through the cabinet under the sink. From the speed of his movement, Knox found himself with his back to the wall. He looked straight into the cold eyes of his surprised foe as he pulled on his stuck foot.

Knox pressed back into the wall and launched himself up and out, dummying a punch at twin's head. The guy raised his arms to block Knox who pulled out of the punch at the last second. Then opting to grab the back of his adversary's head before slamming it forward into the mirror. A loud smash of glass and a painful cry later and he was leaving a shattered crater in the mirror, one now decorated with cracks spanning the full length.

Still holding onto his head, Knox kicked down hard into the back of the guy's knee, dropping him down like a sack of shit. He pulled him back once more and followed the action through, this time driving his face straight down into the sink, hitting him one more time for good measure.

"Who do you work for?" Knox demanded, hearing a depth to his voice he only reserved for controlled rage. He then let the dazed and confused opponent fall to the wet floor.

Knox opened the guy's jacket to reveal a Kramer Horizontal Shoulder Holster with double mag pouch. This guy was seriously packing, which begged the question, why didn't he pull it on him? Knox reached for the pistol as two flailing arms pathetically tried to reach it before him. Knox hit him square in the nose, knocking his head hard onto the urine soaked tiles. Knox then pulled out a Springfield XDM.

"You're not F.B.I mate… That's good, don't want them catching up with me." Knox said knowing that their field agents were now issued with the Sig Sauer P320, moving away from the Glock 22 and 23.

Knox tucked the Springfield muzzle down in the back of his waist band and pocketed the two mags in his jacket.

"Finder's keeper mate…" Knox said patting the spark out Mr Semi Pro on the cheek.

Knox then stood up and just as he picked the guy up by the shoulders, two clubbers walked in joking and laughing about something in Spanish. Their faces dropped at the carnage in front of them.

"No problems guys, my friend here just slipped on his piss… shit Spanish, Knox. Sin problemas chicos se deslizó sobre su mear…" Knox said nodding his head repeatedly, wide eyed with a crazed gin.

. . .

"Si usted lo dice señor..." One of the Spanish clubbers muttered a rapid 'If you say so' as they both cautiously backed out of the room, bouncing off the door frame and walking into each other.

"Come on lad up ya' get, you're scaring the locals," Knox said, straining as he lifted the guy into a cubical, his dead weight landing with a hard thud. Even Knox winced, as that was most certainly going to throb in the morning.

He walked out of the toilets and Knox pulled out his wallet to count out fifty Euros. Notes in his hand he looked first to the attendant and then back over his shoulder towards the door he just walked through.

"Hell, of a mess in the cubical Smiles. For your time and for your trouble." Knox counted fifty more Euros and put the bundle of notes into his silver tips tray.

Knox made his way back up the corridor pulling out his flip phone and hitting speed dial. Just as he heard the dial tone the door leading back into the club filled with a figure.

"Knox, Freeze! Put your hands in the air!" Barked Mr Semi Pro, who must have suspected his colleague was taking too long.

"Hands up Knox! I will put a cap in your knee, last warning." The guy said, walking sure footed and progressively towards him. Knox lifted his hands and said nothing, locking eyes with the over confident gunman.

"Good, good now turn around and put your hands on your head. Slowly, slowly." Semi Pro's voices calmed down with an air of relief that told Knox that he was sure he was in control of the situation.

Knox did as he was instructed, his arms lifted exposing the Springfield tucked in his waist band. Knox then looked at a not so smiley African, who quickly grabs his money. Knox smirks and grants him a cocky wink.

"Is that my partners gun Knox!? Where is he? Is he alive? Knox! Answer me." Knox said nothing even when he felt the cold blunt barrel end of a silencer pushed against the back of his clammy neck.

"Show me where he is, start walking you son of a bitch! Or I swear to God I will shoot you where you stand." He demanded as he pulled his partners gun out of Knox's combats.

"And you, don't you fucking move! I'm watching you." Semi Pro shouted over to the attendant.

Knox slowly started walking but still said nothing. With every step forward the pressure of the barrel on his neck didn't let up. Smiles gave Knox the slightest of looks. As Knox got closer, blocking the gunman from seeing the attendant, Smiles looks down with his eyes, motioning to Knox to look at his hand. In it a spray bottle of breath freshener. Yep, that would do nicely Knox thought with a satisfied grin. He drew level with Smiles and stopped walking.

. . .

"I didn't say stop! Keep walking. Walk!" He said as he struck Knox with the hilt of his gun. Knox fell to his knees and quickly grabbed the bottle from Smiles' hand, knowing he had to take the hit.

"Get up you girl! Did my partner soften you up? That was nothing! Get up, hands on your head." The guy laughed as he grabbed Knox by the scruff of his jacket, pulling him up. But when Knox reached his full height he spun quickly and sprayed the bottle straight across his eyes, before ducking into a crouch and out of the way.

Three rapid thuds, each followed by a sharp ring as they sounded into the air, puncturing holes in the walls. But he fired off his weapon in vain as Knox just hooked his right arm up between Semi Pros legs in a swift motion tripping and flipping him up and taking him down hard. The asshole found himself face down, eyes burning and lungs struggling to inflate from the impact from one of Knox's favourite wrestling moves...he swore that shit would never get old.

Knox stood on the guy's wrist, his full weight making his shaking fingers span open. Knox kneeled pressing his other knee into the middle of Semi Pro's back just below the neck.

"Softened up enough for you lad? Who do you work for? Who sent you?" Knox said picking up the CZ P-09 and checking it over.

. . .

"Fuck you, Knox! I'm telling you nothing!" He said as he gasped for breath, wincing.

"Christ mate a P-09? 19 rounds plus one in the barrel, do you miss a lot?" Knox said as he mercilessly hit the back of the guy's head, knocking him clean out.

"Thanks for the help friend, you really saved my bacon. It's really…" Knox said as he stood up and turned to face Smiles pausing mid flow as he saw him.

Sat still as stone, Smiles slumped in his chair head resting back on the blood splatted wall.

"Ahh, shit." Knox posture slumped as he shook his head walking over to Smiles.

"I'm sorry friend." Knox's fingers stroked closed the lifeless glass eyes that were looking up at him, then he pocketed the 100 euros out of the tips tin.

Knox knew he had to get out of there and sharpish. Picking up the Springfield and tucking it away with the P-09. He then hit speed dial on the flip phone again. Calmly walking out of the corridor back into the booming club, passing the security on their way to the toilets the phone connected.

"It's Knox, the heat is too hot. You need to call her in and now." Knox said looking over at the woman dancing provocatively with some guy. Before Knox reached the exit the entourage around the woman all looked at their phones within moments of each other.

"Well, that was efficient…" Knox said pushing through the doors and giving a nod to the redhead who now had sexy Susie to keep her company. Company who made the 'phone me' sign at him, letting him know that he would get to taste that company.

"English man! You! Stop!" A strong accented voice demanded of him, from the now lone doorman that had stopped him entering before.

"Got to go pal, see you later." Replied Knox before feeling a heavy hand grab his shoulder.

"You go nowhere English man," growled the doorman, Knox snapped.

In the blink of an eye, Knox grabbed the doorman's wrist, twisted it in a painful lock as he spun around to face his opponent. Knox swiftly kicked out, targeting the inside left knee of the doorman. The sound of snapping bone and tendons ricocheted off the buildings as the colossus buckled to the floor. This combined with his own weight broke his wrist when he dropped with a stomach twisting crunch on the ground.

"Oh and, I'm Scottish pal," Knox said before stamping his heel into the doorman's jaw, simultaneously yanking up on the broken limb, until his arm popped out of its shoulder socket.

· · ·

Walking away opening his phone Knox scrolls through his contacts, stopping at Southern Belle xxx, he tapped call.

"Hey darlin', I can't get to the phone right now so ya'll leave me a message and I'll get back to ya'll. Kisses."

"Susie, it's Knox... I have a bottle of scotch if you fancy a night cap... Call me."

Cause God knows, *he certainly needed it*.

3

THOUGHTS

Knox woke in a cold sweat, this wasn't anything new, but tonight was better than some. This time at least he hadn't awoken to his own gut wrenching sound of the names of brothers long gone. The hum of the air-con filled the room with a monotonous white noise. It was a comfort to Knox who could never relax or sleep in the quiet stillness. He pulled the white cotton sheet off himself and sat on the edge of the bed. The cold large marble tiles a welcome feeling as his feet met the floor. Knox reached over to the side table, fumbling about until he half opened his eyes to help find the glass of water that was eluding his fingertips.

With a long exhale before standing, Knox looked at the empty glass in his hand swearing it was full before he went to sleep. He walked across the room to the en-suite, the half open blinds cast stripped shadows along the floor thanks to the full moon.

Knox flicked on the shaving light over the mirror, after a flash of blindness his irises adjust to the sudden, almost painful light. Splashing water over his face Knox took a moment to look at the reflection staring back at him, as if the water was cleansing, not just the cold sweat away but the reason for it as well.

Knox felt the bruise on the back of his neck from the butt of Semi Pros gun, then his right shoulder where there must have been something on the toilet wall he had threw himself onto. He reflected on how he evaded being taken in, twice, or had their intentions been more of the permanent kind. It was clear to him that whatever was going on around this woman he was on their radar now, and that meant his ability to watch over the woman was compromised.

Knox thought about catching the next flight out of Malaga or buying one of the many unused midlife crisis boats filling marinas up and down this coast line. That could be a more viable stealthier exit out of Spain, lay low somewhere in the Med before picking up more work suited to his talents. There was always good paid work sooner or later, Dani took care of that. It's not like you could go sign up at an agency for his kind of work. You had to know the right people, whether you were hiring or touting your services. If you didn't know the right people you were pissing in the wind.

Knox shrugged his shoulders before shaking his head. No, he would stick it out a bit longer. After all, the money was better than most and so far, nothing had happened he couldn't handle. He gazed into the mirror as he ran two fingers over the seven-inch scar across his left oblique then down a few more inches to the crimson healed bullet hole and round to where it had existed. Rubbing it as if remembering the pain.

Knox's body was a time line of history, each scar a biography telling its own story of pain. His early military career and following years of strength and weight training had sculpted his body to athlete standards. A sportsman would know the time, dedication and sheer will power to achieve the physical level that adorned them in medals and success. But they wouldn't know of the blood spilt or what it was like living with the horrors Knox's training prepared him to succeed in. Knox's medals were not for first place or runner up. His medals were for putting his life on the line for others, survival and valour. For as much as Knox honoured and respected them, he would trade everyone he was awarded in a heartbeat for the lives of his fallen brothers.

Knox was drawn back from his thoughts by two long beeps combined with vibrations. Knox's flip phone had a text message. A rare event as almost no one had his number.

Making a girl wait? Not very gentlemanly Mr Knox. Stay safe and talk soon. Dani x.

Knox's mind filled with thoughts of Dani. He had only met her twice, but that had been enough. He wanted her full stop. He would never admit it to her, never mind say it aloud, putting the words out there to be heard by a protentional enemy. Dani was the only woman Knox new would be trouble. She is the one that would make him lose his edge, his focus, which was a dangerous combination in his line of work. There wasn't one thing he would change about her. Dani had an influence on him he couldn't understand, let alone handle. He wished it could be different. He wished he could let her in, but Knox new she was too good for him and he would only hurt her.

Knox still couldn't shake how she affected him. He wanted to see tears of desperation in her eyes. Those fucking eyes! Those eyes could bring him to his knees, yet his deepest desire wanted to see them looking up at him whilst she was on hers. He wanted to see them widen as she struggled to take his full length into her perfect warm lips. To grasp a fist full of her long blonde hair, bringing her back up to his level when he needed something more. To bend her body back under his and take her hard because he knew there was no other way for him. Knox's eyes narrowed as they looked back at him in the mirror with undiluted hunger.

"Hey... honey pie, get your fine ass back in this bed." Said the sleepy sweet southern belle Susie.

Knox looked down at the lower part of the mirror to see the bed sheets pull away to reveal the lovely lush and round ass lifting and rocking in a slow rhythm as if reliving their earlier pleasure.

"Don't you know it's rude to keep a lady waiting." Susie giggled as she pushed her hand down between her legs letting out a quiet moan as her body arches in pleasure.

Knox fully aroused from his thoughts of Dani walked into the bedroom and stood over the temptress lay before him. Susie's rich warm dark skin tone contrasting against the starched white cotton sheets.

"My, my delicious, I do love a man who stands to attention," Susie said rolling onto her back biting down on her finger as she opens her leg before Knox.

Knox without a word, grasped her ankles pulling her to him, Susie playfully tried to get away turning onto her front pulling at the bed in vain. Knox pinned her down with one hand around the back' of her neck the other grappling her hip. She lifted and pushed back into him as Knox knelt over her and bit down where her neck met the shoulder, followed by an aggressive unyielding thrust, he entered her...

Lay nonchalant their skin glistened in an amber glow of the morning sunrise blead through the blinds. The cool chill of the air washed over them in a wave leaving a wake of goose bumps.

Susie reaches for Knox's cigarettes lighting one before placing it in his lips followed by a light kiss on his cheek. She took a second cigarette for herself then slipped off the bed and walked over to the large double sliding doors that lead onto the balcony. Knox watched the dark curvaceous silhouette pull the blinds too before sliding the door open. Susie stretched and twisted before leaning on the balustrade. She had a body to make grown men weep. Knox admired the view as he smoked, a view that got better as Susie turned around resting her elbows on the rail behind drawing Knox's eyes to her pert natural breasts.

"Well, that was intense..." Susie said before exhaling a stream of smoke up into the morning air.

"You seemed like a different man... Who is she?" she said looking right at Knox.

"Who is she? Not sure what you mean Lass." Knox said with a puzzled look.

"Who you were thinking about, it's okay honey I don't mind. It was wild, I liked it." Susie grinned with that big, get anything she wanted smile.

"What can I say, you got me all hot and bothered," Knox said as he got up and started getting dressed.

"Was it something I said? Hey, I won't bring it up again." Susie turned away looking out onto the sea view. Malaga port in the distance to the right with a car ferry being loaded. Empty beach in front with a quite dual carriageway between.

Knox once dressed, walked over placing one hand on Susie's shoulder the other pinching her butt cheek.

"I don't know about you but you gave me an appetite, I am going to run down to the shop, and when I get back I'm making you breakfast. Bacon and eggs with me or do you like pastries?"

"Bless your heart you are spoiling me, be careful Lucas, I may just have to stay if you treat me this well. But I have a better idea, let's go back to bed, it's an ungodly hour. I am sure I can help with that appetite of yours." Susie said as she turned and wrapped her arms around Knox's neck as she kissed it before looking up at him.

"So very tempting, but you haven't tried my eggs," Knox replied with a wink, stepping back.

"Come on sugar, don't make me beg, I want more." Susie's tone sounding a little annoyed and with a look in her eyes that was a little desperate. She grabbed at Knox's waste band and pop his top button.

"Okay…" Knox grabs both of Susie's wrists, her eyes lit up as he leads her back onto the bed laying her down. He stood back and placed his fingertips on his popped top button waste and teased. Susie smiled and bit down on her lip, Knox smiled back as he did it back up.

"Right you wait here and I am going to go get a few things, plus I need cigarettes. I won't be long and I am sure we will have time to have more fun…" Knox winked and slapped her butt as he headed straight to the door.

"Fine but your loss… I need to leave soon anyway… Croissant, no Danish pastry!" Susie's got louder the further she heard Knox walk away, shouting the last part as the outside door shut to the apartment.

Walking into his local small convenience store, Knox nodded and gave a little wave to the old woman working behind the counter. One who recognised him instantly. She smiled back and said "hola" as she picks out two boxes of Marlboro Red off the shelf behind her.

Knox smirked to himself as he thought 'I clearly spent too much here'. Walking down the aisles picking out what he needed, Knox spotted a young lad. The normal black hoody covering most of his face, with headphone leads hanging down and skinny jeans that Knox would never understand. Somehow, they could still be worn with a saggy arse, showing off most of his boxers. This was a pet hate of Knox's. Harmless enough but this kid had looking shifty down to a fine art.

Knox walked passed, looked him in the eyes and nodded before reaching for a jar of jam just in front of the lad.

Now, why would a lad like him be looking at jars of preserves? Killing time waiting for the right moment, Knox hazarded a guess, he would keep an eye on him.

Reaching the counter with everything he wanted Knox made small talk with the old lady. This lady was sweet but she couldn't look anymore stereotypical. Like any number of retired women walking out of church after mass, taking an afternoon walk or better still sat on a bench in a group staring at everything and everyone. Spanish elderly women just had a look about them that made you wonder, will all the beautiful young Spanish women end up looking like that and if so... how? Just as Knox handed over his cash the hooded lad walked passed at pace.

"No tan rápido chico... Estas olvidando algo." Knox said asking him 'not so fast had he forgotten something' then took a grasp of the lad's arm causing the clinking of bottles.

An eruption of Spanish at a million miles an hour fired out of the old woman's mouth, as she waddled around to give the lad a slap around the head. The young lad struggled and two bottles of booze fell out from under his hoody. Knox let go of his grasp of the lad, catching the first bottle easily. Seeing there was no time to catch the second Knox puts his foot under the falling bottle breaking its fall, as the young lad made a swift get away.

"Conozco a tu madre, Conozco a tu madre." The woman shouted over and over. Knox smiled at her after she said she knew his mother, then she turned her attention to him. Reaching up and cupping Knox's cheeks thanking him one moment and blessing him the next, he felt good but also a little embarrassed.

"Really no trouble at all, my pleasure... Damn Knox Spanish. Realmente ningún problema en absoluto no era nada realmente. Necesitas obtener CCTV," Knox said again in Spanish then adding that the woman needed CCTV as he pointed up to the corners of the ceiling. But Knox was sure his words fell on deaf ears, due to the woman's lack of stopping for breath. Now she was telling him he must come for dinner and is welcome anytime. He couldn't help but accept and he would confirm next time he was in. Picking up the second bottle and placing in on the counter with the first. He placed his euros next to them and then spent the next few minutes trying to get away from the sweet, grateful store keeper.

Returning to his apartment Knox paused a few meters from his door. The door and frame had been damaged and it looked like it had been pried open with a crow bar. Placing the bags down, Knox muscle memory kicked in and he felt for the gun in the back of his waist band, but it wasn't there. He had left it in the apartment. School boy error Knox thought to himself... although in his defence he didn't usually go to the store packing.

Knox moved in closer and listened at the door. It was ajar by a few inches but he heard nothing. Slowly removing his belt Knox wrapped it around his fist making a loop. Stepping forward he used the front of his boot to push the door open, slowly rolling his foot as he stepped into the door.

Knox's mind raced, as Susie was in there when he left. But was she still in there, was she okay, was she dead? Knox pushed the thoughts away and cleared his head. With the door fully open, he surveyed the short hall of the apartment. Signs of a struggle were evident with artwork knocked off the walls, with the glass shattered in the frames on the floor.

Knox stepped carefully, missing any glass, and looked to an internal door to his left which was the toilet, and then the kitchen door to his right. He checked the kitchen first, it was clear, so he made the most of it. Knox pulled out the largest blade from the knife block. After he placed his belt down Knox moved back to the hall, holding the knife with the back of the blade running along his outside forearm.

A breeze was blowing through, the balcony door must still be open. Knox could now faintly hear random tapping as the bedroom blinds flitted in the wind.

The main room, was open plan and sparse, and therefore easy to see it was clear. But now with the added mess of what little furniture there was turned over. What did they think they would find? Unless of course setting it up to look like a burglary. Knox owned very little just a large carry all which he didn't really unpack. Renting fully furnished apartments meant no stress, no worry, leave at a drop of a hat type living.

Moving over to the dining table Knox put a hand under as he kept his eyes on the door way to the only room he hadn't been in, the bedroom. Feeling the smooth plastic tape over the hard edges of a handgun, he carefully pulled the gun from its adhesive binds.

Knox felt better now being armed, letting out a silent yet deep breath. Checking the Springfield XDM was still loaded, he had hidden the weapon, yes, but assumption was the mother of all fuck ups, one Knox couldn't afford to make and old habits die hard.

Traversing the door to the bedroom, Knox knew this would be the most dangerous point, known as the fatal funnel. Standing at the side of the door way Knox lightly pushed with his boot the door wide open then took cover back behind the wall. No sound was heard other than the door knocking against a door stop on the floor.

Bringing the gun to a close contact firing position at his chest, his eyes down the barrel. Knox scanned the available field of vision, mentally cutting the area he could see into sections of a pie, working at clearing each part.

Three, two, one... Knox stormed the room point to point, always moving never standing still...but nothing!

Susie wasn't there, her clothes gone but bag left. Knox checked it, emptied it out onto the bed. Purse, makeup but no phone. Bed sheets on the floor half way towards the door, looked like she was dragged out of bed. No blood, nothing damaged in the room. But the door was forcefully broken so she would have heard it, so she couldn't have been surprised in her sleep. The apartment had been turned over but nothing was taken.

Knox considered and scrutinised every detail. All the signs said she was taken, they screamed it in fact. And that didn't feel right... was it too obvious?

"Time to get the hell out of here," Knox said under his breath as he put his weapon in his waist band before packing up his small number of things.

Knox left the apartment with his helmet and keys to his Triumph in one hand and his bag in the other. Reaching the road outside where his Bike lay waiting. Just as he was about to place the canvas carryall down on the bike, Knox spun around to the sound of wheel screeching. Hard revving alerted him as a white van skidded to a stop right in front of him. The side door flew open revealing two tactical dressed men, with black ski mask covered faces holding Susie gagged, arms behind her back with a gun pointed to her temple.

"Knox, get in the van! Now!"

4

THE NEST

"Let the girl go," Knox said to the masked men, with a calm tempered voice laced with deadly intent.

"She has nothing to do with this, she's just a barmaid I picked up."

One of the men threw a pair of rigid handcuffs onto Knox's lap, motioning with his head to put them on. Knox picked them up and cuffed one of his wrists clicking it as tight as he could, showing compliance before moving his arms behind his back.

"No! In front Knox." The gunman said pressing his Sig Tacops hard onto Susie's temple.

"Okay guys, easy now," Knox said cuffing his free hand in front of himself then holding his hands out for them to check and tighten.

"Susie, it will be all right, I promise," Knox said as he looked her in the eyes with a little smile nodding his head.

The masked man frisked Knox taking his newly acquired Springfield, along with his wallet, cigarettes and lighter. Dropping everything on the seat next to him the masked man then checked over the gun in fine detail to which Knox looked on puzzled.

"It's for sale if you want it, mate. Come on guys you got me, how about we drop the girl off. She hasn't seen your faces, I will do whatever you want, no trouble." Knox said as he looked at the two men trying to see some reaction.

Susie pulled her arms from behind her back, pulling the gag out of her mouth.

"Jesus Tom, you didn't have to press so fucking hard." Susie gave the gunman a look like she was ready to hit him as she clenched her fists.

"Just trying to make it believable boss, like you said." The gunman said holding his hands up after holstering his weapon.

"Right, do it again and it will be the last fucking thing you do," said Susie with no trace of a southern accent. Knox looked on, his heart sank at the realisation of the situation unfolding in front of him.

"Shit, fuckin' idiot," muttered Knox.

"Oh, don't be too hard on yourself now sugar," said in an exaggerated southern accent by Susie.

"Just a barmaid? Honestly, Knox that hurts a little." Susie smirked after kissing her teeth and just as Knox was about to speak, she issued another order.

"Bag him." Susie then elbowed the masked man next to her.

"With pleasure. Night, night." He said putting a black hood over Knox's head, swiftly followed up with a hard punch into Knox's lower side before pulling back for a second strike to the head.

"Take my gun Bitch?!" He said as he pulled back for a third hit but Tom grabbed his arm, restraining him back.

"Easy Greg, the Brig wants to talk to him," Tom said pulling him back onto his seat.

"You got your precious gun back, now chill out!" Tom added through his gritted teeth as Greg struggled.

Then out of nowhere, Tom dished out a punch to Knox's other side and said after getting a raised eyebrow off Greg,

"What? I didn't knock him out like you would have."

"Now, now boys, play nice!" Susie shouted half laughing as she crawled over her seat on to the back row, where a bag of gear was waiting for her as she started to strip off.

"If I catch you looking he won't be the only one that kicked your ass's," Susie said as she laughed pulling her camo vest off.

Knox winced in pain as his body's core struggled to hold himself upright as the moving van made its way through the back streets. Controlling his breathing and heart rate Knox listened, there wasn't much more he could do other than wait. With the speed of the van now holding steady along with its engine note, it finally meant smoother movements from left to right Knox knew they must now be on the main road. Outside traffic and the local noise was getting quieter if any at all, so Knox believed they must be heading out of the city.

Ten or fifteen minutes of driving and no one said a word, then the silence was broken.

"Right boys look sharp, we are here." said Susie as the van started to slow and turn a few times before coming to a halt.

Knox heard the sliding door of the van open and the men brushed passed him getting out. He heard three or possibly four male voices all speaking at the same time.

"This the guy? Brig is waiting in the NEST, take him through." Knox could just make out before being pulled out of the van, pushed and shoved in the direction they wanted him to go in.

"Sit!" Echoed around the room, Knox thought it was the gunman Tom from the van but wasn't sure. He should have been harder on Semi Pro and his twin as it didn't take a genius to know that's who the masked men were. A mistake that had obviously cost him.

The room filled with the sound of boots walking in and around the room. Knox took a few deep and slow breaths, trying to keep a grip of his nerves and steady his heart rate.

He had been in this situation before, worse in fact, as he wasn't exactly close to hyperferremia, bleeding, or on the edge of starvation. And if they wanted him dead he wouldn't be sat here waiting. So, overall, the odds weren't that stacked against him.

But why was he here? What did they want? Silence fell upon the room and soon after a door opened and shut a distance away. Steady footsteps made their way across the room their echoes getting louder. A chair scraped on the floor before creaking a little. Tapping of files and rustling of paper followed then by nothing, prolonged silence…

A click of fingers, moments later the hood was taken off.

"Brigadier this is…" Tom said standing next to Knox on his right but was cut short.

"Captain Lucas Knox, yes." The Brigadier said looking down and opening a file.

A seasoned looking army man with grey hair, weathered skin and a hint of aged scarring to the left side of his face, near the ear, faced him. He was sat looking over the file, a file that Knox could easily guess what it contained.

"I am Brigadier Carter, commanding officer of Tactical Intelligence Unit Seven. To your right is Lieutenant Thomas, your right Lieutenant Gregory. I believe the three of you have met before. You gave the lads a bit of a schooling, one they are both thankful for…" Carter said pulling closer into a desk not looking up once as he flicked through the brown card file marked 'Knox' in red print.

Knox looked up to his right then left, to find Mr Semi Pro and his twin looking a little bruised and a tad pissed off. Knox's mistake confirmed.

"Hey, boys no hard feelings eh?" Knox said with a smirk.

"Asshole." Muttered Lieutenant Gregory in response making Knox grin harder.

"This is my second in command Major Harris who you haven't met." Carter points over his shoulder to a tall slender black man with a beard. He was dressed in army fatigues with a commando green beret, telling Knox all he needed to know about Harris…He probably quietly ate nails for breakfast and shit out two by fours.

"Hello, Captain… A pleasure." Harris said as he nodded at Knox, to which he returned out of respect.

"Well it's been fun, meeting you fine folk but unless you're gonna break out the tea and biscuits I don't really see what I am doing here."

"I told you who we are," Carter said like this would be enough of an answer.

"That's all well and good for you guys but I've never heard of Tactical Intelligence Unit," Knox said in a disinterested cool manner.

"No, well I should bloody well hope not. Officially, we don't exist Captain." Carter said acting smug.

"I'm not a Captain, not anymore. Just get to the point, why am I here and what do you want? And what is wrong with an invite anyway… Bait and grab bit old school, cold war, isn't it?" Knox looked right at Carter.

"Knox, I understand you were one hell of a soldier. That's what I have read in your military file. Joined up at sixteen and rose the ranks of The Black Watch, Royal Highland Regiment. Served in Iraq in 2003 as part of Operation Telic… Basra, wasn't it?" Carter lifted his eyes from Knox's file to gauge his response. Knox shrugged his shoulder in acknowledgement. Carters eyes dropped down to continue once more.

"Based at Camp Dogwood you were awarded the Military

Cross. Hellhole that camp 'Triangle of death'." Carter shook his head before carrying on.

"2005 you were in Afghanistan, this time you were awarded the Conspicuous Gallantry Cross, twice! And rounded off your tour there with a Victoria Cross." Carter paused for a moment as if he was mulling something over in his head. Knox fidgeted with a little unease hearing his record of medals.

"And that Captain brings us to your SAS selection which saw you serve in countless operations in Iraq, North Africa and Afghanistan. Notably being part of Task Force Black working alongside American Delta Force." Carter slaps the file down as he sits back in his chair tapping his fingertips as he collected his thoughts.

"The recommendations from your commanding officers, quite frankly make shoving sunshine up your ass an art form. So, tell me, Knox, why did you leave?"

"I like Tapas and the sunshine." Knox's commented dryly.

"I doubt that. By all accounts, it would have been nothing but promotion after promotion for you." Carters eyes squinted a little as if he was focusing on Knox that bit more waiting to judge his answer.

Knox could see where this was going and he didn't have to tell him anything, he knew this. But what was the harm, he already had his file and they were some arm of the British government. No doubt thought up in some office in Westminster by two old boys drinking subsidised Brandy and smoking cigars sat on old Chesterfields.

"It was my choice and they wanted me out in five years anyway. Private consulting work and security pays well and a relatively low chance of getting my arse blown up or shot." Knox stared at Carter without a single blink.

"But enough about me let talk more about you and the reason I am here. Because as lovely as it is to hear about my short glittering career I do have a schedule to keep." Knox said raising his voice as he hadn't gotten answers the first few times of asking.

"Major, uncuff the Captain. Come with me Knox, I want to show you exactly what you're doing here." Carter stood and started walking off back to the door he came in from.

"You won't be doing anything stupid, will you?" Said a deep but softly spoken Harris as he un-cuffed Knox's aching marked wrists.

"No need to worry, I'm not without a shred of self-preservation, Harris... but wait... you're not...?" Knox looked at Major Harris side on with a questioning glance. To which Harris chuckled.

"Your Harris's little brother?"

"Yeah, you served with my brother in Iraq."

"You must be six inches taller and a higher rank," Knox said laughing.

"What can I say, I got the brains as well as height. Best not keep the Brigadier waiting, he gets a bit... *grumpy.*" Harris winked as he leads Knox to the door Carter exited through.

Knox walked into a hive of humming banks of servers, cooling fans, masses of cables leading everywhere around a frame work of screens and work stations manned by operatives. The operation hall had no natural light, which made working out how big the warehouse was near impossible, as it was mostly in shadow. The functional strip lighting over the centre of the hive of space-age tech illuminating only what was needed.

"Welcome to the NEST Captain, if assets on the ground are the limbs of the operation, then this right here, is the heart and brains. Cyber surveillance, bank accounts, credit cards, phone monitoring, live CCTV streaming. You name it!" Carter said standing proud.

"Any form of modern network accessible technology they can find, monitor, track and take over, that's what we can do. Christ, they know how long a target sets their microwave for. The perfect tool to support assets on the ground. I never want my teams in the dark." Carter added, walking around like a strutting cock.

And why not, it was a hell of a setup. Knox had seen similar with the SRR but nothing this big or as mobile. Catching sight of one of the screens, it was playing back footage from Sala Gold. Carter spots Knox looking at the footage.

"Making that go away is only scratching the surface of what my team can do." Carter gestured to the operative at the work station. He watched all the footage of himself fighting Thomas in the hallway, Gregory in the toilets and even outside the club taking down the doorman. But with rapid fingers tapping over a keyboard and a few clicks of their mouse, all the footage of Knox ever being at the club was wiped.

"Handy… I liked the moves on the doorman, very brutal but in an effective way of course." Carter commented before he walked away heading over to a glass walled tactical room. He waited for Knox.

"Please Captain, take a seat." Carter pointed to a stool next to a planning table, on it lay files and photos of Knox.

"I am touched, always wanted a stalker," Knox said sarcastically, picking up a photo of him stood by his Triumph at the beach, watching the woman swimming in the sea.

"Knox, I am just going to come out with it. We have been watching you for some time. You were recommended to us in fact, by a few sources. And then we find you working close to one of our targets." Knox looks at Carter.

"The woman, she's one of your targets? The rich, spoilt bitch? I haven't seen her do anything other than spending money on herself like it was water." Knox scoffed.

"Isabelle Pérez, but we are more interested in her father Marco Pérez. She's a side target. Look, Knox, I want you to join my team. You are a fine soldier, assists of your calibre we just can't get." Carter said direct and to the point.

"I am flattered but I'm retired and I have been out of the game for some time," Knox replied looking through photos of himself drinking coffee at a café, getting off his motorcycle outside his apartment. Photos all taken from street cameras, ATM machines and even what seemed like people's camera phones.

"Out of the game… don't bull shit me, Knox." Carter pulled a file from the table and opened it in front of him.

"We got this from your 'Broker' she has been most helpful, even if you have passed on every one of our job offers." Carter flicks through the pages of the file showing Knox's private contract hire work.

"Very colourful… 'work' shall we say. Clearly, they are not all easy private security jobs for oil workers in the Middle East." Carter said putting his index finger down on a page detailing a mercenary contract in South America.

"You can hire, take your pick of anyone in the 22nd, so why me?" Knox's turned away and looks out over the NEST, thinking to himself this was the work Dani wanted to talk to him about. But she hadn't mentioned anything about turning job offers down.

"It's true and I have already acquired some for my team in fact. But you have been out of the army for a time and with it, you have lost the airs and graces the military usually instils in a man. We need that Knox, we need your skill set, to blend in. And besides, you took out two of my best men like they were recruits on their first day at Harrogate for God sake."

"I must have caught them on an off day." Knox replied

wryly, when in fact, what he wanted to say was 'Jesus Christ, those were your best?!'

Carter didn't look convinced and so he shouldn't, as those two were sloppy at best. But Carter has an Ace up his sleeve and he soon shared it with Knox. He pushed a photo of himself in Iraq stood with a Delta Force Soldier, his friend... *Mac*. Knox's cocky demeanour soon dropped as Carter spoke.

"Your first job would be to help us find our missing man or ascertain what happened to him. I believe you two served together, you saved each other's lives countless time I imagine." Carter said passing Knox Mac's T.I.7 file.

"He was my best asset, the complete soldier, perfect and professional." Carter sighed as he moved to look out over the NEST. As if he was talking about a lost family member.

"Was? You sound like you have resigned yourself to him being gone." Knox snapped back, pissed off with the term asset. No longer were they men, sons, brothers, husbands or fathers. Fucking assets! Hell, a gun was an asset. A name on a wall in some government building if they were lucky and their closest loved one gets a clean crisp folded flag for their loss, for the blood spilt, for the pain.

"Damn you, Knox! I remember everyone under my command that didn't make it back, their faces and names etched in my memory. Even the letters I wrote to their families. My burden Knox, the burden of command. Mine alone, it's a role I chose for queen and country. And I would do it all again. Wouldn't you?" Carter spewed out a nerve touched by Knox.

"Help us identify what happened to McCarthy, join my team and you will have support and intel like you never had before." Carter pushed with a quieter dogged manner.

"How much?" Knox starts to crack.

"How much?" Carter confused.

"How much? Yeah, you want my help, I want cash. And a lot of it." Knox pushed to see how Carter would react.

"And here was me thinking that knowing about your friend, brother! That would be enough." Carter said with a high almighty tone.

"I am sure Mac knew what he was signing up for, and he sure as hell wouldn't be doing it for free. Your offers have been turned down for a reason, what's your new offer?" Knox coolly looked at Carter.

Carter took a moment looking over the NEST, turning back to face Knox, Carter nodded.

"Okay Knox, what is your price?" Carter said with a stare that could cut glass.

"Your last offer to my broker, double it and you have a deal." Knox had no idea what that offer was, or if Dani had turned it down not because of the money but the job its self. In truth, Knox was getting more cut up thinking about his brother Mac, and if the money wasn't the best it will do until he gets the job done and he can move on.

"God damn, it Knox, double?" Carter looked away. And just as Knox was about to speak Carter beat him to it.

"Okay, you have a deal." Carter agreed in a slightly beaten way. He then made a call.

"Captain, he is in. Bring his bike around. Clean up his apartment, and sort his shit out."

"Bring my bike around? Sort my apartment?" Knox looked puzzled.

"Well if I am paying you double you are starting right away. Welcome on board Captain." Carter held out his hand to which Knox shook it, wondering what he had gotten himself into and more worrying yet… what was Dani going to say?

"Right Captain, you have no time to meet the team or have a briefing."

"I don't?" Knox questioned.

"Well, you have got an appointment to keep, after all," Carter said with a slight smirk.

"You know about..." Knox paused and looked back at all the surveillance equipment in the NEST. Then he turned back to Carter and said,

Of course, you do...

5

DIABLO & SON

Twenty-five minutes later, Knox rumbled along a fast but dull stretch of A-7 between Velez Malaga and Torrox a coast line motorway. Cutting through the hill side fruit plantations and villas now mostly owned by expats enjoying sea views and Mediterranean life. Knox travelled at a pace, sitting between eighty and ninety, the sound of the Triumphs exhaust notes in its sweet spot. Riding on auto pilot his mind was occupied, not on the meeting he was close to being late for, but on Dani, T.I.7 and the job he just took on.

Pulling off at the next junction the Triumphs exhaust note roared and popped as Knox slipped down the gears using the engine to brake as much as his right foot pushed down on the pedal. Reaching the traffic island at the base of the slip road, Knox shot across an oncoming vehicle. The startled face of the dirty looking Spaniard in a pickup truck loaded with crates, a testament to how close a call it was.

. . .

Banking hard around the island, the scrapping of foot pegs told Knox to stop, he was on the limit. As Knox and the bike levelled out the hard-effortless acceleration lifted the front wheel slightly, Knox hankered down ready for what lay ahead of him, the mountain road ascent.

Taking the twists and turns steady, Knox eased back and enjoyed the views up at the mountain range of the Parque Natural Sierras de Tejeda. As the road aggressively rose meter by meter, he found more road barriers snaking around hairpins. The metal is all that separated Knox from the perilous drops into the gorge. It was then, on a short two-hundred meter straight that cut through rugged rock, it happened.

Repeated sounding of a car's horn shrieked its banshee discord in Knox's ears. A low, almost florescent green, Lamborghini Spyder with its roof down, tore past. She cut defiantly across his front wheel and pulled away, the sexy boom and rasp of the quartet exhausts echoing back from the rock face which bordered the road.

It was Isabella Pérez, Knox now knew her name. A large tight-lipped smile crossed Knox's face as he watched the back end of the Italian bull pull away. Dropping down two gears and rolling his wrist back, taking a firm grip of the bars, Knox went after her. 45, 60, 75, and he still wasn't gaining but she wasn't pulling away. Christ, she knew how to drive Knox thought to himself. Knox adjusted himself on the bike and took to the challenge. The building whine of machinery on the brink of torment tore at his eardrums. Knox dragged out every available horse power from the Triumph inline twin. Hard acceleration only matched by the eye tugging braking before each turn.

He was gaining, 50 meters, 40, 25! Now he could just see her glamour screaming sunglasses in her rear mirror. The good road was running out. One of those exclamation marks that the Spanish use to denote danger flashed by on his right, followed by a red triangle with a lightning bolt shape arrow telling you the road ahead was very twisty.

This was perfect for Knox. The bike carried more speed through the hairpins and bends. Around the next turn, the road declined slightly, there was a church spire, a tight cluster of white houses of a small village nestled on the hillside almost defying physics. They shot past another road sign for an S-bend. Both slowed down 80, 50, 30.

Knox watched her tail-lights briefly blaze, he saw her right-hand flicking down on the paddles, almost simultaneously with his left foot changing down. Then they were in the S-bend, he had to brake as he enviously watched the way her four-wheel traction side drifted around the bend. Knox's body hung off the side of the machine, his knee almost touched the road surface as the back wheel hopped and skittered. He held on with gritted teeth, taking the British engineered motorcycle to its limits.

Isabella slowed to a parade like speed through the village, loving the attention she was receiving. Knox slowed, seeing it as ungentlemanly to overtake now. With a brief wave of her hand as she smiled and dropped her glasses, their eyes met in the rear mirror. Hankering down for a split-second before the

Italian bull found traction, it rocketed up the long straight rise at a blistering pace out of the village.

Knox had lost fifty or so meters, the race was back on. Knox gained a little on the bends but losing it all to the straights, he had to concede to her nerveless driving. Now Knox wondered about her destination and debated with himself whether he should forget about the meeting and hold back.

That decision was taken out of his hands, as two bikers on black and orange KTM Super Dukes pulled off a side slip as if they were waiting for the Lambo to pass. They were not looking back so they didn't take notice of Knox coming up behind them. Their V-twins snarled as they took an aggressive approach behind the super car.

Knox instantly knew they were not weekend bikers out for a ride.

The two riders had what at first looked like small black bags at their sides. But all became clear when the lead rider took his hand off the handlebars and picked up not a bag, but a CZ Scorpion Machine gun.

"Shit!" Knox barked.

Riding in hard and too fast into the next bend, Knox cut across the tail rider. Hitting his brakes hard he forced the rider to lose control and the KTM dropped onto its side. The rider fell away from the bike and slid hard into the metal crash barriers. Knox looked ahead. He had lost ground on the lead rider. Thankfully the Lambo was clear out of sight. With dogged determination, Knox hunted down the now lone Duke.

The rider had noticed he had lost his partner. Looking over his shoulder at every opportunity. Spooked by Knox gaining he let out a short burst of gun fire towards him. Bullets ricocheted off the road surface and rocks. They missed Knox as he narrowly weaved and accelerated through the fire. Knox unhooked a thick chain wrapped around the underside of this seat. He had one chance to take out the rider, as he was more than out matched with a damn machine gun blasting away at him.

Riding up alongside the rider, Knox spun the chain like a lasso, and with a well-timed throw launched the chain into the workings of the KTM's chain and rear wheel. It locked up instantly, the bike flipped the rider over the handlebars and off the cliff edge swiftly followed by his machine.

Knox slowed and pulled over close to the roads edge and took stock. He then watched the motorcycle roll end over end and down the sheer drop. There was no sign of the rider. Knox's ears pricked to the sound of revving followed by exhaust blips and pops. Ones, which could be heard up the mountain road in the distance, meaning Isabella was away.

Leaving what he hoped was the danger behind, he pulled onto a white stone gravel entrance. A large green solid metal gate with gold deadly spear, Arundel finials running along the top, closed off the drive way. Flanked by 9-foot-high white rendered walls with ornate terracotta tiles and two motorised CCTV cameras bold as brass covering every angle. Well, it looked like someone certainly liked their privacy.

Knox had no idea what the property was like on the other side of the gate, grand and extravagant most probably. The details for the job of watching who he now knew was Isabella was done right here on the stones. Knox was sure who he'd spoken to was a middle man of a middle man. He didn't like to do his business this way and not knowing the name of the person you are charged with protecting was not a normal way to do thing. But the money was too good to say no to, and he had a feeling he would have to prove himself to gain their trust. Clearly, Isabella and his employers were very high profile.

Knox checked his time piece. He had a few minutes to spare, shaking his head in disbelief, he reached for his Marlborough's. And just as he was about to strike a light, the cameras moved into position, like he knew they would. They locked in on him and the sound of steel cogs rolled on a tooth rail, as the gate opened.

"Please enter Mr Knox. Ride up to the garage and wait with your motorcycle. I will meet you there and give you further instruction, thank you." A voice sounded out over a crackling speaker. Knox looked up at the cameras and nodded as he fired up the 1200cc engine and rode up the sweeping long drive. Pulling up to a six-door garage, one door started to roll up. Standing behind the lifting door stood a short silver haired

Spanish man, smartly dressed in white. He pointed to the centre of the garage and Knox pulled in.

"Thank you, Mr Knox. My name is, Juan, I am Mr Pérez's Butler, El Jefe likes all vehicles to be hidden…" Juan paused and pointed up.
"The sky has eyes."

"Good to meet you, Juan, you don't do tune ups by any chance?" Knox smirked as he looked over to the array of tools and equipment.

"Come, Señor, this way. El Jefe is waiting" Juan smiled as he ushered Knox to the door. El Jefe meant The Boss.

Knox walked out onto a large sun terrace with an infinity pool making the most of the far-reaching views, all the way down to the sea. A million euros added to the property value from that view alone.

Juan pointed to the far end of the terrace where a large wood frame pergola stood. Thick vines blooming with flowers cast a welcome cover from the hot Spanish sun and under it sat alone man in a linen suit reading on an iPad. A small black coffee with a brandy on the side was his only company.

. . .

"Welcome Mr Knox, please join me and take a seat. Would you like any refreshments? A cold drink, coffee or maybe something stronger perhaps?" The man placed his device down as he welcomed Knox, motioning him to sit. Knox sat and the second he did, he could see that the man wasn't alone like he first thought. In fact, he had two well-dressed armed personal body guards stood in the shadows to the left and right of him.

"Ay, a coffee with milk would be grand, thank you," Knox said looking over his surroundings.

"Mr Knox, I am Marco Pérez, you may or may not know who I am. But I know who you are and it seems that I am humbly in your debt." Knox didn't say anything, as he wanted to see what this guy knew first. It was always easier to win the game when everyone's hands were on the table before his own.

"It has come to my attention that you were hired by my son in-law to watch over my greatest achievement, my precious daughter Isabella," Pérez said as he gave a look to Juan who slipped away.

"She is your daughter? You will forgive me for asking, but you seem to have all the help you need…" Knox nodded to the two shadow guards before continuing.

"Which doesn't make sense seeing as I have been watching your daughter for weeks now and I haven't seen any protection like you have here," Knox said just as Juan returned with a coffee.

"Thank you, Juan." Said Knox as he looked to Juan.

Pérez nodded again to Juan, who then picked up an ornately carved box off the table Pérez and Knox were sat at. Sliding the top panel open to reveal perfectly presented Davidoff cigars and cigarettes. Knox smiled, and Pérez grinned.

"Please Lucas… may I call you Lucas?" Knox nodded.
"Help yourself." Pérez clicked his fingers and Juan held the box in front of Knox and then picked up a large silver cube lighter with a depiction of a Matador confronting a formidable bull skilfully engraved upon it.

"My lungs will feel spoilt. How will I ever go back to my cheap smokes? But let's not worry about that now, you have good taste." Knox said before he picked up a cigarette, which Juan lit as soon as Knox was ready.

"Good, good. If you are going to kill yourself slowly, do it with the very best, no?... After we have negotiated Lucas maybe these will become more… how shall I put it? Your regular brand eh?" Pérez said before he took a cigar from the box, cut and lit it himself. He took three fast inhales then one long deep drag before taking a moment to enjoy the fine aroma in the plume of smoke.

Knox thought for a moment as he took a sip of his coffee which was as smooth and luxurious tasting as the Davidoff between his fingers.

"Isabella, she's as strong willed as me but as stubborn as her mother, God rest her soul. She will not have bodyguards, she point-blank refuses. Men I assign to her, she gives the slip or makes their jobs impossible by putting herself in dangerous situations. Not surprising then that they quit…She kneed one in the cahonis, nearly landed me a law suit in my lap…Wilful women eh?" Pérez said shaking his head with a chuckle.

"I can believe it, she certainly knows how to push that Lamborghini to the limits it was engineered for," Knox said almost feeling sorry for the guy. I mean hell, he dreaded to think what she had been like as a teenager!

"I am a man with many enemies Lucas in business and in life. It is impossible to have what I have without doing so. It has always been a strong possibility my Isabella would be drawn in and used against me. And now it would seem that fear is coming true." Pérez stood up and turned to look out at the hot hazel draped view over the sun scorched terraced hill sides, straight down to the turquoise ocean.

"I am in your debt Lucas, you stopped her kidnapping, and un-doubtable the same again in that blasted club she insists on going to. I lost her mother Lucas, I cannot lose her too. If anything were to happen to her… I just… I…" Pérez took a deep breath and composed himself.

. . .

"Well I think I should tell you now, whoever is interested in your daughter Senor Pérez, they are stepping up a gear. I intercepted two men on motorcycles waiting for Isabella as she drove passed no doubt heading here. I was in the right place at the right time." Knox finished his coffee and stood as he extinguished his cigarette butt.

"Two men? On motorcycles you say? What…! Juan, Juan my phone." Pérez face and body language turned to pent up anger. Juan rushed over with a phone already dialled. Pérez nodded a thank you to Juan.

What came next was a rapped blast of Spanish that Knox found impossible to follow. Only picking up the odd word… 'worry', 'stupid', 'car', 'not telling'…shit like that. His tone went from aggressive too soft and tender in an instant. And with a few almost whispered words he hung up then turned to Knox.

"Walk with me Knox, I want you to tell me everything," Pérez said before he started to walk along the terrace. His guards moved from the shade, ready to follow at a distance, well trained, so as not to overhear.

"My daughter is a great concern to me. She has her own issues, and reasons for why she won't listen. And I have spoilt her, so the fault is mine, I know this."

"She was lucky, this wasn't the same as the clowns at the beach. The men at the club, the bikers just now, they are packing some real fire power. I don't know what their plan was, but it wasn't going to be pretty." Knox told him, being brutally honest as he needed it. Pérez winced, no doubt thinking about the horror of what could have happened.

"I can help you, I have worked with women like your daughter before in private security. You may not like my methods, but they work." Knox was blunt and to the point. Pérez looked over him with intrigue when hearing the term 'His methods'.

"Where are the men now? And if your methods work maybe it is what she needs. I have tried and failed but she still needs to be kept safe." Pérez said looking thoughtful.

"One ended up kissing a crash barrier at speed, and the other took a cliff dive off the edge along with his bike. No witnesses but I am sure it's being investigated by the local police, if not the Guardia Civil. But don't worry, shouldn't be any ties to me, you or your daughter." Knox reassured with a glint in his eye.

"Don't worry about the Police, I will make all that go away if there is a link to you, it will not be for long. I have…" Pérez stopped mid flow as his eye was drawn away. Knox turned to see what had distracted him.

Strutting down a spiral stone staircase leading from a roof top sun terrace was Isabella, with a glare that could burn through ice. She sauntered down in a long, floaty and almost see through summer dress. It danced in the warm breeze as if in harmony with her dark hair.

. . .

"Father, you summoned me like one of your staff…" Isabella kissed the air around her father's cheeks as she scornfully leant in.

"Come, come don't be like that. You cannot blame a father for worrying and loving you too much!" Pérez's face lit up at the sight of his daughter, a large grin matching his wide-open arms asking for a hug. One Isabella walked into, then turned her back spitefully so as her father ended up hugging her from behind instead. He kissed her shoulder and Knox rolled his eyes unnoticed, or so he thought until Isabella cut him a look.

"Isabella, my love, don't be like that… this is…" Pérez was interrupted.

"The cutthroat brute my fiancé and you hired behind my back father?" Isabella snapped.

"Isabella, hermosa. I didn't have anything to do with Mr Knox's appointment. But after everything that has happened, I am so glad that Malcolm hired him. Isabella, you owe Mr Knox gratitude, if it wasn't for his action, Heaven knows what may have happened to you." Pérez said his voice turned sterner towards the end.

. . .

"If you've come here to look after me, Mr Knox, thank you, but no thank you. My father has bodyguards, my fiancé has thugs and I don't need any more testosterone around me..." Isabella sneered as she started to walk away. Both Knox and Pérez follow her.

"The killers out there don't care about your father's bodyguards let alone your fiancé's thugs. They don't care about you or what they do to you, they just want his wealth and most of all to hurt and break your father. And right now, you are making it easy for them." Knox cut back at the princess.

"That's every man within a 1000-mile radius. Including you, work for free, do you? That's why you're here... You think I can't do it. You think I'm going to screw up. Or get myself killed... I am tougher than all of you think." Isabella almost stomped her foot as she folded her arms starting to walk a little faster.

Knox took hold of her arm, pulled her back and around to face him. Her look of shock and horror turned to disgust, with how dare he, as her eyes burnt into Knox.

"I think running around here like a spoilt brat makes you think you're more than you are. Mean people like me, take one look at you and see an easy target." Knox gripped harder, shook her a little and started walking pushing her backwards. Isabella without thinking walked back in compliance.

. . .

"I think you think your money, your father's money, can buy your way out of any situation. I think your mouth and manner is more likely to get you into trouble than out of it. Men, strong like me will do far worse than grab your arm and push you around and make you walk backwards Miss Pérez!" Knox let go, she took a few more steps back, she turned to her father with an aggrieved expectant look. Pérez nodded and looked away.

"You are wrong… You don't know me, in fact, that will be your biggest mistake" She telegraphed a big swing to slap Knox's face. A slap that Knox caught without a blink. They locked eyes like in the mirror that evening at the beach. But this time her eyes were filled with hate and fury.

"My mother was pushed around and her people, but I won't be. Get your hands off me. Some say this family, the blood in my veins is cursed. Living up here in the hills in this Eden, with all this wealth you think you would be free. But no, just like my mother I am being pushed around like a prisoner in a golden cell." Isabella said dramatically and her father looked in pain by the verbal slap in the face.

"Isabella? Is everything alright?" A voice carried over from behind Knox. Everyone turned to see a slender man in a suit, no tie walking over.

"Darling, I see you have met your saviour. A real hero some may say. I think you can forgive me, he may be my best and most important secret I have ever kept from you." The man slipped his arm around Isabella, pulling her into him for a kiss. A kiss that looked forced with just as forced a smile afterwards.

"Lucas Knox, my son in law Malcolm Howard." Pérez placed his hand on Malcolm's shoulder as Malcolm held out his hand to Knox. Knox shook it as he sized him up. Isabella looked at her father with a scowl.

"We are not married yet father. Now if you don't mind I am tired. I am going to go lay down." She said pulling away from her fiancé who took hold of her hand to hold her back a moment.

"I will come check on you in a few minutes, I just need…" Isabella cut him off.

"Yes, yes fine whatever you want." Isabella frowned as she slipped away.

Pérez returned to the table, followed by Howard and Knox.

"Well Lucas, shall we negotiate?" Pérez passed him a cigarette, as Howard helped himself.

"Yes, let's get this wrapped up as I am sure you are eager to get started, isn't that right old sport," Howard said to Knox with an

English private school boy accent. One Knox had heard many times before from officers born to the right parents.

"What I was hired to do was watch over a woman, keep my distance and step in if need... *If*... I was needed too. Minimal risk job." Knox said as he sat back in his seat.

"I think we can all agree things have escalated well passed minimal risk. She is a target and by the looks of it, someone's main target. My question to you is where do you want to take this and are you and her ready for the level of what is now needed?" Knox finished by lighting his cigarette.

Pérez looked over to Howard, Pérez gave a signal and Howard stood up and walked away.

"Mr Knox, you have our full attention. Malcolm did extensive research and referencing into your background, past work and skill set. We have already seen for ourselves you are the man for the job. But tell me, do you want the job?" Pérez stared at Knox and Howard returned to the table with a tan leather briefcase.

"I have only two conditions," Knox replied.

"And they are?" Pérez asked coolly.

. . .

"I answer to one person and one person only, it keeps things clear and simple." Pérez nodded and then asked.

"And the second?"

"All matters of security and safety, I call the shots, it's my way or I walk," Knox said with a tone that brought no argument. Both Pérez and Howard spoke at the same time.

"Agreed."

"Now the only thing left is investment. Malcolm open the case." Pérez nodded to it, directing his future son in-law. Howard placed the case in front of Knox, rolled the combi-lock to the correct combination 0812 to the left 2016 the right. A crisp double clip sounded and the latches popped open. Howard lifted the lid. Knox's eyes lowered into the case, then lifted back up to meet Pérez and Howards.

"One point five million euros Lucas, it's yours if you take the job. And a very handsome wage each month." Knox had to work hard to keep this cool, calm, collected look in place when Pérez asked,

"So, is that enough investment to keep my daughter *safe*…?"

6

DEPOSIT & BRIEF

Outside the Banco de España building in Malaga hours later, Knox found himself walking through black iron gates before making his way up the wide stone steps leading up to its tall double doors. The grand facade of the building, six imposing sixty-foot stone columns made the building stand out along the Paseo del Parquet. Knox stood in the lobby and made a call from his phone.

"Well, hello stranger," Dani said and the second he heard her cheerful voice he felt a strange weight being lifted from the heavy rich bitch burden that was Isabella. He even found himself taking a moment to drink in the sound of her voice before readying himself for the barrage of words that Dani usually fired at him.

"I got your text. It was a little tricky with the time you gave me, but I worked my magic as usual and got it done. So, handsome, are you impressed?" Dani asked in her usual flirty and upbeat manner.

"Thanks for that Dani, life saver as always. I really didn't want this kind of cash hanging around. But..." Knox was quickly cut off.

"But...? I don't like it when you say 'but', Lucas. You're not going to break my heart now, are you?" Dani held her breath and Knox hated himself for the way he enjoyed the idea of her worrying about him.

"Dani..." He dragged out the sound of her name in a comforting way before telling her.
"You worry too much, Lass. As if I would break your heart."

"No?" she asked questioning him and Knox imagined her with her hand at the delicious curvature of her hip before it met the perfect handful of an arse he just wanted to bite into. He smirked knowing his answer and inwardly calling himself a bastard for enjoying their sexual banter, one he knew could never lead to the bedroom like he wanted.

"Well sweetheart, you would have to give it to me first." Knox smiled when he heard a small sigh being released, one she no doubt tried to hide. He could almost see her biting her lip and onto the end of a blue pen that he knew she did often out of habit. He couldn't believe it was possible to envy an inanimate object like he did that day he first met her. But seeing the way her lips subconsciously sucked and nipped at its plastic end… well shit, he had been having dreams about them paying the same attention to his cock almost every night since. Even thinking about it was getting him hard and this was his cue to reel back to reality and get down to the reason he called.

"No, it's about work. Oh, and you can breathe now, I wouldn't want you going lightheaded on me again," Knox said unable to help himself with one last tease.

"Again…? In your dreams, Mr Knox. Anyway, work is what I wanted to talk to you about yesterday. You had an offer come in and…" said Dani but was quickly interrupted.

"Would it happen to be for a British government department by any chance?" Knox asked.

"Er… yes, how did…" Dani said with an inquisitive tone as Knox jumped in again.

"The one where they have made a few offers but you turned them down?" Knox's smile grew as he waited for Dani's response.

· · ·

"Okay, so... Have you been spying on my computer, are you watching me now?" Dani half laughed with a touch of confusion and was that also hope he heard underlining her voice?

"Well now, that would be telling. The funny thing is I have accepted the job offer from them. I started... well this morning in fact," Knox said as he braced for a backlash.

"Hold on... but... how... what? I am really confused here Lucas, so time to fill me in." Okay, so if Knox found himself getting hard before, hearing her say this was causing him to have to readjust himself.

"Did they go to you direct and cut me out? Bastards! They can't do that, we have rules and I am going to..." Dani said as her confusion turned to outrage. Knox cut in quickly, smirking at the feisty side he hadn't seen from her before.

"Hold on, I can't get past 'fill you in'..." Knox chuckled.

"Lucas!" she scolded but it didn't work in removing the grin from his face, nor the idea of her squealing his name like that as he hoisted her over his shoulder and slapped her arse.

"It's not what you think, Darlin'. Something I was working on down here meant I crossed paths with that particular department and they pulled me in. We had a chat and well, I kind of took the job." Knox knew this wouldn't go down well.

. . .

"You bloody did what?! Guess that's me out of a job then, oh well, I always have my painting to fall back on," Dani said with a put on sad voice. Knox rolled his eyes knowing he would never be able to let her go and if she thought he would, then she was a damn fool. Even if he wasn't prepared to risk taking their friendship to the level he wanted, he knew he wasn't able to walk out of her life for good. But instead of saying any of this, he decided now was a good opportunity to pry and see if she had any idea of what he had been up to.

"How is the painting going, sell anything lately?" Knox asked, knowing full well he had bought two of her paintings last month under his pseudonym name, Ethan Connelly. Something Knox had been doing since he found out Dani sold her paintings. She was talented, well Knox thought so, as her style and subject were on point with his tastes. At first, he had been surprised to find out this side of her. Not the fact that she could paint but more the likes of *what* she *did* paint.

Sexual, moody, and dark BDSM had not been what he had expected to see on her private website, one he had some difficulty finding at first due to the pseudonym she used. But he was a man who liked to know all there was about the people he worked with and Dani had been no exception. In fact, it had quickly morphed from a professional necessity into the realms of unhealthy obsession.

. . .

Of course, finding out that she lived out her secret submissive fantasies through her artwork, was like waving a red flag in front of a Dom like himself. He'd bought around thirty of her pieces so far and had no plan on ever stopping. In fact, he couldn't actually say what his favourite piece was, as they were all ones he could see himself re-enacting in person with the artist herself.

The only sad part was they were all kept in a storage unit in the U.K. along with other sentimental possessions. One of the down sides to having no fixed address and being in his line of work, always moving around to where the jobs took him. Although he wasn't sure if he had them displayed that he would ever get any work done, not with bound beauties painted in black and white that all looked ripe and ready for the taking.

"Actually, I will have you know I sold two last month," she said with sass that sounded a lot hotter coming from Dani than it had from the now knowingly fake 'Susie'. Knox smiled to himself hearing the confirmation he needed to know that Dani had no clue who kept buying all her paintings.

"I have regular clients you know… but don't change the subject Lucas, what financial package did you negotiate? I turned down their first two offers but their last offer wasn't bad and that's what I was going to talk to you about." Dani was clearly back into work mode.

"Well, I don't really know," Knox said then laughed but as Dani said nothing he started to feel a twinge of guilt for teasing her, no matter how much he enjoyed it.

"Dani... what I mean is I asked for double what their last offer was or I walked. I had no idea, I was just winging it," Knox said elaborating on what she wanted to know, something he now wanted to know himself.

"Whoa, let me get this straight...You asked for double... And, and they agreed?" Okay, so Knox was taking this as a good sign for a payday.

"They did."

"That's fantastic! Wow, you must be good, Lucas," Dani said in utter shock.

"If only you knew," Knox muttered under his breath without thought and referring of course to his sexual obsession.

"Sorry, I didn't catch that?" Dani asked and Knox cleared his throat.

"I said, 'so you see, it's not all bad' and of course, it's all still going to go through you, that was my one other demand. You are my broker and I wouldn't want it any other way," Knox said easing Dani in for the next bit of news.

. . .

"Well, I should think so too. So, do you want to know what the deal is then if they are giving you double?" Dani's voice got excited.

"Yes... but there is more. I took on a second job too. And that's why I needed this account sorting." Knox knew this wasn't going to go down well.

"Lucas..." She said his name in her usual scolding tone and before he could start to explain she started,

"Really! A second job? I think I am too scared to ask. The deal you have made works out at £250k a year, so you now have no excuse for not buying me dinner, Lucas. What is this second job and how can you do both, do you have a twin I know nothing about?" Dani added with cheekiness.

"I have been paid in advance up front, and I need you to clean it. Taking your normal cut of course. I am going to deposit it in the account you have setup..." Knox sat down at a bench and told Dani all the details, the job with T.I.7 and the offer by Marco Pérez and Malcolm Howard. Of course, he left out the part about 'Susie' and the whole bait and grab part, not wanting to give her an idea of how ruthless T.I.7 could be when they wanted something.

But Knox found himself easily getting lost talking to Dani and his only annoyance was that he wasn't doing so in person. He enjoyed chatting with Dani more than he wanted to admit to himself but as he offloaded and she listened, he found it harder and harder to get off the phone. After a time, Knox felt a tug of guilt pull on his conscious. He had taken up too much of Dani's time and in truth, he knew he was heading down a slippery slope and in doing so dragging her down with him.

So instead of doing what he wanted to, which was continue talking to her, Knox congratulated Dani on the sale of her paintings as well as her windfall in the form of the commission she would be earning.

"Thank you, Dani, as always you are a true pro. Talk to you soon," Knox said without showing he didn't really want the call to end.

"It's my pleasure Lucas, stay safe don't get yourself killed. I really don't fancy having to find someone else to broker for, it's a pain in my arse to vet, interview and set up their accounts," Dani joked before adding her usual nickname for him, one he didn't mind in the slightest.

"Bye handsome," Dani said and with the same thoughts of not wanting to show she was sad to be ending the call, she hung up. However, not before Knox caught the sigh of disappointment, one no doubt warranted, because, for all her hints, Knox still hadn't asked her out for that dinner.

. . .

Knox sat for a moment deep in thought as he closed the flip phone, and with a mental slap across his face, he stood and walked over to customer services. He placed the tan briefcase down on the desk which made the bank assistant look up and take note.

"I would like to talk to the manager about making a large deposit," Knox said with a smile.

Knox pulled up outside T.I 7's warehouse. The last time he arrived here he had been cuffed, hooded and sore. Now though, with two short beeps of his bike's horn, a door opened next to a large roller door and out popped a scruffy man. He looked over to Knox from the doorway before going back inside, closing the door behind him.

"There's nothing like friendly service," Knox muttered to himself and seconds later the roller door lifted and Knox rode inside. You could be forgiven for thinking it was a working garage. With two Land Rover Defenders that looked mean in dark gun metal grey and black hardware, bonnets lifted as guys worked on them. The other side of the Defenders sat three Jaguar F-pace, of course, black with tinted windows. Knox strolled over to one of the black cats, placing his hand on the driver's door handle.

"Nice isn't it…" The deep voice of Harris sounded from behind Knox.

"Go ahead it's open. The other two are the 2.0-litre turbo,

but this one is the 3.0 litre supercharged…" Harris said with a big grin as he walked past Knox and held his arm out to invite him to open the car's door.

"I have to admit I am a fan," Knox said as he looked over the interior of the luxury SUV.

"It's a far cry away from Panthers, Foxhounds or the most uncomfortable way to travel around the desert slowly cooking your arse off, Snatch Land Rovers," Knox said as he gave Harris a telling look, one which Harris smiled and nodded as he remembered the military vehicles all too well.

"Come on, let's get to the briefing, you can meet the team. They have been waiting," Harris said hitting Knox in the shoulder as he walked off.

"Briefing… Been waiting… wait how did you know I was coming?" Knox said as he caught up to Harris.

"Well, clearly we put a tracker on your bike. Anyway, it's not like you weren't going to take the job, right?" Harris said with a smirk.

"Captain, come in…You know Gregory, Thomas and of course, Captain Ellis." Carter said standing next to a tactical board. Captain Ellis looked at Knox with an emotionless expression, a look that couldn't have been more different than that of the sexual need only twelve hours ago.

"Captain..." Knox said as he took up a position next to Ellis. She said nothing.

"Good, you are all a team. And I expect you to act like it and fast. All history I want dropped. Am I making myself clear?" Carter barked as everyone said Sir, all but Knox who looked at Carter and nodded.

"Patricia Miller, my team. Team, you will extend Miss Miller every courtesy. She is here at our invitation, she is representing Langley's interests." Carter said introducing Miller, stern faced, with an almost grey complexion matching her suit. Late thirties, single, married to the agency type. She took a long drink from a take-out coffee cup as she met everyone's eyes with her own before saying "Officers". If anything, she looked pissed off at being there.

"Now we are all acquainted... Operation 'Hail Burn' people, that's why we are here. Langley and River House have been completely railroaded off this. Their top brass believes they have dirty operatives. So, they have come to us for intel and to enforce. Miss Miller if you would," Carter finished and directed Miller to address the room.

. . .

"Currently, we have a joint operation between the US and the Brits collecting intel on two new fringe outfits. They want to join the big boys of the middle east. They're chasing international arms in an area of the world that is way beyond their comprehension. It's crazy, to say the least. This new player is operating in a highly incendiary region, and we would all hate to see that run out of control." She paused and looked around the room for expectant looks of agreement before continuing.

"In my view, it should be placed under a pure intelligence jurisdiction, acting on a political brief, but with what has come to light with both our departments, that simply isn't going to work. You must nail these people, they have the funds and the backing. Fail on this one and we could be seeing a major power shift in the region," Miller said with a tone that was straight out of the book on 'how to address your team' guide.

"In this new era of Parliamentary, States' Congress accountability and transparency, River House and Langley will be keeping a close eye on us. I, for one, am not happy about it but it's the cards we have been dealt and we have a job to do," Carter said as he cut Miller a look of disdain, one she equally returned.

"So, tell us about Hail Burn. I am new to the party," Knox piped up.

. . .

"Hail Burn is an ongoing anti-illegal arms operation based in Washington and shared intel with River House. A standard tracer operation, it's been running just over a year," Miller responded.

"Who are you going after?" Knox asked

"The key player we believe to be one Marco Pérez. Director of Hail Trans corporation and we think he has a hell of a lot more on the side. His areas of international crime are vast. Drugs, people trafficking and weapons being his main trade. But it has come to light that he has gone into a new venture," Miller said before taking a sip of her coffee.

"And that would be?" asked Captain Ellis.

"He has gone into moving money," said Miller.

"Moving money, he has gone into Banking?" Gregory queried with a confused look on his face.

"Of a kind, yes, but this money is the drug lords' and cartels'. You see, the kind of money they have they can't move through banks from one country to the other. It's traceable, we can intercept it and there is just too much of it to hide. So, they have taken to smuggling the cash in massive amounts. And we believe that Pérez, through his Hail shipping company, is the major player," Miller said before moving over to a control panel. Displayed on the tactical wall were photographs of Pérez at a meeting in Madrid with two known cartel bosses and a Syrian war lord.

"The four were discussing a future arms deal, as well as funding. Our op on the inside died getting that information out to us. And that is where our operation is compromised and why we have come to you," Miller finished and took a seat.

"Where are the arms coming from, who is Pérez buying off...?" Knox looked to Miller then to Carter.

"Marco Pérez is buying arms under the counter from British and American arms companies. People on the inside are aiding and abetting, fake MOD end-user certificates, fast-tracked orders. Clearing certificates and doctored serial and account numbers. And they are getting paid royally to do so," Carter said with a less than impressed manner.

"And Marco Pérez has the US and British contract to export all their legit arms deals. Hail Trans Corp, therefore, has export licenses granted, they can ship when and wherever they want," Carter finished off.

"So, there we have it, people. Our job is to gain the intel needed. Knox give us an update, you deposited a sum of money today. I take it your meeting went well?" Carter said looking at Knox like he and everyone in the room knew, but did they know he had one point five million in a bogus account. Of course, they tracked his motorcycle and most likely tailed him on local CCTV, as he was very careful no-one had tailed him. But if they knew the amount he was pretty sure they wouldn't be so cool about it.

. . .

"Yes, I am now the personal security to Isabella Pérez, all aspects of her safety are under my control as well as the security of the households. So, I am in the door, if she has any information I will get it. I would be surprised if she has any involvement. But I think I can get close enough to Marco and Malcolm. It looks as though I will be on double pay," Knox smiled.

"Make the most of it Knox, and drinks will be on you when we nail these bastard's balls to the wall. That's all everyone," Carter said as he dismissed the group.

"Knox, go with Major Harris, we have some kit for you," Carter said almost cracking a smile.

"Yes, Sir…"

7

TECH WIZARDRY & NAKED MISERY

"Captain, this is Olivia Rose. Miss Rose this is Captain Lucas Knox." Major Harris introduced Knox to a small, young woman, who looked more like she was on work experience. With her messy, honey blonde hair in a bun, she was dressed in an oversized suit that looked bought more for comfort than for size or style. Knox could imagine that the part of the job she hated most was having to look professional. In fact, he could just picture her shedding her clothes the second she walked through the door and put on some cute, colourful pyjamas, that Knox would have only found sexy had they been torn off her.

"Hello, it's pleasure to meet you, Miss Rose," Knox said, then smiled as she looked up from over her laptop screen. Rose looked lost in thought as if she had been woken from a daydream, with what seemed like foam from her coffee on her top lip.

. . .

"Oh... yes... erm... Hello... Sorry miles away," Rose smiled awkwardly as she adjusted her glasses and stood up, knocking her coffee cup but catching it just in time before it went over. She shoved her hand out to Knox as if it was some kind of unnatural reaction she had forced herself to learn. Knox promptly shook it noticing her hand was covered in notes, scribbled on with a biro.

"Not a fan of post it notes?" Knox smirked.

"Post it notes...?" She looked around herself for clues and then looked at her hands, making the internal light bulb flickered to life.

"Oh right, yes, of course, my notes. I can't lose my hand," Rose said looking at Knox as if it was the most normal thing in the world. He tried to hide the smirk.

"Miss Rose is our head of special ops support, everything you need in the field, she is your route to getting it," Harris said trying to emphasise the importance of Rose's role, even if she didn't portray it herself.

"Please call me Olivia or Rose. Miss Rose makes me feel like a school teacher," Rose said before she erupted into laughter as if she had said the funniest thing she'd ever heard. Knox and Harris looked at each other with raised eyebrows.

. . .

Rose adjusted her glasses again before she noticed the coffee foam on her lip, unembarrassed and with no awareness that Knox and Harris had noticed the foam on her lip, she wiped it away.

"Right, let's get you all kitted out, that is why you are here right? *That is why you are here...* You are not with SIS are you?" Rose looked around as if she was expecting someone to turn up.

"Yes, the Captain is here to get his kit. For his undercover operation that you were informed about... *in my memo to you."* Harris kindly reminded Rose. Rose looked at Harris for a moment as if she was racking her brain to remember. She looked at her hand to see '*Knox*' written in the blue mess of notes, then the lights switched on again.

"Yes, yes of course... Come, come it is over here. I have everything ready for you," Rose said as she led the men over to a large matt black metal cabinet that was on wheels like most things around there. It reminded Knox of a professional mechanic's tool box, brushed aluminium edged handles running the width of the draws. There were a few of them in the area, but this one was pulled out from the rest.

Rose lifted the top surface up, it was a lid the full width and length of the cabinet. On the inside of the lid and tray below were dark grey moulded foam inlays, which held an array of weapons, hand guns of different calibres and sizes, close quarter shotgun, submachine gun and an assault rifle. Rose then pulled the top draw out to reveal just as big an array of knives, tactical military, folding, throwing and survival.

"And that's about all your, cold killing, brutish man toys to choose from, but here is my favourite," Rose said after first turning her nose up at the tools of his trade, then her face lit up as she pulled the next drawer out. In it lay gadgets like smartphones, GPS trackers and locators, listening devices and cameras. And a whole host of other things Knox had no idea what they did, but he was sure he was soon to find out.

"An exploding pen?" Knox mocked with a smile as he picked up a pen from the tray, clicking it repeatedly to the annoyance of Rose who slowly took it from him as if he was a child.

"This is not a toy and it is not an exploding pen, really this isn't Q-branch in a fictional novel, Knox," Rose said looking at him over her glasses before pushing them back up her cute button nose.

"It is an electronic bug detector. It can detect anything that is electronic and transmitting, recording sound or vision. Simply turn the lid to the right until it clicks like so, then hold over an object or area you wish to check for bugs. If there is the tip will flash red, it is accurate up to one metre." Rose said, obviously in her element as she moved on to picking up a black smartphone.

"Now this looks and has all the functionality of any modern smartphone. The difference is this smartphone has a few added features that you can't get from the local Apple store," Rose said as she showed Knox the phone.

. . .

"I have to warn you, I tend to break these modern phones," Knox said looking unhappy with the large screen. Rose simply took the phone from him and hit it on the corner of the metal cabinet hard, over and over before holding it out to Knox. He took it from her hand with a shocked look on his face.

"My phones are not just smart they are tough, so unless you plan on getting blown up, I can assure you the phone would survive better than you would."

"Well, thanks for the vote of confidence, Darlin'," Knox said with a laugh.

"I doubt a man like yourself needs any more confidence, a bullet proof vest perhaps, but that is up to you… Now, where was I…? Oh yes features…" Rose said which made Knox smirk and wink at her making her cough and clear her throat. It was a pleasant surprise seeing geek girl with a bit of spunk, as in this place and dealing with us military dogs, she would need it to survive the job.

"With this phone, you can clone any other sim card network phone. Listen in on their calls and read their text messages and emails…etc. You can also make calls from their number and such but you get the idea, I'm sure," Rose said with infectious enthusiasm.

. . .

"This tracking device is magnetic and only the size of a small coin so you shouldn't have too much trouble hiding it. It links up to an app on the phone so you can then follow it on the ever so handy, Google Maps," Rose said clapping her hands at the integration with Google Maps.

"The listening and filming devices can also be monitored from an app on the phone. And to make it easy all the information is sent wirelessly to the NEST," Rose said as she looked very pleased with herself.

"How do I turn the devices on and off?" Knox said as he picked up one of the listening devices.

"Simple answer, you can't. They are always on, battery life in all of them is around sixty days. So, the only way to switch them off is to render them inoperable," Rose said looking at Knox as if to say why would you ever need or *want* to turn them off.

"I have a document with instructions on how everything works. Would you like me to email it to you? PDF work for you?" Rose pulled out her phone and started tapping then waited for Knox to reply.

"Email...? Maybe best you print me out a copy, I will need you to set me up an email as I haven't one." Knox smiled as Rose looked at him as if he was from the dark ages. He wanted to laugh out loud as her mouth actually dropped open.

"Uh…but you…you must have…" She started to stutter, pushing up her glasses again and nearly tripping over herself as she took a step closer to him. He wouldn't have been surprised if she started poking him in the chest to check whether he was real or not.

"It is okay, Olivia, I am sure we will soon drag the Captain into the twenty-first century. Now if you will both excuse me I will take my leave," Harris said before nodding to both Knox and Rose then turning and walking away. Knox thought for a moment, then followed Harris and caught up with him at the door.

"Major, may I have a word?" Knox said as he reached Harris.

"Yes Captain, go right ahead." A puzzled Harris looked back at Knox.

"This Olivia lass, how old is she…she is a section head?" Knox whispered to the side of Harris' head.

"That's irrelevant Captain, trust me, you wouldn't want to be in her firing line. Now get back to it.," Harris said in a tone that wasn't to be messed with. Knox accepted what he was saying with just a look, and headed back over to Rose.

. . .

"Everything okay, Captain?" Rose asked with a hand on her hip and attitude written all over her face.

"Yeah, sure, so, where were we?" Knox said looking a little sheepish.

"Oh, for fuck sake, you trigger happy types are all the same! Listen, Captain, I may look like I am just out of Uni. But I will have you know I never went to Uni or much of school for that matter. I was hacking government networks, power grids and NASA to name a few, for fun! I could do more damage sat in my pyjamas watching SpongeBob SquarePants than you with your little dick and an 'I need to shoot a big gun' complex, could ever dream about. Have I made myself clear?" Rose said turning into a hot-headed firecracker with a look in her eye that said back off or I will scratch your eyes out with my super computer. Knox instantly respected her. She may have been little and cute but she was tough and he liked it.

Knox held up his hands.

"Hey, easy there. I am sorry for any offence taken and look, I am a bit old school, a blunt weapon okay. I know I need to get with the times, so forgive me," Knox said humbly. Rose relaxed and broke her intense look with a sweet smile.

. . .

"Apology accepted Captain. Now let's get you kitted out and up to speed," Rose said acknowledging Knox's sincerity and moving on after having made her point. She turned around and Knox smirked once more, knowing he had been right about the pyjamas.

It was the morning of the next day, Knox pulled up to the imposing green gates of the Pérez residence. He looked up at the CCTV camera which trained onto him. Within moments the gates opened. At a slow pace, Knox made his way up the winding driveway, passing groundsmen working on the pristine tropical gardens. Pulling up to the same garage as before, Juan stood waiting. He pointed over to an area which had recently seen building work and the only evidence was the swept-up floor covered in the last bit of building dust. A small car port had been built.

"Please Mr Knox, it is now your parking area," Juan said. Knox smiled, rode over and parked up in the welcoming cool shade.

"Bring my blasted car around!" Howard said as he stormed out of the main house entrance. Knox looked over and watched Howard talk on his phone, irate and agitated as he paced around. Howard spotted Knox, he hung up the call and walked over to Knox with purpose.

"Lucas, so you came back and didn't do a runner with my money," Howard said in his 'my shit don't stink' way.

. . .

"Well, the Boss' cigarettes were too good to not come back." Knox smiled as he looked at a button half hanging off Howard's blazer jacket.

"You may want to give your tailor a ring, everything okay?" Knox added, motioning to the button.

"Bloody Hell, yes it seems I will." Just as Howard replied, Juan, pulled up in Howard's Bentley Continental GT in stunning bright Aegean blue metallic paint. Knox sucked air through his teeth.

"Very nice, try not to pick up any speeding tickets," Knox said as he got off his bike and headed to the house. Howard sort of forced a smile out before he got into his car and then looked out his open window at Knox and said.

"Knox, Isabella wants to go shopping today. Make it happen, there's a good chap," Howard said with his normal smug expression. As Knox made his way through the house, armed Armani dressed guards showed him to a staircase and pointed up. At the top of the stairs, Knox found a single door on a large landing area. The door was half open but Knox knocked anyway, then walked in.

Isabella sat at a vanity unit facing a large mirror, she was all but naked, only wearing purple lace French knickers. There was that toned slender back Knox had admired on the beach. Knox and Isabella's eyes met in the mirror. Knox' eyes dropped to her breasts, raising an eyebrow at her blatant and brazen attempt to get attention. She turned instantly to look at Knox.

"The door was open, I thought you would be dressed," Knox said unapologetically, not flinching or showing embarrassment by any means and therefore not playing into her games.

But then it was clear that Isabella had been crying, black mascara running down her cheeks. She stood and walked over towards Knox intently, looking him in the eyes. She picked up a robe and covered herself, also showing no sign of embarrassment.

"I will wait for you downstairs," Knox said bluntly.

"No, it is fine. Give me a moment and I will be dressed." She walked into a dressing room and slipped on a dress. Knox could see Isabella in the dressing room from a full-length mirror that was positioned just right. Isabella came back out and walked over to her balcony.

"Coffee...?" she asked as she walked out and sat at a table with breakfast and fresh coffee waiting. Knox looked sceptical wondering why she was acting nice to him and not trusting it, even when he joined her.

"Again I..." Isabelle cut Knox short.

. . .

"Forget about it, but you listen to me. I don't care who sees me naked. I do care who sees me crying. You tell no-one you saw that, is that clear?" Isabella said with a manner as if she was talking to one of the poor overworked maids. Knox almost rolled his eyes as the bitch re-emerged, strangely feeling more comfortable dealing with her this way. Any other way and he simply wondered what she was planning.

"Of course, you don't need to worry about who I talk to. I know the value of privacy," Knox said pouring himself a coffee. Isabelle looked at him as if waiting for him to pour her one too.

"I may be working for your father, but I'm not working as your waiter. Now, if you ask nicely I may do. Otherwise…" Knox said and waited for a response.

"Please, would you be a darling and pour me a coffee?" she said as her eyes narrowed and sarcasm laced her words.

"Wasn't so hard now, was it?" Knox said irritating her further as he poured her coffee. She gave him a forced smile that was obviously through gritted teeth, then decided to get back at him another way when she said.

"I'm going shopping, want to come?" Isabella then sipped at the black coffee smirking, knowing a man like Knox would hate the idea.

. . .

"Ah, I don't think that would be wise," Knox replied confirming what Isabella first suspected.

"No problem, you can wait here and if you are lucky, I will let you carry my bags in when I return," Isabella said as she lit a long thin cigarette.

"That's not quite what I meant." Knox pulled out his lighter as hers was not igniting.

"Yes, I know what you meant which is why I am choosing to ignore it. What do I have to worry about when I have you to protect me, right?" Isabella said as she smoked, with a smirk that was practically begging to be wiped off her face. Knox didn't rise to it, no matter how much he wanted to.

"Shopping... No problem, in Malaga?" Knox coolly replied.

"No... Granada." Isabella stood.

"Enjoy the coffee and the view, I will get ready," she said as she walked off the balcony back into her room.

Knox took a sip of his coffee, and out of the corner of his eye, he watched Isabella pick up her phone before she swanned off into her bathroom. Knox pulled out the smart phone he had been kitted out with. Flicking through the apps he found the one Rose had shown him to connect and monitor nearby phones. He locked onto Isabella's phone and waited.

Knox's instincts were right as a text message alerted on his phone. It was Howard messaging Isabella. Knox paused for a moment, then opened the message and read it.

Howard: Will you and your new shadow be going out today? I am sorry we fought.

Isabella: Going shopping in Granada, don't care about my shadow. I am buying something nice using your credit card. It will be a more meaningful apology.

Howard: Why am I not surprised? Have fun, doing what you do best then. I have a late meeting tonight. See you tomorrow.

Knox forwarded the message to the NEST. If Howard was having a meeting it would be prudent for T.I 7 to tail him. Being Pérez's right-hand man, he would have to be involved. Knox waited and enjoyed the picturesque view dominated by an old church tower. When the coffee had gone cold a check of his watch showed over an hour had passed. Knox stood and walked inside.

. . .

"Isabella, will you be much longer? You will be losing shopping time. Won't that be a shame?" Knox said and he muttered the last part to himself.

"I am ready now, you can't rush beauty," Isabella said from her dressing room.

"I will go get the car ready, meet you there," Knox replied as he walked to her bedroom door and just as he opened it and was about to walk through, Isabella strolled in, arms across her chest holding up a bright Ferrari red little dress.

"Be a dear and zip me up," she said turning around showing Knox her bare exposed back. Knox remained where he was stood, looked at her expectantly and waited. Isabella looked over her shoulder annoyed that Knox hadn't jumped to her request.

"Please…" she said with a sigh.

Knox walked over, looking down at the impossibly small chrome zipper, his eyes being drawn to the small of her back. She was wearing nothing under the dress. He pinched the material below the zip and with the other hand pulled the smooth action zipper up. He paused for the smallest of moments at the sight of the hairs on Isabella's neck stand on end as goose bumps sent a shiver down her spine once he reached the top. Isabella flicked her hair when she felt he had finished. Knox took a step back.

. . .

"Shall we go?" Knox said extending his arm to the door. Isabella strolled past in her fast becoming trade mark impudent manner.

"You know it wouldn't hurt to tell a lady she looks nice. Come, let's go. I have shopping to do," she said before stopping in the doorway and looking back at Knox, speaking to him like he was some guard dog.

"You don't need to worry about bringing the car around, haven't they told you?" Isabella looked at Knox's facial expression indicating no-one had told him anything. Her smirk, however, told him everything.

"No? Well if you're going to take care of my safety, I suggest you keep up to date with my travel arrangements, Lucas..." Isabella said pausing as an unmistakable sound grew from in the distance closing in on the property.

The sound of a helicopter.

8

LUNCH WITH A BANG

Knox looked down over the Sierra Nevada Mountains, finding it hard to believe that they would be covered in snow in just a few months. The Airbus H160 cut effortlessly and whisper quiet through the air even at 185mph. Knox looked around the interior, upholstered in rich leather with wood and metal accents. All customised to Marco Pérez's specifications, logos of his company and family crest stitched into the soft Nappa leather.

What a different world it was. A far cry from heading into covert missions in Wildcats and Lynx army helicopters, that was for damn sure. The deafening sound of blade-vortex and engine rumble, metal rattled and sounded like every nut, bolt and rivet holding the choppers together were under strain, moments away from failure. This world had pilots and air crew in a different kind of uniform, clean cut and drenched in expensive cologne and perfumes, champagne and canapés served with a smile.

Isabella sat with her long legs crossed as she filed her nails with a pout you could hang a jacket on. She looked bored and that pissed Knox off. He took a breath and calmed himself down, telling himself she didn't know any better, that she was born into it. And her father admitted to spoiling her rotten and letting her get away with everything.

Knox's thoughts were broken as he was brought back by the captain's voice, one which informed them over the intercom that they would be landing in five minutes. Granada city grew on the horizon as the H160 started its smooth descent.

"Where would you like to shop first?" Knox said to Isabella

"Hugo Boss or Canali, I need to sort something out," Isabella said in a drab tone, without taking her eyes off her nails.

"Something to sort out? You have to return something?" Knox jibed knowing full well Isabella would return nothing and would not think twice about putting something that didn't fit in the bin, no matter how much the price tag said that was left on it. Maybe it was something of Howards, Knox thought to himself.

"If I am to be forced into being seen with you then we need to sort out this whole, 'I buy my clothes from the second-hand Army store' look," Isabella said as she waved her hand up and down at Knox's attire.

"What's wrong with what I'm wearing, Lass?" Knox said pretending to be affronted when in actual fact Knox didn't give two shits what she thought of his 'attire'. No, in Knox's line of work it needed to be practical and that was that. Besides, a suit in this weather was damn hot and in his opinion not exactly what he would call 'inconspicuous'.

Alright, so maybe it would fit somewhere like New York walking into an office building, then he would blend just like the rest of the sheep. But somewhere filled with half-dressed tourists all loaded with bags, kids and cameras? No, Knox didn't think so. Besides, Knox hated trying to hide his gun in a suit. He was too bulky as it was to even get them to fit right, let alone loose enough to hide his Sig P26.

"Nothing at all if you work at a biker bar, but you don't, you work for me," said Isabella bringing Knox back to the conversation and realising she had answered his question.

"I work for your father, not you," Knox said as he held his calm.

"And you now represent him, and frankly you are making me look scruffy. The Pérez family has an image to uphold. So, you are getting new clothes. Don't like it? Then quit." Isabella said knocking her sunglasses down from her head as her pout grew bigger. Knox knew he had to let her have this small victory, or what was his argument with Pérez going to be, without sounding like a whining little bitch like his daughter.

They circled the helipad before making the final approach, a black car was parked waiting.

"When we land you wait here until I give you the all clear, understand?" Knox said sternly.

"That is my normal driver, he is harmless. I use him all the time." Isabella said with attitude. Knox decided not to bother arguing as he would bound and gag her if it meant he could do his job the way he intended…actually, it was sounding like a good idea if she kept this hissy shit up.

After they had safely landed, Knox got up and stepped out. Isabella waited for her door to be opened. Knox stopped the flight crew before they reached the aircraft's door.

"She stays in the chopper until I have checked over the car," Knox shouted to the ear of the ground crewman. Isabella looked on with a scowl. Knox smirked before he turned, head down and headed over towards the car, one hand gripped on the gun holstered to his belt at the back. After checking the driver and the car over he gave the all clear. By this time, the chopper had cut its engines and wound down. Isabella was helped down by the ground crew and she swanned over before she stood by the rear door and waited for Knox to open it.

"Hands stopped working?" Knox said as he got in the front passenger side. The driver, with a look of panic, got out and rushed to open her door.

"Charming, who said chivalry was dead?" Isabella mocked as she sat down. Knox ignored her and looked out over the airfield.

"I am here to protect you, not pander to you," he said as he looked over his shoulder, which Isabella ignored as she now looked out of her window.

"Why haven't we left already?" Isabella said to the driver, who in turn looked to Knox.

"Isabella… seat belt, use it then we will leave." Knox turned back to face forward and waited. The driver looked as if he was going to shit bricks, Knox saw his discomfort and winked at him.

"I have all day…" Knox said as he relaxed into every inch of the plush Mercedes-Maybach's luxury seat, and flicked the seat massage switch. With a huff, Isabella buckled up.

"Driver, let's get going," Knox said as a smile slipped out over his lips.

Hours dragged by and now with a car boot full of shopping bags, Knox was ashamed to admit, a lot of them were his. Isabella went to town and she purchased a suit for every day of the week and a spare, all courtesy of Howard's credit card. If Isabella wanted to let her fiancé know she was pissed off, she was going the right way about it. But Knox wasn't totally convinced it was all about Howard hiring him. No, it was deeper than that. One thing Knox did know, no matter how super rich they were, family drama was still the same as any other.

Knox fidgeted in his seat pulling at the starched stiff white shirt cuffs, under the new dark grey suit. He was hot, uncomfortable and pissed off.

"Knox, I am hungry, take me to lunch. I fancy something hot and spicy. Driver, you know where," Isabella said from the back seat, texting on her phone.

"Hold steady Felipe, is this a regular restaurant you go to?" Knox said having taken the time to find out the driver's name earlier in the day.

"Yes, I always eat there, the food is fantastic and they look after me *well,*" Isabella replied in a tone that said she didn't like being questioned in front of the driver.

"No good, forget it, it's predictable and they will know you may be there," Knox said looking back at Isabella.

"You are paranoid and this is so stupid! I can't even eat at my favourite restaurant now?!" Isabella bleated.

"No, you can't," he told her sternly before turning to the driver.

"Felipe, do you recommend anywhere good that would be up to Miss Pérez's exacting standards. Oh, and easy for you to drop off and pick up would be ideal," Knox said putting his hand on Felipe's shoulder giving it a squeeze telling him not to worry about upsetting the boss lady.

Felipe made a call on the vehicle's hands-free system, he spoke to a concierge as though he knew them well. He booked a table and told them he would drop the VIP clients off in under ten minutes.

"Thank you, Felipe you are a gentleman," Knox said as he wound down his window and put his sunglasses on, Isabella stared at him in the mirror.

The sleek black Maybach drew up outside the Hotel Palacio de Santa Paula, located in the historic centre of Granada. The five-star hotel staff were waiting at the door and kerb side.

Knox looked to Felipe, who shrugged his shoulders back at Knox.

"They know who she is, it's to be expected," Felipe said coyly.

Knox gave him a look and then got out of the car. The doorman opened Isabella's door and Knox walked a half step behind and to the side of her as he scanned the surroundings. They met the hotel manager who stood waiting at the sliding smoked glass door entrance. They made small talk with Isabella who couldn't have been less interested if she tried. Knox gave the manager a sympathetic look.

As they walked from the main lobby of the hotel they found themselves in a grand open-air courtyard. Isabella cut Knox a look, one which made him smile as he saw she wasn't expecting it to be so nice.

"What... you haven't been here before?" Knox said with a knowing grin, Isabella cracked a smile.

"Careful now, I wouldn't want to think you are enjoying yourself." Knox pulled a chair out for Isabella as they reached the table reserved for them. She looked unsure at first then sat.

"I wasn't born in a barn," Knox said as he pushed her chair in.

"Let's just eat, shall we," she replied picking up the menu.

"You want me to eat with you?" Knox said, standing next to her.

"Well I don't want to eat alone and as good as you look in the suit, you will make me and the other guests feel uncomfortable stood watching over me," Isabella said as she looked Knox up and down.

"Plus, you must be hungry also, please sit," she said with a softer tone.

Knox nodded in agreement and sat to the side of Isabella at the fully set table with his back to the wall. As they looked over the menu Isabella texted on her phone, Knox looked at his from under the table.

Howard: How are you and the shadow, getting along?

Isabella: I can't even eat at my favourite restaurant. Should I even bother going out of the house?

Howard: It is for the best we want you safe. And you will have to learn to like it.

Isabella: Well I am sat in a hotel with a more handsome looking shadow now, thanks to our little shopping trip. So, it is not all bad.

Howard: Hotel? That's not funny Isabella.

Isabella: Yes, this hotel is beautiful. Shame you would rather work than take me nice places like he has.

Knox rolled his eyes as his attention was drawn by the waiting staff. He ordered a still water whilst Isabella ordered some bottle of pink fizz that cost more than he would spend on a meal for two.

Knox wasn't interested in eavesdropping on Isabella's churlish attempts to make Howard jealous, no doubt he would have the backlash of that at some point. He would have called him a poor bastard but he was a stuck up, toffee nosed twat and as far as he was concerned, they obviously deserved each other.

Knox went back to the job at hand and kept his mouth shut, only speaking to order food, and thank the waiting staff. As the time passed and as they were eating Isabella became more frustrated.

"Well, isn't this stimulating?" she burst out.

"Excuse me?" replied Knox.

"I am bored, did they not have conversations at the family dinner table in England?" Isabella said with a sarcastic tone. Knox put his swanky cutlery down hard on the modern designer tableware.

"Let's get a few things straight, I am not here for your

entertainment. I am here to do a job. Also, I am from Scotland Lass, and you couldn't handle a conversation around a Scottish family table." Knox said looking Isabella direct in the eyes.

"You are so rude, don't talk to your employer in such a way," Isabella said cutting Knox daggers.

"Fire me, oh that's right your father employed me to look after your bratty arse. Now finish your food or I will call the car and we will go," Knox coolly said with a manner that was letting Isabella know not to push his patience.

"How fucking dare, you speak to me like that! You just got yourself fired," Isabella said standing up and throwing her napkin at Knox, which made him smile.

"Isabella, sit down," Knox said as he too stood.

Just as Isabella was about to speak, Knox heard and saw a commotion from behind her in the lobby. Knox placed his hand on his hilted gun and walked around to Isabella, who screamed at him. Knox put himself in front of Isabella and the advancing disturbance.

"Isabella, quiet!" Knox said firmly as he backed Isabella and himself towards cover behind a wide stone pillar. Shots fired in the reception lobby area, this incited the other dinner guests into mass panic and hysteria. Deep male voices yelled and shouted from the lobby. Knox crouched down pulling Isabella with him. As she was about to scream he covered her mouth with his hand as he drew his gun with the other.

"Shush…" Knox whispered as he stared into Isabella's eyes.

"Do everything I tell you to, and I promise you we will get out of this," Knox said calmly as he released his hand from her mouth, then turned and put Isabella's hand on his back.

"Keep your hand there until I say otherwise. I move, you move, okay?" Knox said and Isabella, fear stricken, nodded in small fast actions.

Knox moved to better cover around the pillar and tucked

Isabella down. Reaching for his phone he tapped frantically before pressing a panic alarm application. No sound was heard as the screen went red. Two armed men burst in through the doors leading into the courtyard from the lobby. 'Pérez, Isabella Pérez!' Bellowed one of the two African mercenaries'. Both were wielding AK47's that they fired into the air. Bullets ricocheted off the high walls of the stone courtyard as dust and small stone chips showered down around them.

Knox watched as he glanced from their cover to see the other guests, some dropped to the floor crying, others frightened into silence. The men searched the few who bravely or stupidly ran for the doors, pushing their assault rifles into their faces, only checking the women. They knew their target but what they didn't know was that they would have to get to her over Knox's dead body.

Knox tucked back down and signalled to Isabella to stay put. He then stooped low and made his way around the outside of the courtyard behind tables, plant pots and trellis panels until he was level with the two gunmen. The gunmen were losing their patience letting off more shots into the air, yelling 'Pérez'. This was when Knox spied his chance.

The furthest man was empty, his AK rapidly clicked giving Knox his opening. He jumped into action, Knox picked up the closest dining chair to him. He then hurled it straight at the gunman who was reloading his weapon. Knox followed up with three rapid shots, one in the head of the second gunman. The next two into his shoulder and chest as he turned to see where the chair that hit his comrade had come from.

"Don't move! Freeze!" Knox roared as he trained his gun on the last man who walked towards him ready to fire.

"For the Bull!" The gun man pulled out a knife as he dropped the empty AK and ran at Knox. Two shots fired and echoed off the walls, each bullet casing dropped to the floor, ringing out as they bounced. A deadly silence fell on the room, Knox's breathing was all he could hear. Knox looked over the two men. One had a small Algerian flag on his belt buckle. Knox took note of this as he strode past them making his way back to Isabella.

Knox knelt by Isabella who was sat cowering, her head clutched in her hands. She jumped as Knox touched her arm, she looked at him like a scared child.

"Is this real enough for you now?" he asked in a soft voice, praying this time she would understand the severity of her situation. She nodded quickly, tears streaming down her face.

"You're safe, come with me and let's get you out of here," Knox said as he took her hand but she was a dead weight as she wouldn't move. Knox had seen this enough time to know that shock and fear had taken over.

"Isabella, it is okay. You are safe, but we have to get out of here," Knox said with a calm reassuring tone. Knox saw she was out of action so he scooped her up in his arms and headed towards the back of the courtyard. The smoked glass doors which matched the entrance operated on motion sensors but they were not opening. Knox turned around and as he did saw a third Algerian walk into the courtyard from the lobby.

"Pérez!" The Algerian man yelled.

"Fuck!" Knox said as he ran for cover behind the nearest pillar, bullets bounced off the floor and up the edge of the stone column. The glass doors that were inoperable shattered in a cascade of tiny diamond snow. Isabella screamed and Knox pulled her tighter into him. Four more shots fired but they didn't sound like the same weapon, there was no sign of bullet impact around them.

"All clear! Clear," shouted two British male voices. Knox looked around the pillar, his eyes were met with the sight of two tactical dressed men. Thomas and Gregory. The Algerian man on the floor, dead in front of them. They spotted Knox and signalled, sileantly asking if he was okay. Once he nodded they then signalled for them to leave.

Knox did not need to be told twice as he hot-footed it out of there, Isabella in his arms. Bursting through the rear fire exit which led out to an alley, sirens could be heard as they closed in. Knox knew Felipe and the Maybach were parked up in the adjacent street to the alley but Knox couldn't trust the driver or anyone else around the Pérez family. So, he headed in the opposite direction down from the alley and into a small square. He gently placed Isabella down on a rustic bench that looked as old as the historic city itself. At first, she didn't want to let go and he had no choice but to pry her fingers from his jacket.

"Isabella, you're safe, everything is okay," Knox said as he crouched down, gently lifting her chin with one finger so their eyes could meet.

"Come on, talk to me Lass, you're alright now," Knox said as he rubbed the tops of Isabella's arms.

"Who... were they, why...?" Isabella said before bursting into tears as she nestled her head into Knox's shoulder. Knox looked a little uncomfortable but put an arm around her. And with the other hand took his phone and made a call.

"It's Knox, I need wheels and I need them now!" Knox said sharply and straight to the point.

"We have your location, go to the road three hundred yards to your east. Transport will be provided," said a cold clinical almost robotic female voice before the call cut off.

"Isabella, we have to move. Hold my hand and don't let go," Knox said as he took her hand. Isabella nodded as she stood, taking a deep breath.

"That's it, brave girl, let's get you the hell out of this nightmare. Hold on and run." Knox smiled before turning and heading in the direction he had been given.

They reached the road and Knox looked up and down the street as they ran down, and just as he thought, no vehicle. He heard tyres squeal from the next street, then the source of the noise came into view, one of the black Jaguar F-Spaces. Major Harris was driving the SUV and it skidded to a halt beside them.

"All yours, Knox," Harris said as he got out the car, leaving the driver's door open for him.

"You're a true Gent. Oh, and don't worry, she won't get a scratch." Knox said as he opened the passenger door for Isabella who looked confused.

"There better not be, now get out of here," replied Harris.

"Whose car is this? Where are we going?" Isabella asked.

"I will explain on the way, now get in please," Knox said eager to get going as he shut the door. Once Isabella was safe inside, Knox walked around to the driver's side.

"Harris, the hotel?" Knox said quietly as he passed the Major.

"It's being sorted, don't worry, now go. Oh, Knox, nice threads," Harris said with a smirk, Knox smiled as he took off his suit jacket throwing it onto the back seat.

As Knox stepped into the driver's side, the ground shook with the sound of a massive explosion. The boom reverberated around all the buildings. Knox looked to the direction of the hotel to see rising thick black smoke.

"Lucas, what was that?!" Isabella called out to Knox, he sat in the car as he slammed the door behind him.

"A bomb... one that was meant for you."

9

KNOCK BACKS

After a one and half hour drive from Granada to La Caleta, Malaga, Knox and Isabella pulled up outside his unassuming apartment block.

"Is this your place?" Isabella said as she looked out the window her eyes scanning up and down at the building.

"For now, it is yes. Come on, let's get you inside," Knox said as he got out of the car. He looked suspiciously up and down the road when Knox spotted the T.I.7 van parked at the end of the street. The van had started to tail Knox when they merged onto the A-45 an hour out of Granada. Knox saw it as a good thing having extra eyes on them, as it could only help with any unwanted visitors.

Knox and Isabella walked up to the front entrance of the apartment block and Isabella had to run a little to catch up with him. She linked her arm in his, smiling as she almost snuggled it. Knox awkwardly smiled back, hoping this wasn't turning into what he thought it was turning into. He had seen it before when women had made it through something traumatic with the help of a man.

The main entrance to the building and his apartment front door had no sign of any break in and, other than the smell of fresh emulsion paint, you would never have known only a day ago it was broken into. Knox was in an extra careful mentality and drew one of his two guns before pushing his key into the mortice lock of his door. At the sight of the gun, Isabella backed away a few steps.

"It's just a precaution, stay behind me," Knox whispered as he saw Isabella's unease.

They entered the apartment everything was as it was the day he had moved in if anything it was cleaner. It was all clear so at least Knox could relax for the moment.
"Please make yourself at home it's not the biggest apartment but it serves my needs and has a magnificent view," Knox said with a smile as he made the sign for 'drink?' as he walked into the kitchen.

"I think it is lovely and I would love a drink, thank you," Isabella said as Knox observed her walk elegantly over to the balcony doors to take in the view. She thought about opening the sliding doors, her hand even lifted and started to reach out for the lock. But she stopped herself with the thought of being watched. Finally, it was sinking in that someone wanted her captured or worse... *dead*.

"Here, this always gets me relaxed and settles my nerves," Knox said as he handed Isabella a gin and tonic on ice.

"Thank you, what is it?" Isabella said as she took the drink from Knox.

"It's a stiff gin, Christ knows you deserve one after today," Knox said as he clinked his glass to hers before taking a seat.

"Lucas, why...whoever it is out there, why do they want me?" Isabella asked in a quiet voice, before taking a big sip of her drink.

"Do you know what your father is involved in? His business, the deals?" Knox said, calmly, not letting on he knew exactly what her father was involved in.

"My father loves his business, it's his life, more than his own family," Isabella said looking at the ground.

"He owns one of the world's largest export and shipping companies." She walked over to the window and looked out at the view again. Her slender frame casting an even slender shadow across the room, as the evening sun began to set orange contrasting against the black shadows.

"He built that port over there, built it up to what it is now and it is the smallest one he owns." Isabella pointed to the Port of Malaga which dominated the horizon view from Knox's apartment. Immense container ships, ferries to and from north Africa all sailed daily which contrasted against the super rich's mega yachts and the sandy palm tree littered beach front, with its array of bars and restaurants.

"I know very little about his deals, only what I have read and seen in the news." Isabella's body language dropped and she looked as though she was talking about a father who had died, not one that gave her anything she wanted with no thought to cost. What she really wanted, what she needed, was her father's time. Knox was sure that stemmed back to when she was very young. The loss of a mother is hard on a child of any age, Knox knew that all too well. But it must have been doubly hard to not have your father also, even though he was in plain sight. Neglect like that over time can do more damage than the pain of bereavement.

"So, you never go to his business meetings or on work trips with him?" Knox said before taking a swig of his drink.

"I have travelled with him sometimes to various places, normally if they are exotic or wonderful places to shop," Isabella said disinterestedly, as she sleekly crossed her long legs after sitting down in front of Knox. A view most men would lap up but she was doing nothing for Knox.

"But I am always left with a chaperone... normally a bodyguard or the son or daughter of one of the businessmen my father has met with," Isabella said pausing to take a drink, a drink she obviously liked more and more. She held out her glass.

"May I have another?" she softly asked giving Knox a look he was sure she used on her father when she wanted something.

"I don't see why not. One or two more won't hurt," Knox said as he downed the last of his drink and made his way to the kitchen. Shaking his head at the thought that if she was someone else, he would be happy to offer them another drink and it tended to take the nervous edge off most people. But Isabella, well now that's the last thing he needed or wanted.

"One thing is for sure, your father has pissed someone off or maybe a few people for all we know," Knox said as he took ice out of the freezer and poured two more drinks.

"You think there are more than one after me?" Isabella's voice turned fearful.

"I do yes, but I need you to do something for me," Knox walked back over to Isabella as he spoke.

"What do you want?" Isabella said with a confused look on her face. Knox knelt in front of Isabella and placed her drink in her hands, firmly cupping his own hands around hers as she held the drink.

. . .

"I want you to remember that I am here to protect you, I won't let anything happen to you. But I can't do that if you don't trust me and you keep things from me," Knox said as he looked directly into Isabella's eyes, speaking in a strong 'I mean what I say' kind of manner.

"I am not keeping anything from you," Isabella said with attitude. Knox, with a knowing smile, took a moment before saying.

"Listen I am not pushing you, I didn't mean it like that. I mean if you involve me in all your day to day decisions, then it makes my ability to keep you safe easier." Knox stood back up as he spoke.

"Trust me, I don't enjoy or want to sound like a control freak who wants to know when, where and for how long on anything, let alone shit like when you drop the kids off at the pool," Knox smirked knowing full well Isabella would have no idea what he was talking about.

"Drop the kids off at the pool? I don't have children Lucas, you know that. Does this look like a body that's borne children?" Isabella looked at Knox like he was crazy. Knox looked back at her almost fully displaying her body, and he thought to himself, it's a shame she didn't have a kid. It may have brought her spoilt arse kicking and screaming into the real world. But Christ what if the kid turned out as spoilt or worse. That was a hard one for him to call.

. . .

"It's a saying my mother used to use. I will tell you what it means one day." Knox knew she would not be able to let it lie.

"Tell me, Lucas, I want to know. Tell… me", Isabella crossed her arms and pointed her toe at Knox to emphasise the 'tell' and 'me'.

"It means going to the toilet," Knox said before he erupted into a roar of laughter. Isabella looked at him with utter disgust at first, but Knox's laughter boomed and was infectious, so she couldn't help but laugh herself. They talked for a few hours. Isabella told Knox of her childhood in private schools and the places she had been. Knox listened and kept the conversation away from him and his history. It wasn't that Knox was ashamed of his history, but almost twenty-five years of military life and the last twelve years of it special operations was a life of pain, loneliness and being paid to kill…not a conversation most women could handle.

It was getting late and Knox wanted Isabella to sleep not lie awake thinking about what could have happened earlier and getting her a little drunk was sure to help with that. He stood up and went into the bedroom and returned with a blanket and pillow.

"Are they for me, Lucas?" Isabella asked in a 'she really hoped not' way.

. . .

"No, for me. I will sleep on the sofa. Please take the bedroom, the sheets are fresh and you have the en-suite. Towels are on the bed for a shower when you want one, sorry no bath here," Knox said as he put the pillow and blanket out on the sofa.

"Are you sure?" Isabella sounded unusually concerned.

"Yes, it is fine. I will not sleep much anyway as I will be keeping you safe remember?" Knox winked as Isabella got up to make her way to the bedroom. She stopped and turned to Knox.
"Lucas?" Isabella paused.

"Yes." Knox turned to look in the direction of his quietly spoken name.

"Thank you." Isabella looked at him with a genuine look of sincerity.

"You are welcome, go on, go get some sleep. See you in the morning. Night Isabella." Knox nodded and smiled.

Knox made himself a coffee, sat out on the balcony and looked out onto the Mediterranean. The ocean was as still as a mill pond. Knox could barely hear the waves washing ashore. He was wired, thoughts played in fast forward over and over in his mind. The Pérez family, Marco's T.I.7 file, Isabella's lack of understanding of what her father was into. Agreeing to work for T.I.7 and the team, the money, what he could do with it. And as always making her way to the top of his thoughts was Dani.

Knox did what he always did when he needed to clear his mind and relax. He took out his gun and laid it on the table in front of him. He stared at it before picking it up again and stripping it down as fast as he could. Once stripped and laid out in perfect order, each bullet lined up in an arrow straight row. He took a breath then reassembled, and repeated, again, and again until he was doing it with his eyes closed. It was almost a ritual, like meditation. Of course, he wouldn't be risking it if he didn't have his back-up, Sig P229 nestled safely in his holster.

"Lucas... Lucas." A soft whispered voice called to him pulling him back out of his meditation... it was Isabella. Knox opened his eyes and turned to see Isabella stood in the doorway, naked in all her glory.

"Isabella is everything alright?" Knox said as he averted his eyes.

"I didn't have you down as the shy type. I can't sleep." Isabella began walking over. As she reached Knox she slipped onto his lap and leant in whispering.

"Come to bed with me, keep me company." Isabella kissed Knox's ear as she finished the last words.

. . .

Knox held her firm and pushed her back a little. Isabella looked at him, shocked at first, then a big smile crossed her face before she leant in again to kiss him.

"No! Isabella, you are confused," Knox said as he stood up taking Isabella with him.

"No! No?" Isabella shrieked, all affronted at the nerve of anyone saying no to her.

"It's not that I wouldn't love to, you are very beautiful. Any man would give a limb to be with you," Knox said as he turned away not looking at her.

"But I don't work like that, you are my client. You are a job and I don't mix pleasure with business.

"Bull shit Lucas, no one turns me down. Who is she?" Isabella said stamping her foot as she slapped her hand on his back.

"Who is she?" Knox repeated as he looked back at Isabella.

"Yes, you heard me, who is she? There is only one reason a man would pass up a chance of being with someone like me. They are a fool in love," Isabella sneered.

. . .

"You don't know what you're talking about, now go to bed, Isabella," Knox said as he turned away and listened for a response which never came. Instead, he felt Isabella's hands slide over his back and round to his chest.

"Please Lucas..." Isabella whispered as she leant into him, Knox could feel her soft breath on his neck. Knox turned to face her, their eyes locked and Isabella's face lit up with a big smile at getting what she wanted. Knox took hold over her wrists, moving her hands back down to her sides.

"Isabella, I said no!" Knox said as he picked her up over his shoulder and took her to his room. She didn't know what to think. Shocked at being picked up, the only sound she made was a squeal as she kicked out her legs. Knox put her down on his bed with a small amount of force before pulling the sheets over her. Then walked out without saying a word.

Shutting the door behind him, the sound of the door latching was followed by a scream and a thud as something hit the other side of the door. Knox smiled and shook his head at what had just happened. It was true that almost any red-blooded man would have jumped at the chance. But Isabella, for all her model looks and money, left Knox feeling cold. He could never be with a woman like that, even for just one night. Knox could just see it. She would be as selfish, demanding and pouty in bed as she was in her everyday life. For Knox that would not just be a turn-off, but a disaster in the making. Isabella had got something right though, it was another woman on his mind... *Dani*.

Knox's eyes slowly opened and adjusted to the morning light flooding into the room. The sound of running water could be heard.

Isabella was taking a shower. Good, she needed a good cooling off. Knox made coffee wondering just how shitty she was going to be with him this morning after receiving his knock back. Right on cue, after Knox poured two big mugs of coffee, in flaunted Isabella. Her hair wet and wearing nothing but one of Knox's t-shirts, one that was well over sized on her, but only falling just past where her arse cheeks met the top of her almost never-ending legs.

"I hope you don't mind, but I didn't want to put my dirty dress back on," Isabella said as she sat at one of the two stools the other side of the kitchen breakfast bar.

"No, not a problem, but we will need to sort you something out, as we can't be taking you home in just my Biffy Clyro T-shirt," Knox said still weighing up what mood Isabella was in and feeling a niggle at seeing her in his T-shirt. This was a sexy look Knox liked and could only envision Dani dressed this way. But in his fantasy, Dani would be in his Led Zeppelin T-shirt. The black would complement her long thick natural blonde hair, but even more so the luscious curves of her behind. Isabella may have a model's body but Knox liked more meat on his women.

He liked the feel of something to hold onto when forcing himself into the comfort of a woman's body, one he could dominate.

"Biff, ro... who?" Isabella looked at Knox as though he was speaking a different language, thankfully bringing him back to the room, away from dangerous fantasies about Dani.

"Never mind, is that the shower I can hear running?" Knox said looking to the bedroom.

"Yes, I left it running for you. I thought after being up all night you would want to freshen up," Isabella said before sipping at her coffee.

"I could cook us some breakfast while you shower." Isabella looked coy as she took a second sip.

"You cook?" Knox asked unable to keep the shock from his voice as he headed to the bedroom.

"Yes, my mother taught me," Isabella called out to Knox as he disappeared into the shower room and Isabella walked around to the kitchen.

As Knox finished up in the shower he heard the loud buzz of the intercom panel. Someone was at the entrance to the building.

. . .

"Leave the door, Isabella, I will see to it, just got too dry off," Knox said as he rushed to cover himself with a towel and not slip over on the wet floor. Meanwhile, Isabella was looking at the small black and white screen on the intercom panel. Seeing a woman stood waiting, Isabella buzzed her in and both women walked over to their respective sides of the apartment's front door.

"Isabella, wait!" Knox shouted as he made his way to the door in just a towel, but he was too late. Isabella had already opened the door to none other than Dani.

His Dani...

10

DANI

"Dani! What... when did you...?" Knox said shocked to his core to see the object of his desires, his sexy blonde cyber guru artist stood at his door.

Dani stood speechless at first as she looked Knox up and down, covered with just a towel around his waist. The hard lines of his body were gently being licked by the beads of water from his shower and Dani's mouth went dry. However, that sexy sight alone wasn't enough to drown out the sight of Isabella draping herself over Knox's shoulder. She pretended to hide behind him coyly, as the T-shirt she was wearing lifted just enough for Dani to see her bare ass cheeks.

"Well, I was here to make sure you were okay, and I can see you are, so I won't keep you from your... *job,*" Dani said waving her finger at Isabella with an obvious look of disgust. Knox frowned at Dani, seeing something different in her...she was hurt, that was clear, but the way she looked at Isabella was nothing short of loathing and then it hit him, *she was jealous*.

Dani felt like screaming at Knox, but at the same time desperately trying not to show how devastated she felt. She had been so worried about him when she had seen the hotel explosion on the news, that she hadn't even thought about it. She just booked the next flight out to Spain, and all for what, to find him screwing his *work!* She had tried so hard to keep Knox as what she had convinced herself he was, just a client, but what she saw in front of her hurt her enough to know that he was a lot more than that. The hurt that she felt deep in her guts told her that much.

"Darling, you didn't say you were expecting visitors. I thought you wanted to run everything by each other." Isabella said smirking as she looked Dani in the eyes before she pulled a little pout. Then she ran a finger down Knox's chest and Dani had never wanted to break someone's finger so much in all her life.

"Right, I won't keep you." Dani turned on her heels and headed down the hallway. Knox grabbed Isabella's wrist and with every ounce of control he had, refrained from doing something violent to her.

"Get your arse back inside, *now!*" He told Isabella, surprised he had managed to keep his tone from murderous. Then he turned from her and tightening his towel around his waist and made after Dani.

"Dani...! Wait," Knox called.

"Lucas, how dare…" Knox stopped, turned back to Isabella and saw her stood there with a cocked hip as if she had the right to issue orders to him. So, he stormed back towards her.

"You! Stay in the apartment!" he growled as he pushed her back behind the door and shut it. Isabella let out a huffy squeal. One he didn't give a shit about. He had more important things to deal with than the childish games of some disgruntled bitch who didn't like feeling second best. In reality, he wouldn't have touched her even if she had daddy dearest pay him too!

"Dani hold up, hold up," Knox said as he rushed up to her taking hold of her hand. Dani stopped dead in her tracks at the feel of Knox's warm hand taking hold of hers and she hated how much his touch affected her.

"Don't Lucas, it's fine. Look, I just want to go… it's none of my business," Dani said not turning around but instead looking to the floor, the door, the walls anywhere other than turning to face the man. A man that without hesitation she came running at the thought that he was hurt…or worse, *dead.*

"Dani, please. It's not what it looks like," Knox said with a soft warm tone Dani had never heard before. After that, Dani couldn't help but turn to face him. With a scowl that would put fear into even the largest of rugby prop forwards, Dani's anger boiled over.

"Don't give me that bullshit line Lucas, I'm not some love-sick teenager, how do you think it looks?" Dani pulled her hand away as she lied through her teeth. She stood back putting the same hand on her hip, she looked Knox up and down and loathed how she had fantasised about his body. Now in the flesh that fantasy was put to shame. Jesus, but she couldn't even count the number of muscles on the man's torso! And once again she found herself wanting to lick the beads of water still running down him, which were fast being merged with beads of sweat.

"I was just taking a shower, she wasn't meant to open the door. We were…" Knox said calmly as Dani interrupted him.

"Getting cleaned up…yeah, I get it! Listen what you get up to is your own affair, I don't have anything over you for Christ sake…! To think I was goddamn worried about you!" Dani said in annoyance as she turned away. Knox took hold of her hand again and placed his other on her shoulder. Touching her skin almost felt electric. If only she knew how wrong she was. She had a massive hold over him, one like no other, Knox thought bitterly, knowing that he couldn't just make her his. He could tell her right now how he felt about her, this could be his one and only chance, but he knew that was a dangerous line he would be crossing...for both of them.

"Worried about me... why... that's why you are here?" Knox questioned, the words just coming out of his mouth. The wrong words, he knew as he mentally kicked himself for not saying what he really wanted to. In fact, it was probably a good thing that Isabella was in his apartment right now. Knox didn't think he had it in him if given the opportunity, to hold back in doing what he really wanted to. Which, looking at the blonde beauty in front of him, was to put a shoulder to her waist, hoist her up and carry her back to his bed where he could spank the anger right out of her. Then he would make her his in a way she would have no doubt about his feelings towards her.

"The bomb! Been too busy with trout lips to see the news? The hotel in Granada, Lucas?" Dani erupted and Knox had the beginnings of a smile building on his face he was trying so hard to hold back. Seeing this side of her was bringing things out in him that he couldn't control.

"What are you smirking at?" Dani said before she paused and Knox couldn't help it as his smile broke free. Between Dani calling Isabella trout lips, and how cute she looked all angry and feisty, Knox just wanted to grab hold of her and shut her up by force, his lips to hers.

"When I saw the news and after trying to get in touch with you, I hacked the hospital records and found details of patients that matched you and your rich tart, listed as casualties. And by the time I arrived that status had changed to fatalities!" Dani said, which Knox barely heard, as his focus was drifting away, but soon got pulled right back into the firing line.

"Knox, are you even listening to me?!" Dani said, her nerves being tested.

"Details of me and her as fatalities?" Knox looked on with

confusion before it hit him, T.I.7 had set it up so whoever was after Isabella would think she and Knox were now dead.

"Yes, why else would I have caught the first flight out here? Spent six hours travelling and booked into the shittiest hotel in town," Dani said punching Knox in the shoulder.

"Shitty hotel?" Knox questioned.

"Yes Lucas, it's the only one with rooms because it's August and everyone and their mother are on holiday here!" Dani said exasperatedly.

"Where are you saying? It is not safe for you to be here." Knox became concerned as his tone and manner changed instantly. There was no way he was having Dani staying in some dive hotel in a bad area of town, not when he could do something about it.

"Sure, it's not more like I am cramping your style and fun? You don't need to worry about where I am staying," Dani snapped back.

"Tell me now where you are staying, I am not going to ask you again," Knox said in a strong yet unaggressive way without raising his voice but commanding obedience. Dani instantly stood up a little straighter and without even a question or thought she blurted out.

"I am staying at the La Casa de Enfrente," Dani said, unsure as to why she gave in so easily.

"No. That is no good as you won't be safe there," Knox stated slipping easily into a more comfortable dominating presence a sub like Dani would instantly recognise. He knew this when she started to say,

"But I..." He cut her off with a look and said,

"It's not secure enough for you. Have you checked in yet?" Knox asked in a serious manner but with genuine concern for Dani's safety.

"No, I haven't yet, I was going to do so once I had been by

here. I needed to check on you first but I wasn't expecting to find what I did," Dani's voice softened with a touch of sadness.

"Come into the apartment and let me get dressed. I can explain and put things in a clearer light." Dani turned away but Knox wouldn't allow this for long. He reached out, gripping her chin gently so that he could pull her gaze back to his. Then he leant in closer and waited until he knew that he had her full attention before he spoke again.

"Nothing...I repeat, *nothing*, is going on between her and me. It's not what you think Dani." Then Knox took hold of both Dani's hands with a firm but tender grip. He looked directly into Dani's striking sapphire blue eyes so that she could see the truth in his. Knox couldn't help but pause and lose track of all thoughts as her hypnotic gaze took a hold of him.

"Lucas...I shouldn't have come," Dani said with a sudden nervousness coming over her, tearing her eyes from his as she couldn't look at him any longer. It was too dangerous, as she was falling quicker being here with him like this and falling quicker only meant one thing...falling harder when he broke her heart. And he would, as she knew a man like Knox could never be satisfied with someone like her. What could she offer him but the next job? Some lonely cyber geek practically married to her computer. Not exactly the glamorous and exciting piece of ass he had waiting for him in his apartment, no matter how much Dani thought of her as a skank. In a man's eyes, it didn't make her so.

"I am glad you did, it's good to see you," Knox said and he lifted her head up as he hadn't finished admiring her gaze.

"Lucas... I..." Dani spoke before she was interrupted.

"I don't want you staying at the place you have booked. Give me ten minutes and I will have a room for you at the Gran Hotel Miramar. I insist," Knox said with a smile and then she went and did it, she sucked Knox in by returning his smile with her own heart-warming one. Hiding the inner turmoil his concern over her was causing.

"So, I am a little parched, are you going to invite me in?" Dani said with a touch of that trade mark cheekiness she had in their phone calls.

"Yes, please come in. And Dani, Isabella is an acquired taste. One even I haven't developed yet...and I have been forced to be in her company for far longer than you," Knox said as he nudged Dani a little.

"Well, I can't say she made the best of first impressions. You in the towel, however..." Dani tried hard to hold back a giggle as she tugged the wet white cotton.

"Come on my wee doll, let's get you that cuppa. All that travel and crappy flight food, you must be gasping," Knox said as he was about to knock on the door, one he had no key for, for obvious reasons. The door swung open with Isabella standing with an unimpressed look on her face.

"What do you mean I am an acquired taste, one you haven't developed?" Isabella said as her trade mark scowl upped a notch.

"You, go get out of my T-shirt and put your dress on. I don't appreciate the shit you just pulled," Knox snapped as he walked past Isabella with Dani in tow, who gave Isabella an awkward smile followed by a 'whoops' look.

"What, can't your friend take a joke? Who is she anyway?" Isabella's bratty response fell on deaf ears.

After getting dressed and brief introductions, Knox made Dani and the pouting Isabella, who sat with a face like a slapped arse, drinks. Knox brought Dani up to speed with the events in Granada after he had made a call, sorting out a penthouse suite at the Gran Hotel Miramar...Hell, he had the money, money he was more than happy to spend on Dani.

"I think it's time you got me home, Lucas." Isabella piped

up as she had been listening to Knox and Dani talk and hadn't been able to get a word in.

"About that, a bit of a change of plan," Knox said a little annoyed at Isabella cutting into his and Dani's conversation.

"Change of plan? No, I need fresh clothes and I have my personal trainer coming today." Knox and Dani gave each other a look.

"Don't be alarmed okay, but after the bombing at the hotel…" Knox said bracing himself for the bratty aftermath but was cut short.

"Yes, yes I know I need to be more careful. I will, I have you to look after me and I will do as I am told," Isabella said as she gave a fake smile to Dani. A smile Dani rolled her eyes at.

"If I could finish…" Knox said as he stared out Isabella, who tried to stare back but masked turning shy at Knox's gaze, by huffing and motioning him to speak as she looked away.

"The news has jumped all over it, and there are reports that you have died in the blast." Knox looked at Dani and mouthed 'wait for it'.

"I have what! No, no, no. I need to let people know I am alright and I am not dead! Malcolm, Daddy, and…" Isabella stood up dramatically as she said this, but then oddly stopped herself as she was about to name a third person. She fell quiet and sat down.

"Okay, listen, Isabella, it's not such a terrible thing now. The people that are out to get you will no longer be after you, which buys us a bit of breathing time," Knox said as he walked over to Isabella and then looked to Dani as if to say he wasn't quite expecting Isabella's reaction.

"I need to call my father and Malcolm, I need to let them know I am okay at least," Isabella said quietly in a subdued way.

"No!" Knox barked, to which Isabella and Dani jumped.

"Sorry... look I know it's hard to understand right now and yes, they will be worried and distraught, but until we can rule out there being a mole around them, you will only be putting yourself back in danger again," Knox said as he placed a hand on Isabella's shoulder.

At the sight of Knox's hand touching some other woman, Dani had to look away. She told herself to get a grip, confused at the strength of her emotions being in Knox's company. Up until now, he had just dominated her thoughts, ones that could easily be forgiven for deceiving her. Hell, it wasn't like they had spent much time in each other's company. Just enough for Dani to discover how handsome Knox was in that perfectly rugged way and how the sound of his accent could do strange things to her aching body. But now, well that was a different thing altogether.

"A mole? You think there is a traitor?" Isabella dramatically alleged as if the possibility of it was impossible.

"How else do they know your movements, where you are and the perfect time to strike?" Knox looked Isabella in the eyes as he raised his eyebrows as if to say wake up.

"Bastardos!" Isabella whispered through gritted teeth.

"Bastards they maybe, but effective and good at their job they are," Knox said as he walked back over to Dani.

"I have been thinking about it most of the night, and I have an idea," Knox said as he winked at Dani.

"You do... who... Who do you suspect, tell me?" Bratty Isabella was back.

"Soon enough, but first we have to lay a trap." Knox grinned and Dani knew it was a dangerous sign. Just looking at the way his biceps stretched out the material around them, she knew that when he put his training into gear, he could be lethal without even giving it much thought. It was like tapping into a different side of him, one she didn't ever want to witness in real life.

"Now that sounds interesting," Dani said as she leant in and reacted as though she wasn't afraid that he could get hurt, but trusted him enough to take care of himself above all else. Okay, so she knew that this wasn't exactly true as he was clearly the type of man who wouldn't think twice about putting himself in front of a bullet if it meant saving someone else. But Dani had to have faith that he would come out of all this in one piece. After all, he had lasted this long on his own.

"How are we to set a trap?" Isabella asked, as she too leant forward, excited at the idea.

"I need to work out the details and logistics of it. I have some 'friends' that can help with that, but I will need to leave to see them first," Knox said as he pondered their next course of action. Dani gave him a look as if to say she knew exactly what 'Friends' he was referring to.

"Maybe I could go and get anything you may need?" Dani said looking over to Isabella as it was obvious that she needed clothes, underwired bra being top of the list, Dani thought to herself. Knox looked to Dani and his first feeling was no, he didn't want to let her out of his sight.

"Not so sure that's a…" Knox began to say before Dani jumped back in.

"Let's face it, Lucas, she can't be going around in just a dirty dress or one of your T-shirts. And I can't lend her skinny ass anything of mine." Dani looked at Knox with a come on now look, as she ran her hands down her hourglass figure, emphasising her curvy hips. Hips Knox wanted to grab hold of as he did unspeakable things to her. Being bound to his bed with hemp rope being top of his list.

"I will go check in, then head out and pick her up some

things," Dani offered. Knox begrudgingly agreed with a nod. Isabella's ears pricked up at the thought of shopping.

"Shopping, I am up for that," Isabella said not engaging her brain or a thought for the real situation.

"How about we put a big bullseye on your back while you are at it?" Knox said questioning whether Isabella had any common sense. Dani giggled, to which Isabella took offence but kept quiet realising how stupid she must have sounded.

"Right I will get going, I will message you when I am on my way," Dani said putting her coffee down as she headed to the door. Knox came over and put his hand on the small of her back.

"Promise me you will be careful," he said leaning closer to her ear and not wanting the brat to come in between their moment.

"Knox, I am always…" he stopped her right there and gave her arm a warning squeeze without even being aware of his actions. He didn't know what was wrong with him, as being around her just brought this darker side out in him.

"You're not leaving until you say the words, Dani," he told her firmly. She swallowed hard and wished they were alone. She couldn't help but wonder what he would do to her if she refused him. But instead, she gave him what he wanted, feeling a different type of thrill knowing that she had pleased him.

"I promise you I will be careful, Lucas." She said his name and he tried hard to quench down the sexual thrust at hearing that breathy voice speak his name in such a way. Now if he could only hear it again and again whilst playing with her body the way he knew would help in feeding his addiction.

"Good girl," he whispered getting closer and when he heard her breathing hitch, he knew it had affected her. Then he let go of her arm before it got to a point of forgetting all about

Isabella's presence so he could spin her around and take her mouth the way he wanted...in a punishing kiss.

"Thank you, Dani, as always you are a life saver." Knox smiled, slipping easily back into his easy-going nature and Dani paused as if his voice had evoked a memory.

"Happy to help, you know me. Plus, I am glad to see you're all in one piece," Dani said as she looked him up and down one last time and imagined him being back in just a towel. Her look said it all and Knox raised an eyebrow at her but instead of mentioning her carnal thoughts aloud for him to hear, she reached for the door latch. Knox beat her to it, her hand grabbed his. Dani's nervous laugh was a sound Knox wasn't expecting to find as a huge turn on, but coming from Dani, he wasn't surprised. She could probably pour him a cup of coffee and he would have found it sexy. Knox opened the door and Dani said bye as she slipped out. Knox watched her walk away hating the sight but loving her curves.

"So, she is the woman," Isabella said as Knox shut the door and walked back in.

"Quiet Isabella, you don't know what you're talking about." Knox sat down pulling out his smartphone.

"I know what I can see and you two have it bad for each other," Isabella smirked as Knox said nothing.

"She is cute if you like that sort of thing." Isabella pushed.

"And what sort of thing is that?" Knox couldn't help but bite.

"Old, and likes her food," Isabella spitefully mocked as she got up and left for the bathroom.

"Got under your skin has she?" Knox smirked as he knew full well that Dani, being only a few years younger than himself, was way too much woman for Isabella to compete with. Dani was everything Isabella wasn't. She had a natural effortless beauty. She looked as good in high heels and a dress as she did in jeans, vest top and flip flops. But the most exciting part of Dani, which Isabella could never match up to, was her intelligence. Now that had Isabella knocked out on the deck before even stepping foot in the ring.

Knox called T.I.7 and Isabella tried to speak. Knox simply held up his finger for her to be quiet and didn't even bother to look at the expression of outrage Isabella was sure to be pulling.

"Captain Lucas, we have been expecting your call. Please hold, transferring you now," said the same clinical cold voice that had answered before in Granada.

"Knox, we need you to get your arse in and on the double," Carter barked.

"Maybe a bit tricky Sir, I have company to keep safe," Knox replied.

"She is low priority Knox, plus everyone thinks she's dead. Leave her at your apartment. We have it under surveillance." Carter said brashly as always.

"Yes Sir, but…" Knox said but Carter cut him off.

"See you at the NEST in one hour, Captain," Carter said straight out before hanging up.

"Who are you calling Sir… and why did I have to get rid of my phone but you got to keep yours?" The irritating Isabella nipped at Knox's ear again.

"Put your shoes on, it's time to go…" Knox said as he tapped the phone in his hand as he thought.

"Go…go where?" Isabella looked confused.

"Gran Hotel Miramar…"

11

DRIVE TWO

Outside the Gran Hotel Miramar, a white and blue Malaga city taxi pulled up. It was opened by the waiting doorman dressed in a full morning suit. Knox slipped the poor man ten euros, in this heat to be dressed like that all day, he sure as Hell wasn't getting paid enough. Isabella followed Knox out on his side as he had instructed her to do. Knox helped Isabella out of the car as he tried to help keep her modesty, with such a short dress it wasn't easy.

They had slipped out the service entrance in the basement of his apartment block, much to Isabella's disdain and complaint. Knox hadn't wanted to be spotted leaving with Isabella by the surveillance van of T.I.7, or be tracked, so he left the smart phone and all his gadgets at the apartment. There was no reason, let alone evidence, to believe that Knox couldn't trust his new team, but still, he didn't. Better to play it safe, after all, there was only one person he could trust… *his Dani*.

Knox didn't know why he kept referring to her as his... well scrap that, yes, he did know why. Because not only did he want to make that statement concrete, but the thought of her belonging to anyone else made his blood boil and the veins on his neck bulge. In fact, just thinking about it now had him grind his teeth, something Isabella misplaced as concern for her safety no doubt.

Knox knocked at Dani's door. The hotel only had two penthouse suites and the other, on the Seaview side of the building, Knox knew was permanently occupied by actor Antonio Banderas, a Malaga born local hero. Dani opened her door and it was her turn to look shocked at the figure stood in her doorway.

Knox as usual and out of habit took note of every curve before walking in followed by Isabella, who was wearing Knox's suit jacket.

"Well, just come on in make yourself at home," Dani said exuding sarcasm, as she frowned when she saw Isabella in Knox's jacket. Knox spotted the frown right away.

"I didn't want her being recognised and well, she did buy the suit anyway," Knox quickly said.

"And you walking around with two guns in a holsters blends right in? I have never seen a shirt let alone a suit bought on your credit card statements, so I assumed as much," Dani said as she shut the door. Isabella looked at her in confusion as to why anyone would look over credit card statements, let alone ones that weren't their own.

"Been keeping tabs on me, have you, Dani?" Knox said as he smiled, secretly loving the idea that his little cyber geek was using her skills to watch over him. He then looked around the room as he always did when entering somewhere new. Checking layouts, exit points and potential dangers as standard.

"Someone has to Lucas, who knows where you would end up left to your own devices," Dani said taking her phone out of Isabella's hand which she had rudely picked up.

"Speaking of which, wasn't I meeting you back at your apartment?" Dani rightfully asked as she put her phone on a side table.

"Change of plan…" Knox said taking a moment to word things right.

"You don't say. I would never have guessed." Dani's tone pointing out the obvious seeing as they were both now in her hotel room.

"Dani, you are the only one I can trust…" Knox started to say.

"Oh, no don't pull that line on me Mr, I am not doing your

babysitting," Dani said jumping in, knowing full well what Knox was going to ask next.

"I know she's a pain in the arse but…" Knox said half laughing.

"I am in the room!" protested Isabella.

"Shush, Dani if there was any other option that was safe I promise you I would have taken it," Knox said as he picked up his suit jacket off the back of the chair that Isabella had dumped it on.

"How long are you going to be?" Dani asked, again giving in to Knox's wishes and he couldn't say how pleased it made him, having her obey in a way she didn't even realise. Knox walked right up to her and grabbed both her arms as the strength of her actions nearly overwhelmed him.

"Thank you just doesn't seem enough but I will say it anyway, thank you, Dani." Dani looked up at him and gave him a look that nearly had Knox doing something stupid…like kissing her.

"I guess my debt is really racking up," Knox said instead, winking at her and then heading to the door.

"Too bloody right it's racking up, that dinner better be la carte!" Dani shouted as Knox left the room shutting the door behind him.

. . .

"Lucas took me to a lovely hotel, well that was until it blew up," Isabella said now lay on the bed flicking through TV channels, eating a packet of nuts out of the mini bar. Dani held her hands out behind Isabella's back ready to strangle her.

Pulling into the warehouse of T.I.7 in the Jaguar, Knox was greeted by Major Harris who had a look on his face that said one thing... 'what have you been up to?'. Knox had taken a taxi back to his apartment, picked up his things and changed out of the suit before leaving in the Jag. The two guys in the surveillance van were certainly confused when they saw Knox arrive considering they hadn't seen him leave.

"As promised Sir, not a scratch," Knox said as he tossed the famous logoed fob into Harris' hands.

"You just gained my trust there Knox, good man. Right the team is assembled ready for a briefing, ready for some action," Harris said as he walked with Knox from the garage area into the NEST.

"Action?" Knox said quietly to himself.

"Glad you could finally join us, Captain. All the ladies keeping you busy?" Carter addressed Knox as soon as he entered the meeting area.

The rest of the team nodded at Knox acknowledging him, other than Ellis. She had a face like a bulldog chewing a wasp.

"Tough job Sir, but I was up to the task. The Major tells me we have some action ahead, have we fresh intel?" Knox asked, thinking best to defect with a joke and move on to what he thought they were all here for.

"Thanks to Captain Knox sending us intel through on Malcolm Howard, Gregory and Thomas tailed him to a meeting with a drug cartel boss," Carter said as he clicked through text messages and photos on the display board. Gregory and Thomas stood looking pleased with themselves. Knox gave them the thumbs up which at first, they weren't sure how to take, before looking even more pleased with themselves. Wow, thumbs up was all it took to make them forget he kicked both their arses, Knox thought with a smirk.

"From that meeting, they obtained audio recording that a container loaded on a waggon is coming down from Madrid and will be heading to Malaga port," Carter explained before playing the audio recording to the team.

"This, we believe, is the perfect opportunity to gain some major evidence on Howard." Carter carried on after the audio had finished.

"Do we know what the container is hauling, Sir?" Knox asked.

. . .

"No, most likely it will be hard cash from drug sales," Carter said as he looked around the room.

"Captain Ellis will lead the team to take control of the container on route. Knox, you will join Ellis and her team," Carter said before turning his back as an operative came in with a printout for his attention.

"Sir, with respect. My team is tight and works well together. Do we really need an extra man on this?" Ellis piped up, taking a momentary break from chewing the wasp.

"I don't see the problem Captain Ellis, am I missing something?" Carter turned to look at Ellis with a raised eyebrow.

"Sir, a private word if I may?" Ellis replied.

"No, Captain if you have an issue, spit it out." Carter turned to Ellis, annoyed that she wanted to question his order to assign Knox to the tactical operation.

"I don't trust him, myself and my team haven't operated with him before. I don't want to be carrying dead weight, Sir," Ellis said straight to the point.

. . .

"Captain Knox is one of the finest soldiers you will ever have the pleasure to serve with. His record speaks for itself. There is no issue so I suggest you get on with the job at hand," Carter said in a way that showed he wasn't interested in hearing any more on the matter.

"Yes, Sir." Ellis barked before walking away. Carter nodded at Knox to let him know he had his back, trusting him until Knox gave him any other reason not to. Then he turned to look back over the paperwork that came in for him.

Knox left the briefing room and headed to kit up with the rest of the team, only to find Ellis waiting for him.

"Knox, a word," Ellis called quietly, Knox walked over.

"Sure thing Lass, I'm all ears," Knox said with a cocky smile.

"You may have Carter in your pocket, but if you put me or my team in any danger I will put you down and I won't give it a second thought. Am I making myself clear?" Ellis said getting right up in Knox's face.

"I don't have a problem with my hearing, Ellis," Knox replied and started to walk off. But his arm was grabbed back by an irate Ellis. Knox paused and looked at her hand gripping his arm. Mentally counting to ten Knox turned his head back to her.

"I don't know what your issue is Lass but if I were you I would let go of my arm. We fucked, you snared me, well done to you, so just forget about it, I have." Knox looked Ellis in the eye as his voice dropped to a deep whisper.

"What's the holdup… why are you two not kitting up?" The calm voice of Harris sounded from behind them.

"Captain Ellis is just welcoming me onto her team, Sir. No issue at all" replied Knox not taking his eyes of Ellis.

"Is that right, Captain Ellis?" Harris questioned, Ellis took a few seconds before she answered.

"Yeah, that's right, just wishing him luck," Ellis said through almost gritted teeth.

"Yeah, what Captain?" Barked Harris, as he raised his normally calm voice.

"Sorry Sir, I mean yes Sir…" Ellis replied bitterly.

. . .

"Go get kitted up the both of you." Harris wasn't in the mood for any shit.

Knox had lost count of how many times he had checked that his kit was fit for purpose and was more than ready to roll, like Ellis, Gregory and Thomas were. They all stood around the Defenders in the garage area of the warehouse, Carter and Harris walked in with purpose.

"Listen up, target is on the move. GPS coordinates have been sent to your comms devices." As Carter yelled the last part, everyone's forearm beeped on mass as the communication device everyone was kitted out with flashed up.

"Ellis, Gregory you are in Drive One, Knox, Thomas you are in Drive Two. Load up and roll. Major Harris will provide backup and assistance if needed in Drive Three. Good luck soldiers and come home safe," Carter said rallying everyone into action as they got into their respective vehicles.

"Hey mate, no hard feelings about the cheap shots in the van, yeah?" Thomas said to Knox as he fired up the V8 Defender's engine.

"No problem pal, never happened," Knox said over the burble of the custom stainless-steel rich sounding exhaust's note.

Harris: *Drive One take the lead, Drive Two follow.*
   Ellis: *Copy.*

. . .

Harris' instruction and Ellis' confirmation sounded over Knox's intercom swiftly followed by Thomas' as they all pulled away at speed in convoy.

Thomas: *Copy.*

"So, Knox you and Captain Ellis," Thomas said with a cheeky grin.

"Honestly Thomas, are you seriously going there?" Knox laughed shaking his head.

"Oh, come on mate, you have got to give me some details," Thomas said as he kept looking over.

"Details on what, pal?" Knox acted innocent.

"Come on you banged her right, you know details," Thomas bold as brass and straight to the point.

"I have been dreaming of that woman ever since I clapped eyes on her... what I wouldn't..." Thomas said in a tone that was way too excited but then was cut off by the sound of the intercom.

Harris: *Drive Two.*

"That's us mate," Thomas said slapping Knox on the arm nodding his head for Knox to answer.

Knox: *Drive Two received over*.

Harris: *Remind Thomas this is an open system. Fifteen minutes to target over*.

"Fuck, fuck it... fuck! Do you think she heard?" Thomas said to Knox holding one hand over his comms mic.

"There is a slim chance she didn't if that helps." Knox slapped Thomas' arm as he cracked up.

"She will have my balls," Thomas said as he grabbed his balls and looked at Knox, then they both burst out laughing.

"Enjoy it pal, it may be the only time she touches them." Knox couldn't help but feel sorry for the poor bastard. Ellis was going to kill him.

"So, Thomas, where did they recruit you from?" asked Knox.

"I was selected for SBS and going through the training when I got called in to meet the Brig, and the rest was history. I never joined SBS and started in T.I.7 a week later," Thomas said with a cheerfulness you couldn't help but like.

"Boss said you were working freelance, what made you jack it in for this?" Thomas said to Knox and he thought about his answer for a moment.

"A friend. I need to know if he is still out there, that or nail the bastard that killed him," Knox said turning more serious.

Harris: *Drive one and Drive Two target in sight. Engage.*

Knox turned to Thomas, cocked his assault rifle, and said,

"Here we go."

12

JUGGERNAUT

Holding steady at the 57mph limited speed of the heavy goods vehicles, Knox and Thomas in the T.I.7 kitted out Land Rover Defender, watched the container truck from fifty or so metres back as they travelled downhill on the dual track A-44. The second T.I.7 Defender alongside them.

Ellis: *Drive One, engaging.*

The second Defender with Ellis and Gregory accelerated past Knox and Thomas just as the road declined that bit steeper. The bright red brake lights flashed up in front of them, the truck attempted to control its speed as the forty-five-ton thunder rolling mass of metal fought against gravity, where the canyon road led onto the first six-hundred-metre-long bridge that stood high, passing over the emerald green water in the reservoir below. Drive One was now alongside the truck, level with the trailer but still accelerating hard.

Knox and Thomas itched to get in the action, both sat leant forward in their seats. Knox's hand held himself up on the dashboard, and if Thomas leant any more forward on the steering wheel his nose would be pressed against the windscreen. Drive One held level now at the tractor unit of the big rig. His window wound down and Gregory's arm was out. He waved at the driver to get his attention before motioning to slow and pull over.

"That's their plan, to ask the driver to pull over?" Knox said to Thomas who looked back at him with an 'I can't see the problem' face as he shrugged his shoulders. Knox just shook his head.

"What?" Thomas questioned.

"You think they're just going to….?" Knox said but stopped at the sound of gun fire.

Drive One swung out to the left, shattered glass from the rear passenger window rained down on the road surface. Ping, chink, tap rapidly repeated over and over as the tiny glass pieces rolled up into the Defender's wheel arches like stones on a gravel road. A second shot rang out and what looked like a sawn-off shot gun fired out of the driver's cab of the now snaking rig.

Ellis: *Taking fire, repeat taking fire. Permission to return.*

Harris: Granted *return fire. Drive Two give support if needed.*

Ellis: *Negative, no support needed.*

"Fuck sake, come on," Knox shouted.

Gregory fired short repeated bursts at the driver's cab. The truck veered hard to the left almost clipping Drive One, before swinging back right. More shots were fired from the truck.

Knox: *Drive One, Drive Two ready to assist.*

Ellis: *Negative Drive Two. Hold back. Drive One pulling forward prepare for a road block.*

"God Damn it Ellis, road block?!" Knox yelled in frustration.

Drive One's shot riddled Defender punched passed the juggernaut with all its available horse power put to full use. The back door swung open on the Land Rover as it pulled in front of the truck's grill. Gregory opened fire on the cab of the truck.

"Jesus Christ, Ellis! Thomas get us closer to the truck," Knox screamed.

"But the Cap hasn't given us the green light," Thomas said as he held his distance.

"If she keeps this mental shit up, her lights will be out permanently. Now get us closer!" Knox said as he tapped on the dash telling Thomas to get a move on. Knox unbuckled his seat belt.

"Okay, what do you want me to do and why are you taking off your belt?" Thomas said as he thought fuck it! Knox outranked him anyway.

"You just get me closer to that truck." Knox wound down his window.

Knox: *Drive One, Drive Three, Drive Two engaging target.*

Ellis: *Negative Drive Two, Drive Two hold back await orders.*

Left then right, the back end of waggon snaked repeatedly across the two lanes. But this wasn't just evasive driving like before, to stop anyone passing, the driver must have been injured in the shooting or more of a problem *dead*. Just what everyone needed was an out of control forty-six tonnes rolling downhill.

Ellis in Drive One had made good distance between them and the seemingly speeding up mass of rolling metal battering ram. Knox knew that at any moment if the driver was fading or dead the trailer could jack-knife or worse go off the road making the metal barriers look as strong as tape on a finish line, sending the rig hundreds of feet down into the deep reservoir below.

Ellis: *Road block in place stand by.*

"What is the crazy bitch doing?" Knox said in utter disbelief.

Knox: *Drive One pull out, pull out. No go on road block.*

Ellis: *Drive Two, Road block in place. Follow orders.*

She is going to get herself and Gregory killed! Thomas get as close as you can to the back end," Knox shouted as he opened his passenger door and started to climb out, hauling himself up by the tubular roof rack.

"Rather you than me mate, and you think Ellis is crazy," Thomas said as he watched Knox make his way to the bonnet on the vehicle steadying himself on the rugged knobbly tyre of the spare wheel that lay flat, fixed to the bonnet. Knox waved for Thomas to speed up and get closer to the tail end. Thomas punched his foot to the floor and dropped a gear just as the trailer swung back from the right to left. Knox was forced back at first but soon righted himself as he leant forward, arm stretched out to grab hold of the container's large metal pole locking system.

As Knox took a grip with only two fingers, the trailer aggressively swung back to the right. Thomas let the trailer pull away a little as he slowed too much in the Defender, Knox was forced to let go as he was almost pulled off.

"Hit it, Thomas! Fucking hit it!" Knox screamed.

"You, mad bastard! Hold on!" Thomas replied.

Harris: *Drive Two what are you doing?*

Ellis and Gregory, five or six hundred metres further up the road, had parked their vehicle across the middle of the carriageway stood in front with their weapons trained on the target. One that was showing no sign of slowing.

Harris: *Drive Two what are you doing? Copy!*

"Knox, I think the Major is getting nervous," Thomas called out to Knox.

"Now Thomas, NOW!" Knox shouted again. Thomas saw

his opening and floored the pedal, the V8 roared. Almost as if it happened in slow motion Knox put one foot on the spare tyre and hauled himself forward and up. Just grabbing hold of the trailer doors, he was just about holding himself up as his feet struggled to find grip. Finally, they found a lip to purchase on, Knox looked back at Thomas with relief and then he started to make his way up the container doors to the roof. Knox knew time wasn't on his side.

Thomas: *Drive three... er... yeah... I don't know. Over.*

As Knox reached the roof and pulled himself up, he crouched down fighting the wind resistance as the truck was rolling downhill at well over 60mph. Knox could see Ellis' ridiculous road block.

Knox: *Ellis, Gregory get the hell out of the way.*
Harris: *Drive One, Drive two, Report.*
Knox: *Drive Three they're going to get themselves killed.*
Ellis: *Drive Three, everything is under control.*

Knox ran forward making his way to the front of the rig. He watched as the rig seemed to steady up and stop weaving. Knox knew it wasn't going to stop for the block, he frantically waved at Ellis and Gregory to get out of its way but it was fast becoming too late. Ellis opened fire, her bullets hitting around Knox, Gregory's all hit on target around the truck driver's cabin.

"What the fuck!" Knox said as he jumped down to the back of the tractor unit to take cover. Seconds later a thunderous crash as metal bent, glass shattered and rubber squealed. Knox braced himself as the jolt almost sent him off the side. Drive One's Defender was rammed aside like it was made of card. Knox could just see the signs of Gregory rolling on the floor as he just made it out of the way.

Gregory: *Drive Three Road block failed.*

Harris: *Drive Two pick up, Gregory and Ellis. Whatever your plan is Knox do it and fast!*

"What did I get myself into?" Knox said exasperated, before taking a second big leap that sent him around to the driver's side door of the tractor unit. The truck driver could be seen in the wing mirror he looked riddled with bullets, but just as Knox was about to open the door the driver looked at Knox in the mirror.

A shotgun barrel appeared out of the driver's window, Knox ducked, jumped and swung on the wing mirror frame, just as the shotgun fired off, leaving Knox with only the sound of a high-pitched ringing in his ears. Pulling his hand gun from its holster Knox fired three shots over his head and into the open window. Pulling on the door handle the door flew open with Knox's weight on the wing-mirror frame. Knox held on for dear life as the driver fell out of the open doorway. If he wasn't dead from Knox's shots when he fell out, he sure was after falling under the left side's nine wheels and forty-six tonne of weight.

The door swung shut as the truck zigzagged, Knox steadied the wheel before crawling through the window. Knox made himself comfortable in the blood-stained bullet drilled seat and carefully put pressure on the air brakes. Knox calmly took control, knowing one wrong move and the back end would jack-knife.

Knox: *Drive Three, Drive Two, I have control of the target.*

Harris: *Excellent job Drive Two. Pull in at the next available layby.*

Thomas in Drive Two pulled up alongside the now slower moving truck and trailer.

"Hell, yeah!" Thomas shouted out of the sunroof at Knox, clenching his fist as he punched the air. Knox smiled as he wiped the sweat from his brow.

"Down to you brother, top driving!" Knox yelled back,

Gregory, looking subdued, was sat next to Thomas and Ellis was nowhere in sight. Sulking in the back seat most likely.

Air hissed with release as the truck pulled into a secluded layby. Knox killed the engine and made his way out down the steps of the truck. Thomas pulled Drive Two Defender up in front.

"That's what I'm talking about!" Thomas said as he got out of the Land Rover first as he cheered, high fived Knox then shook his hand. Gregory got out next and nodded at Knox, walking over and patting him on the shoulder.

"Knox…!" screamed Ellis, who had got out of the rear with her hand gun trained on Knox.

"Ellis, what the fuck!" Thomas shouted as Knox lifted his hands.

"Back off Thomas, and you Gregory!" Ellis pointed the gun to Thomas then Gregory before turning it on Knox.

"Ellis, this is not cool!" spoke Gregory.

"You, fucking hero, Knox!" Ellis snarled.

"You just can't follow orders, can you?" Ellis said with bitterness in every word.

"Orders from a raving lunatic, no I can't. What you thought you were doing I will never know!" Knox said calmly, just as Harris in the Jaguar with lights on full beam pulled up blinding Ellis for a second. Knox jumped at his chance and ran and jumped into Ellis, taking her down. She fired two shots into the air and as they hit the gravel ground hard, Knox's weight winded her as it compressed her with force. She let off a third shot and Knox punched into her side. Thomas leapt onto her gun, pulling it from her grasp. Dragging her arse up, Knox walked her over to the trailer and flung her hard, face first into it. He buried the muzzle of his Sig into the back of her head.

"Knox!" called Harris.

"What the fuck is your game, you crazy Bitch?" Knox

shouted into her ear not giving a damn about the spit from his mouth with it.

"Knox, cool it, Captain!" Harris said calmly, as he too drew his weapon. Harris waved at Thomas and Gregory to stand back.

"Things can get a little emotional in operations, how about we drop the guns and we all talk. Come on, the jobs done," Harris reasoned with Knox.

"Ellis opened fire on me, Sir, then pulled her weapon on me here," Knox called back out at Harris.

"Ask the men, Sir," Knox said as he nodded to Thomas and Gregory.

"Maybe we have our mole." Knox patted down Ellis looking for a phone or anything incriminating.

"Is this true, men?" Harris asked Thomas and Gregory answered without hesitation.

"Sir, yes Sir"

"Fucking get your hands off me Knox, Fuck you." Ellis forced out as hard as she could with her face being pushed into the dusty rust covered container wall.

"Okay, Knox I have you covered. Let Ellis go and back away." Harris calmly ordered Knox. Knox removed all weapons he could see from Ellis and took a moment as he contemplated if he could trust Harris.

"That's an order, Knox," Harris stated and Knox had no choice, he was going to have to. Knox made eye contact with Thomas, he wasn't sure if he had an ally but he seemed ready to help if needed.

"Okay Sir, I'm backing off," Knox called out as he took his gun off Ellis and slowly holstered it, backing away slowly. What happened next, happened in the blink of an eye, Ellis turned, dagger in hand and came at Knox. Bang, bang, bang! Clink, Ching and ring. Shots fired and casings fell to the floor.

Ellis was flung back onto the trailer, three shots into the chest and she was down. Thomas and Gregory ran to her, as she coughed up blood. Knox looked back at Harris as his cold stern look stared at Ellis as he walked over to her still aiming at her.

"Who are you working for, tell me or I will put one in your head and leave you here to rot!" Harris said, emotionless soldier mode kicking in.

"Go fuck yourself…" Ellis said spitting blood as she smirked.

"This is a right goddamn mess, Christ what is going on here?" Knox said as he dusted himself off. He walked over to the Defender and pulled out a water bottle and took a long drink. Harris continued to question Ellis, but she wasn't giving up anything.

"Knox, bring over that Jerry can!" Harris called to over to him and Knox knew where this was going. He unhooked the twenty litre can from the back of the Land Rover's rear frame ladder and walked over to Harris. Knox knew this was going to be messy, hell he had seen it before enough times to know. Harris took off the camo scarf from around his neck and put it over Ellis' face.

"Gregory, Thomas hold her." Harris barked.

"Sir?" Thomas said unsure of what was about to happen.

"You heard me, soldier, do it now," Harris said as he looked to Knox.

"Well, the bitch tried to kill you, right? Get stuck in Captain." Harris held Ellis' head and the scarf in place. Knox took a breath as he hated the smell of petrol, flipping the cap over on the Jerry can, Knox began to pour the fuel over the scarf covering Ellis' face.

Ellis coughed, gagged and wriggled. The sand coloured scarf turned to a pinkish red as the fuel mixed with the blood coming out of Ellis' mouth. More came up as she gulped futilely to get air that wasn't there.

"Talk Ellis and it will stop!" Harris demanded as he signalled to Knox to stop pouring. Harris removed the soaked sodden scarf and Ellis spat and coughed some fuel up, taking in her first gasp of air, even if it was vapour filled.

"Sc...rew...you!" Ellis defiantly spat each word and Harris, not giving up, put the scarf back over her face and Knox poured once more. They pushed it to the very edge of what Ellis could take, the panic for air distracting her from the sting of the fuel getting into her wounds.

"Make it easy on yourself, traitor!" Harris called Ellis for what she was.

"Tell us who are you working for and it will stop," Harris said as he pulled the scarf off again. Ellis took longer to cough up all the fuel, some of it now in her lungs.

"Harris..." Ellis managed to say as a coughing fit took over her.

"What is it Ellis, who... tell me and it stops," Harris said as he leant down to Ellis to hear what she had to say.

"Harris... take your tiny dick and put it in Knox's ass." Ellis mocked and followed it by spitting in Harris' face. Harris stood, wiped the fuel blood mix off his face and drew his gun.

"Last chance Ellis, talk!" Harris said unbelievably calm.

"Never!" Ellis smiled.

"Take cover!" Thomas screamed, as two pickup trucks drove at speed into the layby with men firing off AK 47's in their direction. Thomas pulled Knox with him as he dived under the trailer, bullets missing him by inches. Gregory ran with Harris, just making cover behind the Defender. The pickups circled around for a second pass. Thomas and Knox let off covering fire from under the trailer, Knox took out one of the gunmen firing from the back of the pickup. Harris took out a second, firing off his hand gun.

The second pickup brought heavy fire down on Harris and Gregory's position, turning the Defender into something resembling a colander. Harris got clipped in the shoulder as Gregory called out he was out of ammunition. The pickup was now stationary between Knox's position and Harris, and all their fire was now focused down on Gregory and Harris.

"Thomas, cover me!" Knox said as he got up from his cover picking up the Jerry can, fuel still spilling out. Pulling off a grenade from his belt, he pulled the pin out and ran with the Jerry can over to the pickup. Lifting the clip and wedging the grenade in the handle of the can Knox flung it into the back of the pickup as he carried on running. Thomas lit up the pickup with covering fire.

Boom! The pickup was engulfed in flames like a burning oil rig in the desert. Men covered in burning fuel jumped off the back end and the driver and passenger who threw themselves from the vehicle were shot instantly by Gregory and Knox.

The other pickup sped towards Knox, Thomas spotted it and ran firing shot after shot at the driver, hitting his target and the pickup veered off to one side and crashed. The pickup planted into the rock face that the layby was cut into, sending the gunmen in the rear over the cab head first to their gruesome death. Thomas held a hand out to Knox who took it and pulled himself up. All four men called clear, as they walked around, weapons trained.

"Knox, get down!" Thomas yelled, Knox instinctively dropped to the floor. Thomas fired off four rounds, Knox turned to look in the direction Thomas was firing. Ellis fell to her knees, a blank expression as her life drained away.

Harris: *Drive Three to NEST, Target secure. Request*

medical and back up. Repeat Target secure, medical and back up. NOW!

Harris slumped down as the pain set in. Gregory and Thomas checked over the vehicle wreckages, checking one hundred percent all threats were neutralised. Knox looked over Ellis, closing her eyes with his fingers. He couldn't help but feel shit, yes, she was a mole. He knew she tried to kill him, but they'd had a moment. As fake as it may have turned out, in the end, they still had that moment.

"Thomas, open up the back of that container," Harris ordered, Thomas headed over and broke the seal off the door lock with the butt of his assault rifle. As the doors opened Knox got a feeling.

"Thomas, wait!" Knox called out, but it was too late! Thomas swung open the door as he looked over to Knox, his cheerful face turning to confusion at Knox calling out. Then Knox's guts sank as shots fired and he watched plumes of scarlet mist eject from Thomas as he was riddled with bullets. Falling to the ground Thomas spasmed. The killer jumped from the back of the container, sending rapid fire in Knox's direction. Knox rolled on the ground pulling his firearm and let out every shot in his magazine as he rolled, keeping the gunman in his sight. He tumbled around and around until all Knox could hear was click, click, click.

"Fuck! FUCK!" Knox bellowed into the air, before taking a deep breath as he looked up into the sky. Gregory ran over to his fallen comrade but Knox knew he was gone. Thomas was gone.

"Gregory check that fucking container and kill any fucker in there!" Harris barked in a tone that told Knox he was already bearing the weight of this cluster-fuck of a mission.

"Sir...you have to come and see this," Gregory yelled over to them both. Knox got up and motioned to Harris to stay put.

Knox got to the container and looked at the confused expression on Gregory's face. Opening the door wider on the container and using a flash light next to his now reloaded hand gun, Knox looked inside the unit.

The container was all but empty bar one thing! And it was the last thing that either man ever expected to find.

"What the fuck?!" Gregory said voicing Knox's own sentiments exactly as they both looked at the man sat tied, gagged and lying at the bulkhead. Knox looked harder then it dawned on him as he jumped up and rushed into the container.

"Knox?!" Gregory shouted but Knox took no notice, not now in sight of who he saw in front of him.

His friend and old Delta Force comrade...

Mac.

13

OLD FRIENDS

Back at T.I.7 Knox, Gregory and a patched-up Harris sat looking fatigued and flat. Carter walked into the briefing and everyone stood up in an instant.

"At ease, men," Carter said in a tone Knox was not expecting, calm and mild mannered. Was he not concerned about the 'in Knox's eyes' a total fuck up of a mission, empty trailer, two of his soldier's dead and one of them playing for a different team? On the bright side, one of his team had been found, if not a little worse for wear.

"Harris, I want a full report on my desk by the morning." Carter looked to his Major with a look that said he was not impressed.

"Sir, may I ask, how is McCarthy?" Knox jumped in.

"He will be okay, they had given him a beating and they took off two of his fingers. He is resting up now, he has said he would be up for a full debrief tomorrow," Carter said with a look and tone of relief, as he had resigned himself to the fact Mac was dead.

"They took two of his fingers? Bastards... sorry, Sir." Knox replied sickened at the thought. It was a favourite torture method of the cartel. They would start at the first knuckle and work their way down the finger. The pain of the possible ten cuts to take all your fingers and thumbs was bad enough but the thought of it becoming twenty-eight as they chopped down each knuckle at a time, brutal.

"What Captain McCarthy did say was Malcolm Howard is the major player, doing all the donkey work for his father-in-law, Pérez." Carter looked to Knox as he spoke.

"With the Major injured and considering other events this evening, I am looking to you Knox, to take the lead," Carter spoke in a tone that told Knox he didn't have a choice.

"I will do my best, Sir," Knox said secretly dreading what that may involve.

"We need to pull in Howard and soon, Captain McCarthy picked up that he was being sent to meet up with a container ship coming into Malaga Port," Carter said, and Knox nodded as he thought 'tell us something we don't know'.

"This container ship will have the arms, drugs and cash. We need to pull Howard in when we locate him to gain the intel on which ship it is," Carter said as he turned to the tactical display board. He flicked through lists of container ships reported as sailing in the Med or within two days of the Port of Malaga.

"Sir, if I may, I have another option," Knox said, making Carter and the rest of the room look at him with baited breath.

"Go on Captain, we are all ears." Carter looked at Knox with an inquisitive look.

"What about Howard's computers? He must have information on them that can tie down which ship has the cargo to incriminate the whole Pérez operation? Hack it?" Knox said looking at the room as if to say, 'look at all this tech surveillance you have, how about we use it'.

"Believe it or not Captain it had crossed our minds. We have, in fact, already searched through every computer of his and every staff member of the Pérez company." Carter said as he looked to Knox with sympathy, as he had thought the same.

"The only possibility is Howard has sent a number of emails from a computer on a private network server," Carter said as he showed images and blueprints on the tactical board.

"Is that what I think it is?" Knox asked.

"Yes Captain, the Pérez yacht has a work office that has major computing power, the server room alone could run his whole company." Carter pointed out with a laser pen on the blueprint before pulling the diagrams out to show the impressive mega yacht.

"So why can't we… hack it?" Knox asked again.

"No hard wire, no WiFi and no satellite connection to any network. It's a full off grid setup. It has a sophisticated system that allows selected information to be sent out when a user manually security verifies it." This was all said by Rose as she walked in.

"It is simply one of the most private secure computer systems money can buy," Rose said with excited geek envy.

"Thank you, Miss Rose. So, you see Captain, our only option is bringing Howard in. When we have his location, I want you to bring him in." Carter turned to Knox as he gave him the order.

"Yes, Sir," Knox replied, as he thought to himself maybe this time things could be done his way and fewer people would be killed.

"Right team get some rest, we will be in contact when we have eyes on Howard. Harris, stay behind please," Carter said as he switched the tactical board off and closed the files on his desk. Knox wasn't going to hang around the NEST, not with Harris getting bollocked. Also, Knox for one had to get back to the ladies before they killed each other. And Knox's Triumph hadn't been ridden in a few days, so it was time to take the steel horse out for a ride, one he needed after all the shit. But before he could do that, he had an old friend to see.

"Can I help you, Captain." A quiet almost breathless female voice spoke out in the dimly lit medical unit set up in a tucked away area of the massive warehouse that T.I.7 had taken over. Everything about it reminded Knox of mobile field hospitals, a place in truth he never wanted to have a reason to visit for obvious reasons.

"Hello, Lass. I am looking for my old friend Captain McCarthy. Be a love and point me in his direction," Knox said after looking in the direction of the voice. He found a young medic sat behind a counter out of sight. She was dressed in camo fatigues and a rather tight fitted t-shirt that showed off her assets nicely. Her fatigues shirt was hung on the back of her chair and in this repressive heat who could blame her.

"Sorry Captain, no visitors… Brigadier's orders," she said with a smile and a look that told him that had she found something interesting when looking him up and down.

"Ahh… that's a real shame, you see we go way back and well, the guy saved my life a few times. I think I would cheer the lad up, don't you think. Seeing an old friend and all." Knox leant over on the counter as he looked the young girl in the eyes with a cheeky grin. He didn't know if he was coming across as charming but he gave it a go.

"I'm sorry orders are orders… unless.," the medic coyly said.

"Unless?" Knox asked with a big smile on his face, which the medic reciprocated.

"I could be persuaded to go for a smoke break if you would happen to go see your friend when I am away and you are gone before I come back, who would know?" The medic said with a sweet smile that turned to a cheeky grin.

"And what would persuade you, may I ask?" Knox asked

trying to keep his cool when inside he was thinking shit I hope she's not a bunny boiler. The Medic stood up and stretched purposely showing off her curves, she picked up her smokes before placing a post-it-note in front of Knox.

"Your number," the medic said as she walked around pinching Knox's arse as she walked out. Knox laughed to himself at her ballsiness.

"Improving with the fairer sex I hear, Knox, you old dog, you!" Mac strained out as Knox lifted the heavy canvas sheet at the entrance to the recovery tent.

"Look at you, you look like shit! How did you know it was me anyway?" Knox sat down next to Mac punching his leg, Mac winced a little bit as he smiled.

"I would recognise your skirt-wearing jock voice anywhere," Mac jibed at Knox.

"Listen, lad, if I hadn't told you enough times before..." Knox said but was cut short by Mac.

"Oh hell... like I could forget..." Mac half laughed as Knox now interrupted him.

"We have to wear kilts as our fucking balls are too big for our pants... ay, pal!" Knox said grabbing Mac's face as he pushed it.

"Shit... Knox I don't want to be thinking about your balls," Mac stressed as he pushed the mental image out of his head.

"Sorry, pal didn't mean to get you jealous. That can't be good for your recovery. What's wrong with you anyway, you gone soft, you Yankee pussy?" Knox taunted as he smiled waiting for a reaction.

"Fuck off!" Mac laughed.

The two of them caught up. Knox talked about a few of the paid contracts he did after leaving the regiment and Mac told Knox all about getting recruited into T.I.7 after becoming disillusioned with Delta. Knox knew he was pushing his luck on time so called it quits on their reunion. That or he knew there was a possibility he would get back to Dani and find her currently in the middle of trying to dispose of a dead Isabella in the bathtub.

"As good as it is to catch up pal, there is only so much I can take looking at your ugly mug," Knox said and as he was about to get up, Mac grabbed his wrist.

"Well if you're going to fuck off, can you do me a favour?" Mac whispered to Knox, not that anyone could hear him.

"Ay pal, what do you want?" Knox said as he looked at Mac with a grin, baffled and waiting to hear what banter was coming his way.

"The medic…" Mac said as he nodded his head in her direction.

"What about her?" Knox questioned.

"Are you going to give her your number?" Mac looked serious as he asked.

"Nah… I would break her," Knox scoffed, and Mac pulled Knox closer.

"Oh yeah, got someone at home I reckon, that's what your face is telling me!" Mac may not have seen Knox for a long time but he still remembered how to read him. Knox smiled and it gave him away. If Mac had any uncertainty he didn't anymore.

"Come on Knox, spill. Brunette, Redhead, Blonde…" Mac said watching Knox's face like a hawk. And as soon as he said blonde he saw Knox react.

"Blonde it is, you dirty dog. Serious or is she a fuck buddy?" Mac said as he pushed Knox, getting him back for his piss taking.

"A gentleman never kisses and tells, you know that Mac. Well, no you wouldn't but we can't all have your low morals," Knox cut back at Mac.

"Fuck off Knox, I will have you know my morals have raised." Mac looked at Knox, chin up and proud.

"Oh, right, you don't say," Knox said trying not to crack up at the bullshit he was listening too.

"Yeah, now if they're married I ask them to take the rings off." Mac laughed.

"Oh nice, I take it back… you have definitely hit the giddy heights of morality. You crazy git, I dread to ask if you have been caught yet."

"Knox, you know me. I specialised in evade and capture," Mac said turning serious. Knox couldn't help but chuckle as he shook his head, his sides starting to hurt a little. Mac had a thing for married women. Knox didn't particularly agree with Mac's immoral code, but as a Dom who liked nothing more than to tie his women to his bed and sexually torture them, then really, who was he to call another man's kinks. Besides, he knew that for some soldiers who could never settle down, for obvious reasons, being with married women meant one important fact… *unattachment*.

Personally, Knox didn't know why people just didn't do the sensible thing and meet in a bar for a one-night stand…at least that way, you weren't fucking with anyone's marriage. Of course, this then questioned how many of his own 'one-night stands' had simply taken a ring off for the night? It was a sad fact to face and one of the reasons Knox himself had never married. Because if he couldn't see himself spending the rest of his life with just one woman in his bed, then for him marriage was never on the cards. But if this was the case, then why had Dani's face just appeared in his mind's eye?

"Back to the medic, can you ask her to come in and see me," Mac said straight faced.

"Yeah sure, are you in pain, mate?" Knox looked a little concerned.

"Yeah... yeah, my balls are blue and it's been months. Tell her I need my bed bath!" Mac burst into laughter, as did Knox.

"Right pal, I am off. Good luck with getting that one!" Knox said as he walked out.

"See you around, you old Scottish bastard!" Mac yelled as Knox dropped the canvas sheet.

The young medic was sat waiting, with a look that said she wasn't too impressed that Knox hadn't left his number.

"Sorry Lass but I don't have a phone, I'm a dinosaur," Knox said feeling upbeat from his chat with Mac. The girl sighed and Knox motioned back towards Mac.

"My pal McCarthy did say he was feeling a little unwell," Knox said with deadpan seriousness.

"He did?" The medic asked, who at first wasn't sure if Knox was joking.

"Yeah... he is a bit embarrassed. I said you are a professional and he shouldn't worry. But you know what guys are like, right?" Knox held his hands up and shook his head.

"Yes, relics like you can be a pain to care for." The medic smiled as she stood up.

"Yeah... too true Lass, too true." Knox held his chin as he agreed with her.

"So, Captain what is his problem?" The medic said waiting with arms crossed.

"Well... he has lots of problems but we won't go there. I think you will need to be tactful regarding his current issue." Knox strung it out.

"Spit it out, Captain," the medic said as she was losing her patience.

"He is bleeding," Knox said and winced.

"Badly?" The medic started to walk to Mac, Knox stopped her.

"Yes, Lass... he is bleeding from his anus. The daft git has been hiding it. They really tortured him badly," Knox said and somehow kept a straight face as he acted a little upset, and with that, he patted the medic on the shoulder and walked off with a grin he couldn't stop from slipping out. The medic pulled a face that said 'eww' as she picked up a pair of rubber surgical gloves.

Knox's good mood from catching up with Mac was short lived as we walked past the hospital trolley with Thomas's covered up body lay on it. Knox walked over and stood beside the black body bag and took a moment as he murmured some words as he placed a hand on the body before walking away.

Taking the long scenic route back to the Gran Hotel Miramar, Knox took in the Mediterranean Sea air along the coastal road, air that was still warm even though it was approaching midnight. Knox needed to ride, like sitting and disassembling and reassembling a weapon calmed and relaxed him, so did getting out on the road, the wind in his face, Knox and the machine working as one. This ride, however, didn't work out like that. This time he couldn't empty his mind... Mac, Ellis, Howard and the container ship all of it on fucking replay.

What was Ellis's angle, who was she really working for? Knox couldn't put that one together. Did she know Mac was in the container? One thing Knox knew it was going to be interesting hearing what Mac had to say in the debrief. Knox wasn't going to bring it up with him tonight. Knox knew he may have been a joker, but he was a fully committed soldier and he wouldn't have said anything. This train of thought led Knox onto his other niggle, why did they let Mac live? Why was he in an empty container and more importantly, who was he being sent to?

Knox would have to push his thoughts to the back of his mind for now as he had to deal with what he may find in Dani's penthouse suite. Would it be a bloodbath, Knox smirked at the thought of Dani losing it with Isabella. Then for a second, his face dropped at the real possibility.

"Nah, don't be stupid Knox," he said aloud to himself, as a young Spanish guy on a moped looked over at him. Knox was sat at the first red light of the ride and that was the end of his fun. Knox was now entering Malaga city.

Pulling up just outside the Gran Hotel Miramar on the main road, Knox wanted to have a smoke before he went into the hotel.

The hotel was relatively quiet, as was the city at this time. Knox took off his helmet and pushed the kill switch on the handlebars which cut the engine and the rumbling burble faded away. Knox lit his smoke and as he enjoyed the first deep inhale he admired the architecture of the 1926 building. It looked more like a palace than a hotel. Bathed in bright white lights that only made the white stone seem whiter. It was a hotel of pure Mediterranean elegance and beauty.

Knox took a second to take in the scene now playing out at the main entrance, but his eyes hadn't lied to him. Isabella was making her way out of the hotel. Great just what he needed, Isabella and Dani must have had a cat fight. Just as Knox put his helmet on and was about to start up his bike to head over to 'princess bratty', Isabella stood looking around as if she was waiting for someone. What was she playing at? She hadn't called her private car or worse, Howard, had she? Knox started his bike and dropped his left foot on the gear peg knocking it into first gear.

He checked over his shoulder before pulling off, a life-saving check for all bikers. It was a good job he did as a large SUV shot past him missing him by mere inches. Knox, shocked for a second, put both feet back on the ground to steady himself from the wind force generated by what he could now see was a black, tinted out Range Rover.

Wait! Knox's eyes widened and the penny dropped, it was the same Range Rover from that evening at the beach watching over them. Knox watched on as it swiftly pulled up alongside Isabella. At first, she smiled but as the rear door flung open her smile turned to a worried look. Arms came out at her and dragged her into the vehicle. Before she was fully in, the tyres squealed and its engine redlined as it made a getaway.

Knox followed in *pursuit*...

14

CHASE AND SCRAPE

Knox tailed the black SUV at a safe distance matching its speed. Holding back just far enough so that he wouldn't be noticed, Knox looked on as the Range Rover became erratic, sharp short swerves followed by hard braking. Knox couldn't see into the windows due to the tints, but something was going on inside... could Isabella be fighting back?

They ran a red light, the rear end of the hundred thousand plus euro Range Rover, narrowly missed a night bus. Knox filtered, passed the queue of traffic that had pulled to a stop at the lights. A taxi driver, incensed at what he had just seen, hung his head out of his window, shouting a string of obscenities in Spanish at the reckless driving he had just witnessed. He looked to Knox for confirmation he was right to be pissed off. Knox nodded and as soon as the bus was clear and he saw his gap, Knox launched away, front wheel lifting as he shot through the flow of traffic, giving the other driver more fuel to add to his rage.

. . .

"Loco, loco" the taxi driver yelled.

The rev counter's needle touched the red and Knox upped a gear. The Triumph snaked left to right as Knox weaved past cars as he pushed to catch up with the now out of sight SUV. His right hand rolled forward and the motorcycle slowed, the shift of weight moved to the front, as the engine applied resistance. Knox frantically looked around for any sign.

A mass of red LED's lit up a dark side street and the Triumph's momentum overshot the entrance of the street the Range Rover was down. Knox pulled a U-turn across the main street and pushed it over the double white lines in the process. Knox skilfully got the bike around and pulled up on the other side of the road to the adjacent street. Werp, werp, sounded behind Knox as the local Police patrol car pulled up behind him. They had been parked nearby and witnessed Knox pull the illegal manoeuvre.

"Shit!" Knox said as he watched in the wing mirror as the first cop got out of the patrol car. This was all he needed. Knox turned back to look at the SUV. The lights were off now and they were either parking up or were trying to keep a low profile now the blue roof lights of the patrol car illuminated the whole area, rotating with an almost eye hurting bright blue.

"Apagado, documentos, seguro, licencia," the cop called from behind Knox as he walked up. He didn't have time for this let alone the fact he didn't have the bike's documents on him and he sure as hell wasn't getting off the bike. And just as Knox was about to speak, the Range Rover lit up as it slowly pulled away down the street.

"Sorry pal, holiday, holiday!" Knox shouted pulling away at speed as he cut up an oncoming car, making a beeline for the street across the way. The cop, fumbled trying to draw his weapon but was yelled at by his partner to get back in the car as he pulled up to his colleague.

The people in the SUV now knew that Knox was tailing them if their erratic driving was anything to go by. They mounted the kerb and drove over a reservation, cutting into the oncoming vehicles. Knox followed on his side of the carriageway watching the Range Rover dodging oncoming traffic, palm trees between them and Knox, making the scene look like a flicker book as their speed increased. But Knox had another problem with the Police tailing him adding another two cars to the chase.

A break in the reservation ahead gave Knox the opportunity to cross onto the SUV's side of the carriageway, a mental, crazy ass opportunity but one Knox took. Horns of vehicles sounded long shrieks as Knox passed them. Going against the flow of traffic the police didn't follow Knox, they opted to stay on the right side of the road and follow alongside...their insanity levels obviously not as high as Knox's, he thought wryly.

The black Range Rover slammed on its brakes, it skidded to a halt as its path was blocked by a bus and a heavy good's vehicle. Both of the drivers stamped on their respective brake pedals and the two only just stopped before colliding head on with the black four by four. The rear passenger door of the SUV opened. Out got a heavily built black man who lifted his arms up, wielding a mini machine gun.

"Fuck!" Knox shouted gripping a fist full of brake hard and rapidly coming to a stop with the rear wheel lifting before slamming hard back down. Gun fire tore through the car windows that were caught between Knox and the gunman. The screams of innocent people as they took cover could barely be heard over the torrent of bullets that ricocheted off the roofs and bonnets.

Knox ducked as much as he could before he was forced to drop the motorcycle onto its side and roll himself behind what small cover there was from the nearest car. He reached up, seeing the people trapped inside, and opened the door. He told them to get out and keep their heads down, as they made their way towards the traffic further back.

A second burst of gun fire drilled all over Knox's cover. The Police were now out of their cars and pulled their weapons on the gunman. A second gunman got out of the SUV and opened fire on the Police, followed by the big black guy. They were outmatched and stood no chance as the gunmen's firepower obliterated the two patrol cars. One officer took hits, the other three fled for cover. Knox drew his weapon.

"One, two, three!" Knox said taking in a deep breath as he stood, and started to run for the next closest cover between him and the gunmen. Rapidly firing off his handgun as he ran, he didn't have the firepower but he did have the aim. His first shot shattered the open passenger door glass of the Range Rover, the second knocked the first gunman back as it got him in the shoulder. The third clipped the top of his thigh.

The second gunman turned his attention on Knox as he saw him and Knox knew what was about to come as he launched himself into the air, knowing he had no time. Landing hard on the tarmac road he just managed to get behind a small van as bullets whipped over his head like a mass of deadly shooting stars, sparks danced from the shots hitting the van. The moans of the first gunman could be heard as he dragged himself into the SUV, but then silenced. Two distinct kill shots rang out and the black guy fell to the ground, shot in the head. The second gunman was shouted at to get in, as the black Range Rover started to pull away, mounting the kerb and ramming through the thankfully empty tables and chairs. Frightened people scattered like bugs found under a plate full of food.

Knox stood up and emptied his gun as he fired at the rear of the vehicle, desperately trying to take out a tyre which he failed to do. He ran to his bike, reloading as he did. Knox struggled to pick up the Triumph but just managed it as he started the motor back into life.

Pulling away, Knox looked over to the Police officer down on the ground bleeding out, Knox shook his head in anger and the chase was back on.

. . .

At a blistering pace, Knox was soon back behind the SUV, now on the right side of the carriageway. The one passenger door with the window shot out wasn't shut and swung freely as the Range Rover weaved. Then the door hit the side of a passing car, leaving no hope of it ever being shut again as it was completely mangled. What little glass was left after being shot out hit Knox like tiny razors. They nicked at his jacket and bounced off the top of his helmet as he tilted his head so he wouldn't get hit in his face.

Knox saw a hand holding a machine gun come out of the back window and Knox darted to the other side of the vehicle with the mangled door. The gunman let rip and meaningless bullets shot out in all directions other than at Knox. He pulled level with the broken door and peered inside to see Isabella. Her hands were bound in tape and she had a strip across her mouth. Now, why hadn't he thought of that he wondered.

She stared at Knox with heavy makeup smudged eyes, Howard looked over from the front seat and locked eyes with Knox. Howard said something to the gunman who was half holding Isabella down. The gunman looked to Knox as he trained the machine gun on him and fired over the top of Isabella. A shot just clipped somewhere on the framework of the bike as Knox was just too late in braking hard to avoid being hit. Knox felt something hit his arm and it hurt like the mother of all bee stings.

The motorcycle's handle bars wobbled as if he had hit a pothole or something in the road, sending the bike out of control with tank slap. Knox wrestled the machine, slowing it down as much as possible before it locked up and threw Knox from it. Knox slid to the side of the road as he watched the bike scrape the road surface and a cascade of white-gold sparks followed it.

Knox took a moment as he lay down, looking up at the black starless sky.

"God damn it, Knox!" he shouted at himself, they had Isabella and they got away, he had failed her. Slapping the floor with his hand he took a few deep breaths and got up. Blood was dripping off his fingertips as it ran down his hand from under his jacket sleeve. A leather jacket that was now covered in road rash.

"For fuck sake! I love this jacket," Knox said as he walked over to the total mess that was his Triumph, he kicked at what was left of the twisted front wheel. No time to mourn, he thought to himself as he heard the many sirens that headed towards him. Locals tentatively started to come out of nearby bars and buildings to see what had happened. Knox needed to get out of there and fast. He walked straight into the biggest group of people. The first few spoke to him but with one deadly look from him they made the sensible choice and wisely ignored him. After that, he kept his head down and slipped away through the crowd as the authorities closed in on the area from all directions.

After a long trek, Knox made his way through the lobby of the Gran Hotel Miramar. He looked over all the people he could see as he checked for signs of anyone who may have been a threat. Now, stood in the elevator, the doors closed and Knox could see himself as he stared back at the mess the night had caused.

"Hard night?" Knox said aloud as he winced a little, stopping him from laughing at the state he was in. Knox reached Dani's room and the door wasn't fully shut. Knox drew his weapon, his mind raced…his only thought, Dani!

Knox closed his eyes tight and mentally emptied his mind, visions of Dani being taken, being killed or being tortured flashed vividly before him. Knox knew like this he was no good, so he pressed his gun muzzle into the part of his arm that hurt most. The pain pulled him back and his eyes snapped open when the thoughts had been expelled. The soldier in him firmly engaged.

Knox's blood covered hand slowly pushed the door to the penthouse suite open, the TV was on which provided the only light in the room.

Knox stepped in, his heart raced, emotions built up. He scanned the room, taking note that there were no signs of a struggle. And then the biggest weight lifted from Knox, he let out a breath he had unknowingly held in.

His Dani.

. . .

His eyes widened at the sight of the back of her head, which was off to one side on a high-backed chair. Knox walked over to her, each foot now felt like lead weights were strapped to them. His heart dropped with each step as he drew closer. He stretched out his right hand after putting his gun into his blood stained one. Knox placed his hand on where her neck met the shoulder, he closed his eyes. The feel of her skin still warm.

Thank God, he said to himself...

She was alive...

15

STITCHED

Dani stirred but didn't wake from her sleep. She simply fidgeted and then nestled her cheek onto Knox's hand.

Knox froze as he watched her shallow breaths fill her lungs and her chest move up and down with the smallest of movements. Her face was angelic in a peaceful deep sleep. Relief washed over Knox, to a point it almost overwhelmed him. The realisation of how much she meant to him, hit him like a boot to the chest. Coming off his bike had been nothing compared to this blow. He wanted to stroke the side of her face, he lifted his crimson hand about to do so, then remembered the gun and his blood covered skin.

It pained Knox to do it but he slowly pulled his hand out from under Dani's cheek. If anyone was watching him they wouldn't have thought he was moving at all. He pulled a face as though he was trying not to wake a baby that had been up all night.

Knox found himself sat on the balcony of the penthouse, trying to rein in his thoughts and heightened emotions. He wanted to find out how Isabella had left under Dani's watch. That's if she even knew Isabella was gone, Knox would have it out with her in the morning. It wouldn't make any difference now or later as Knox couldn't bring himself to wake her when she slept so peacefully. Knox had other things to think over in his head, like how he felt when he walked into the penthouse before and after he saw Dani.

Knox sent a large plume of smoke into the air, Christ it felt good. Knox had a love hate relationship with smoking. He loved the act, enjoyed the little hit of nicotine, the ritual of it all. How he could take a moment to stop and think. How it felt with the first cup of coffee in the morning or the taste of it with a drink in the hot sun. What Knox hated was the health risks, the looks none smokers gave him or worse yet ex-smokers. Ex-smokers pissed him right off, smug and condescending.

In truth, he was jealous of their achievement. The real sad truth to it all was men like Knox had a different outlook on life. Former SAS servicemen had an average life expectancy lower than civilians, and with years of being in extreme and dangerous situations where the chances of not coming home were very high, you start to live for the here and now.

"You know smoking will kill you," Dani's sleepy voice spoke out into the night air. Knox turned to see Dani in unbelievably cute little pyjama shorts and top that had a picture of a kitten on it. You can forget all the silk negligees and baby dolls, how Dani looked was perfect.

"Ay Lass, first I need a good woman to give them up for," Knox said as he turned back to look out over the view. Knowing full well if he continued to look at Dani dressed like that, he would have struggled to control himself. Dani walked over and put a hand on his arm, about to speak when Knox winced a little. Dani pulled her hand back in horror at feeling the sticky wetness on her fingertips. She held her hand to the light and saw Knox's blood.

"Lucas..!" Dani gasped.

"What has happened to you, are you alright?" Dani asked in a shriek of concern before she moved around to the front of Knox and checked him over.

"Nothing a bit of warm water and a cloth won't clean up." Knox smiled at Dani and her concerned look. Dani took the cigarette from Knox's finger and threw it off the balcony.

"You know we are in Spain and you could set fire to something, Lass." Knox joked as Dani took hold of his hand and looked at it covered in dry blood.

"We are in the city Lucas, not the campo, now get your ass up and into the bathroom," Dani said with a tone that said she wasn't impressed.

"Have you come off that bloody, dangerous boy toy of yours?" Dani spoke to him like she would a child.

"Well, I would be lying if I said 'no'." Knox laughed as they walked through the penthouse to the bathroom. Knox picked up a decanter and two glass tumblers.

"Sit!" Dani demanded, their eyes met and Dani couldn't help but turn a little shy at the sight of his raised eyebrow.

"Please… I mean please sit." Dani was embarrassed for the first time commanding Knox to do something, it just felt wrong. Knox couldn't help but smile at Dani's reaction and said nothing, instead opting to comply and sit on the edge of the bathtub. Dani took the decanter filled with whisky and tumblers out of his hands. She rolled her eyes as if to question was now the right time for a drink? Knox gave her a look and then said.

"Pour me one… please." Knox gazed into Dani's eyes as she bent down putting the decanter slowly on the mosaic floor. She poured two drinks, picked one up and Knox reached for it. As Dani looked into Knox's eyes, she softly shook her head and pulled the glass away. Knox looked at her as if to say, 'why did you do that'? Dani then put the glass to Knox's lips for him to drink. Knox took a big drink, followed by a big exhale as it tasted good.

"Do you approve, Mr Scotsman?" Dani asked with a little smile across her lips, but her eyes gave him a bigger smile.

"Ay Lass, in more ways than one." Knox grinned back at her.

"Come on, let's get this jacket off you." Dani stood up and helped Knox with the blood-stained, scuffed up jacket. As she pulled the arms up Knox winced but forgot the pain as Dani's top lifted to show her perfect soft white skin and the cutest little navel. Knox wanted to lay his face on her stomach and take in her skin's scent, holding her to him with a handful of her perfect arse.

"Jesus Lucas, that's a nasty cut, what did that?" Dani said inspecting his arm, not sure how to get his grandad top off without getting blood over her hands. Knox saw what she must have been thinking.

"Rip it. I think a ricochet got me when my bike took on gunfire." Knox said as he pulled at his top.

"Gunfire!?" Dani shrieked. Knox gave her a look and nodded down to himself as if to get Dani's mind back on track. Dani gave Knox a worried look but took the hint. She then took hold of the neck material. She looked at him again as if to ask if he was sure. Knox nodded and smiled at how timid she could be, something that contradicted with that sassy personality of hers. This pleased him more than he wanted to admit. Dani ripped his top, the ribs of the material made for a straight tear. Dani's pupils grew as she took in the sight of Knox's large chest. Knox wanted to laugh but instead teased her by simply clearing his throat. Well, at least the sight of battle scars didn't put her off he thought, fighting a grin.

She soon realised she had been staring for far too long and promptly carried on taking his shirt off. She threw the now crimson rags into the tub and ran warm water in the sink. Using the expensive white hotel bath towels she began to clean Knox up. At one point her face leant right up close to Knox's. She turned her head slightly and Knox looked at the shape of her pretty ear, almost studying it. Then he closed his eyes in an attempt to control himself. But this was futile as he took in a deep breath of her aroma and was nearly lost all over again. He wasn't sure what was perfume and what was Dani, but all he knew was it was sweet and he wanted to wake up to it. He wanted to smell it on him.

Dani stopped for a moment, picked up the tumbler and gave Knox a second sip, and then carried on.

"Thank you for doing this, Dani," Knox said almost whispering in her ear. Dani felt his breath and couldn't help her shudder before closing her eyes. She swallowed hard before carrying on. Dani looked to Knox with a look of 'this is going to hurt', then wiped over his wound. Knox breathed in deeply and focused intensely on Dani, admiring the shape of her back and curve of her behind as she crouched in front of him. Yep, could have been worse, Knox thought with a grin.

"I think it's going to need stitches, Lucas," Dani said as she pulled back with a worried expression on her kind face. Knox's attention pulled back from his dirty thoughts and he looked over the wound.

"Yep, you are right, Lass. Swanky places like this will have a needle and thread." Knox looked at Dani as he said it.

"Oh, yes of course... be right back," Dani said after she had looked into Knox's eyes for longer than was needed. Something Knox didn't notice as he had done the same to her. Dani rushed back in with a needle already threaded with black cotton, Knox looked up at Dani.

"I think you are going to have to do it," Knox explained, lifting his arm which showed he couldn't reach.

"No way, I can't..." Dani said shaking her head.

"You are going to have to. Don't worry Lass, you can do it and I will talk you through it every step of the way," Knox said as he placed a hand on Dani's thigh. The moment he did, he knew he shouldn't have. Dani's skin rose up in goosebumps, and the warm silky-smooth skin Knox was enjoying the feel of, felt electric.

"I really don't think I can," Dani said with a soft breathy tone.

"Well if not, it's a trip down the Spanish E.R and that could take hours. And well, let's just say I would like to keep my run in with the police down to a minimum." Knox looked up at Dani and gave her a look that she just couldn't say no to.

"Okay, I will try my best, but you promise not to blame me if it's bad." Dani looked at Knox worried, making him laugh.

"Look at it this way, when I look at the scar I will always think of you," Knox said, which made Dani smile and appear instantly pleased as if it was something sweet. She sterilised the needle in the whisky, then she took a big drink herself.

"Easy now Lass, I don't fancy a wavy line." Knox laughed as Dani pulled a face. It was all she needed to grab his arm and poke the needle through his skin without remorse.

"Brutal... sure you haven't done this before?" Knox jibed and Dani smiled with a touch of a naughty glint in her eyes.

"Maybe, or maybe I find hurting you fun," Dani teased trying to be serious, but the moment she said it, became shy and her cheeks filled with redness. Knox found her blush too cute to handle and he would have paid good money to know what naughty thoughts had obviously just run through her mind.

Knox leant in and Dani stopped breathing. She looked at him then closed her eyes. Knox's lips hovered over hers, a paper's width apart. They could feel each other and with only a whisper away from touching, Knox couldn't stand it any longer.

Knox kissed her, tasted her and savoured every second of it. And Dani kissed him back with a fever that matched his own. She felt his hand wrap around her as he pulled her into him, their tongues tasting each other as if they couldn't get enough. The hint of whisky and Dani made for a heady combination and Knox had to wrestle with himself from simply picking her up over his shoulder and taking her to bed. Blood or no blood.

They paused for a second as they each rested their foreheads on one another, as they caught their breath. Dani's eyes opened and a large smile crossed her face before she kissed Knox again. This time he allowed it to be tender yet passionate, taking their time to enjoy the slow kiss.

"Wow... okay, Mr, I need to finish this," Dani said after she broke away from the long kiss. Knox stared at Dani, and watched her, after first swallowing down the growl that he felt in having her lips taken from him.

"Sorry Dani, I shouldn't have done that," Knox said looking up to the ceiling.

"Why sorry? Don't be, I am not...not in the slightest," Dani said as she pulled down on Knox's chin so their eyes met once more. She gave him a smile and then carried on as she finished off the stitches. She stood up when finished, and held out her hand.

"Come on, let's finish off our drinks in a bit more comfort," Dani said with a brave face and a smile Knox knew she used to hide how she really felt. Knox took her hand and stood, looked over her handy work in the mirror and gave Dani an impressed look. She beamed back at him.

"Lady of many talents Mr Knox, you would be a fool not to..." Dani said and stopped herself short. Instead, she walked out of the bathroom in that perfect way women do when they walk on tiptoes and their arses look incredible... and Dani's was just that.

They sat outside on the balcony and Dani handed Knox a smoke, she even lit it for him taking a drag herself. Knox poured them both a drink from the decanter he'd brought out with him. He looked at Dani, the wind blowing her perfectly messy blonde hair she had just let down. She was pulling out all the stops, and she didn't even know it. Knox was about to speak when his phone rang, making him wince as he tried to get it out of his left pocket. Dani rushed over and leant down, just so Knox's eyes couldn't help but look down her top, and her raised eyebrow told him that she knew it. She slowly ran her fingers up Knox's thigh and walked them to his pocket. Then she slipped his phone out before handing it to him, taking the time to whisper in his ear.

"You only have to ask and I would slip it out for you. You know a good woman can make life a lot easier," she said seductively before she turned, showing Knox her swaying backside as she walked back. She then took her seat and a sip of her drink.

"Knox," said Knox as he answered the call, eyes still fixated on Dani.

"Captain, we have a location on Howard." Carter's voice informed him.

"Really Sir, I had my own little run in with him," Knox said bemusedly.

"Yes, well we have watched your little ride around town after we saw the police reports," Carter said with a tone indicating he was less than impressed.

"They have Isabella, Sir." As Knox said this, Dani looked around as if it only now had registered that she wasn't around... no doubt thinking her still asleep in the bedroom. Knox looked at Dani seeing that she had no clue.

"None of our concern now, Knox. Listen, we have

information that there is to be a big Gala dinner and dance on the Pérez Yacht tomorrow evening," Carter informed Knox.

"Really Sir, I don't think…" Knox said but Carter cut him off.

"Don't think Knox, just listen. He is going to be there so you need to get on board, find him and bring him in. Am I making myself clear, Captain?" Carter demanded.

"Perfectly, Sir. Would you still be interested in the information that's on that boat?" Knox asked as an idea came to him.

"What are you thinking, Captain?" Carter asked, intrigued.

"Killing two birds with one stone," Knox replied.

"I don't have the personnel with the tech ability to spare, Captain," Carter stressed.

"Don't worry Sir, I have my own," Knox said as he hung up, he then looked directly at Dani.

"So how about I take you for that dinner?" Knox said cockily. Dani looked at Knox puzzled at first and then a smile appeared on her face.

"Dinner, Mr Knox?" Dani said with a little excitement in her voice.

"Yes, and Lass," Knox purposely paused to give her an appreciative look up and down her body before continuing,

"You are going to need a new dress…"

16

FISHTAIL & TUX

Knox stirred from one of the deepest sleeps he'd had in a long time. In fact, longer than he could remember. As his eyes focused he looked around for the clock, sure it had been on the bedside table, but it was gone. Knox sat up and his body reminded him of the events of last night, aches and pains in what felt like every muscle and joint. The sun was not high in the sky as Knox looked at the shadows it cast in the room, mentally calculating it wasn't yet near midday. As he fully woke, it dawned on him, that the sun was low but not because it was morning but because it was late afternoon. Shit, how long had he been asleep, where was Dani and when did he get undressed and fall asleep in bed? Knox thought to himself as he looked for his clothes and his things.

Neatly placed on the coffee table in the sitting area of the suite lay his phone, wallet and watch on top of a note.

'Lucas, I think you must have needed your sleep. I couldn't bear to wake you, needed to pick up some things.
I shouldn't be too long. Be a doll and have the housework done and dinner on the table for when I get back.
Oh and... nice underwear.
Dani x ;)
PS. I hid your guns. They are with the clocks in the bedside drawer. Didn't think it fair to scare the housekeeping staff, just in case.'

Knox smiled down at her written humour. He even liked how she signed it with a wink face. Knox looked down at himself. It hadn't even dawned on him until he read the note that he was only in his black boxer briefs. As he looked again around the room he couldn't find his jeans, just his boots. What had Dani done with them? Well, there wasn't much he could do other than wait. Knox made his way into the bathroom to clean up his bloody mess only to find the bathroom spotless. Confused, Knox walked over to the suite's entrance and opened the door, he checked the card that hung on the door handle outside the room and it clearly indicated 'Do Not Disturb'.

Knox walked back to the bathroom, he checked Dani's handy work in the mirror and the stitched wound was still intact. He smiled to himself and thought that wasn't Dani's only handy work, as if ever she needed a side line job, maybe cleaning crime scenes would be a viable option. Knox ran the shower and stripped off what little he had on. He stood in the almost impossibly hot water, and as soon as Knox's skin began to tolerate the heat, he turned the hot water up a notch.

Dani arrived back at the suite and Knox found that he could breathe a little easier once he could see that she was safe. And as most women do after a shopping trip, she walked in with handfuls of bags. Knox walked out of the steam filled bathroom, towel around his waist and a smaller one he was using to dry his head and body. He looked up as Dani stood there watching him like a small woodland animal caught in headlights on the road. She swallowed hard and Knox couldn't help the cocky smirk he could feel rising his lips on one side. It wasn't exactly a bad thing if she liked what she saw when he was half naked, not considering that what he wanted to do to her, often required the lack of clothes. However, the moment broke when she dropped one of the bags.

"Here let me help you," Knox said as he picked up the Massimo Dutti men's clothing bag.

"Sorry it was the only shop close by that didn't scream runway slim fit and was more your, 'Me man, with gun', type of style," she said changing her voice to sound deeper with the 'Me man, with gun' mockery.

"What, do you not think pastel colours and tight shorts are me?" Knox teased back, as Dani eyed up every inch of him. He couldn't help but notice the way she licked her lips as if her mouth had suddenly gone dry. He was half tempted to wet them for her…oh who was he kidding, more than half!

. . .

"Erm… in a word, no. I hope you don't mind, I picked you up a few things, and got rid of the blood-stained stuff, no hotel laundry was going to get that clean," Dani said as she walked through to the bedroom and threw the mass of bags onto the bed. And just as Knox was about to speak, a knock was heard at the door. Knox rushed to the bedside table and opened the drawer, Dani put a hand on his back.

"It's okay, I ordered room service," Dani said with that kind smile of hers that calmed Knox instantly.

"Just a minute!" she called, looking over her shoulder and then back to him.

"Thanks, Dani I will go get dressed," Knox said as he picked up the one men's shopping bag he recognised. Dani stopped him and then handed him another, and another then stopped and thought, then picked up two more.

"That's your lot," Dani said in a way that suggested she was really pleased with herself.

"You really shouldn't have, thanks again," Knox said a little overwhelmed as no one had ever done this for him before. So, with this in mind, he quickly made his way off to the bathroom, as he knew that if he stood around any longer he would make some inappropriate joke to deflect how touched he was by her kind actions.

. . .

"Don't thank me, it was a pleasure. Anyway, I paid on your credit card," Dani said as she winked at Knox when he looked back to her. Dani slipped his card out of her pocket and put it down. Knox smiled and shook his head before walking into the bathroom, as Dani opened the door and instructed the hotel staff to take the food trolley out onto the balcony area.

Knox dressed, now wearing dark blue jeans and black t-shirt that fit perfectly. He held a new leather jacket in his hand, one he couldn't have picked better himself. He walked out onto the balcony to find her sat waiting for him.

"Dani... I" Knox started to say, nodding down to the jacket and Dani saw him struggling to find the words.

"You are very welcome Lucas, come and sit down, the food will get cold," Dani said with a smile as she motioned to the seat next to her. Knox hung the jacket on the back of the chair and sat down. He looked at Dani and then looked at the amount of food.

"Do we have guests coming?" Knox said as he picked up an olive.

"What? I wasn't sure what you would want. And when was the last time you ate something that wasn't junk and had real nutritional value?" Dani said as she put food in front of Knox. He didn't argue with her and tucked in.

"What happened last night?" Knox asked Dani, referring to him waking up in bed in just his boxers. She gave him a coy smile as if remembering the sight of him almost naked then hid it quickly, answering him with her usual sassy way.

"You fell madly in love with me, asked me to run away with you and get married," Dani said casually before taking a big bite of her steak. Knox pretended to choke a little on his food.

"I said no, of course, I mean, I know when someone is just infatuated," Dani said unsure at first how to take Knox choking, as an insult or playful. She opted for playful and winked.

"How did I end up in bed, did you drug me?" Knox teased.

"That would be telling," Dani whispered back.

"I remember talking and having a few drinks out here," Knox said as he looked for the decanter.

"If you class all of the decanter's contents as a few drinks, sure," Dani smirked, and Knox played at looking a little sheepish.
"You fell asleep on the bed and I wasn't going to sleep in a bed next to someone with blood stains over their jeans. So, I

took them off," Dani said as if it was completely normal. Knox raised his eyebrow as he looked at her.

"You didn't stir at all, and well whatever else happened is between me and the bedsheets, now isn't it?" Dani teased as she couldn't hold in her giggle. Knox laughed and he knew it was a testament to Dani at how relaxed she made him feel. This was the kind of trouble she was to him, how he could easily lose his edge. No harm came of it this time but thinking about it now, Knox realised he didn't even check who was at the door when the knock came earlier.

Yes, it was only room service that Dani expected and not some goon squad sent by God knows who. But still, he should have checked and Knox mentally scolded himself. This is what he knew would happen if he let Dani get close to him and his world.

They carried on eating and talking, and no matter how he tried to contain himself he couldn't help but tease her, enjoying her reactions too much to stop. She teased him back of course which only made it more torturous to Knox, as this only managed to imprint images of her bent over his knee and receiving punishment for being so outspoken, in his mind. Of course, he liked her this way, giving her spirited nature the perfect excuse for some Dom/Sub fun.

It came naturally to them and both used it to avoid the elephant in the room, which of course was the kiss last night and where he was nearly desperate for it to lead to. The hardest part of it all was that knowing Dani's secret submissive desires, he could have stood right now, thrown her over his shoulder and down on the bed without a single uttered word of protest.

Once there he could command her obedience, hold her down and demand her come for him over and over until begging him to stop. Only then would he take his own pleasure from her willing, wet body.

"So, it's time for me to get ready," Dani announced as she got up from the table and started to walk off. Knox looked at his watch and secretly adjusted himself thanks to where his thoughts had led him.

"We have at least four hours till the Gala," Knox said as Dani looked back at him with shock.

"Only four hours, it takes a lot of effort to look beautiful for you Mr Knox, I don't just wake up this gorgeous." He doubted this considering she would look stunning if she came back out here wearing only his shirt and nothing else. In his opinion, she didn't need makeup, or hours of hair styling, as in his eyes she was a natural beauty, through and through.

"Will you have time to sort out a tux, that's one thing I didn't get you?" Dani asked with a playfully dramatic tone.

"I'm sure I will manage the task, Lassie," Knox replied making her fight a grin.
"Good boy," she said patting him on the chest before she left the balcony. She then walked into the bedroom and picked up her bags off the bed so that she could lock herself in the bathroom for god knows how many hours, Knox thought, half annoyed that she wouldn't be in his company.

. . .

Three and a half hours later, Knox stood in front of the mirror over his side of the 'his and her' sinks in the luxurious marble, glass rich bathroom. Dressed in a full tux, minus the jacket which was still hung on its hanger on the door. He fiddled with putting in his damn cufflinks. Knox thought to himself, a shave and a tux and he didn't look too bad at all, even if he did think so himself. Knox walked into the sitting room and caught sight of Dani in the bedroom struggling to zip up her dress.

"Unless you are a contortionist Lass, please let me help you," Knox called over to Dani. Dani stopped dead at the realisation that Knox could see her. She took a deep breath and turned and walked over to Knox holding her dress up with her arms crossed over her ample chest. Knox was transfixed, Dani was gorgeous. The way she moved, slightly coy not wanting to make full eye contact as she bravely tried to show confidence. Okay, so Knox had to take it back, hours of hair and makeup certainly made what was always beautiful into something breath-taking.

"Dani, you look…" Knox started saying but Dani quietly interrupted.

"Hold on, wait until you can fully see me," Dani said over her shoulder as he moved the long waves of hair out of the way exposing her naked back. Knox stood and admired it, and felt a tiny bit of sadness that he was about to cover her up. He rested both his hands on her hips, Dani took in a breath as she felt his touch.

Then a startled breath escaped just as quickly as his hands touched her bare skin for the first time. He gathered a small amount of the satin material around the zipper, positioned at the small of her back. He also couldn't help but take notice of the black lace top of her panties. Knox pulled the zip up as slow as he could possibly get away with, running the knuckle of his first finger up the ridge of her spine as he went. Once reaching the top of her neck he rested both hands either side, not yet wanting to let her go. He felt the hairs on the back of his own neck stand on end and all he wanted was to taste her skin as he watched her pulse beat out the faintest of ripples just below her ear.

Dani let go of her hair which swept across like a curtain on a grand stage. Knox fought back his carnal thoughts of what he would want to do to her on that stage. Dani stepped forward and braced herself and turned around giving Knox a spin.

"Will I do, Mr Knox?" Dani said trying to sound playful and not showing how she really felt, a girl that wanted to hear she looked pretty.

"Dani… you look truly beautiful. Honestly Love, I will be the envy of the Gala." Knox said as he looked Dani up and down in the figure enhancing, black, floor length fishtail dress that complimented her hourglass shape to perfection. Applique flowers wrapped around her breasts, snaking up to her neck over a fine black mesh. Knox was taken back as he stood and admired, but the one part he couldn't get enough of was Dani's sapphire blue eyes.

"Thank you, you look very dashing yourself, Mr Knox," Dani said with a delicious blush across her cheeks, one that Knox knew had nothing to do with makeup. Dani gave Knox a little-embarrassed smile at the look he was giving her.

"Oh, I almost forgot," Dani said as she picked up a small clutch bag and went over to her laptop case and pulled out some small USB device.

"We won't be hacking anything without this little bad boy," Dani said pulling a face as she slipped the device into her clutch.

"That reminds me," Knox said as he walked over to his jacket and after putting it on he pulled out a box from its pocket.

"I...well, it's just a little something as a small thank you," Knox said as he opened the box to reveal a bright sparkling diamond encrusted bracelet.

"Oh...my... Lucas, I can't... honestly, you know you didn't..." She started to mumble her protests but Knox stopped her instantly by stepping right up to her and placing a finger at her lips, shocking her to silence. He also gave her no choice but to arch her neck to look up at him, she gasped at the sight of this side of him. He leant down a little and whispered,

"Do you like it?" She started to nod and he couldn't help his tone slip into the realms of demanding,

"Words sweetheart, I want to hear the words."

. . .

"It's…it's beautiful," Dani said in such a way, Knox was once again fighting with himself and his arousal.

"Here, then let me help you," Knox said, happy that he had now got the response from her he wanted, liking even more that he had to demand it from her. He granted her a smile and took the bracelet out of its box and clipped it around Dani's wrist.

"Perfect, just like its new owner is… shall we?" Knox held out his arm for Dani to take.

"Do we even have an invite to this Gala?" Dani asked after clearing her throat and trying to get past the feelings Knox's dominating side had brought out in her. She hoped for a half joking tone to help ease the sexual tension that she could feel electrified the air around them.

"Thankfully Carter organised something."

"Something?" Dani questioned, raising a perfectly sculptured eyebrow.

"In other words, someone is going to miss the party but we will gladly fill in the position for them and take their place. Details are waiting for us," Knox replied putting Dani at ease but at the same time giving her more questions to ask.

. . .

"What kind of details, waiting in a car?" Dani looked puzzled as she spoke, walking into the elevator after leaving the suite.

"Yes, Harris is driving us. And he has the details of our new identities."

"Who are we going to be?" Dani asked excitedly.

Knox smirked at Dani as the doors to the lift closed, that was something Dani was going to have to wait and... *find out*.

17

FINE DINING

Knox and Dani pulled up at the end of the cliché long red velvet carpet. Flanked by red ropes linked to gold stands behind which photographers stood. Harris got out of the car and opened the door for Dani, taking her hand as he helped her out of the Jaguar to a mass of flash photography. Everyone from pop, rock and film stars to royalty, politicians and public dignitaries would be at the Gala and the paparazzi didn't want to miss anyone.

"You look wonderful," Harris said with a smile as he saw Dani's discomfort at all the attention. He then walked her around to an expectant Knox and she linked her arm with his.

"Do you mind if we go straight on board?" Dani asked after she gave a little tug on Knox's arm so that he would know she was whispering to him.

"I want to make a grand entrance and enjoy the moment as much as anyone, but the truth is I hate all the camera attention," Dani said clinging onto Knox's arm tightly.

"Of course, let's go straight in, Lass. We'll have a glass of wine before we order our dinner," Knox said placing a hand on hers. She gave him an amused glance and he thought for a moment then corrected himself.

"Or a cocktail, if you prefer." Knox winked as Dani's face lit up with a big smile, for a moment distracted from the attention. They walked up to the two commissionaires stood at the foot of a grand gangway. They stood beneath a tall gateway which was illuminated with delicate, bright white fairy lights, so many it was impossible to count. They looked at the closest man who asked to see their invitation. Knox hid his surprise when he saw Gregory stood before him who looked over their invite and waved them through with a telling smile.

Knox handed the invite to Dani which she read as they walked up the steep gangway.

"Prince Georg von Habsburg and Duchess Eilika of Oldenburg?" Dani said utterly amazed and laughing.

"And how come you get to be a Prince and I'm only a Duchess?" Dani tried to keep a straight face. Knox shrugged his shoulders and smiled.

"Now you see why I didn't show you before we got out of the car," Knox said will a telling look and they both laughed.

"The food here should be the very best," Dani said as she pointed to a large picture of a chef placed on an easel with a statement that welcomed them to the charity Gala dinner signed by *Alain Passard*. Knox gave Dani a blank look.

"He is one of the best chefs in the world right now," Dani whispered in his ear. However, Knox wondered if he should have eaten more back at the hotel, knowing how small these posh portions could be.

They walked up to a small crowd of other glamorous guests as they bottle necked at the entrance to the Gala. Then Dani's eyes looked on in awe as they both reached the semi open air space. It was a mass of lavish decorations, large bouquets of flowers and large round tables set out with the finest silver tableware.

Waiting staff with drinks and canapes almost floated in between the crowd, as if trying to offer a service without being seen. They were met by the maitre d' who led them through the crowded deck. Knox watched the heads of the diners turn to look at Dani in their wake. The fashionable elite showed their approval with smiles, open mouths and stares and he couldn't hide how proud he felt that she was attached to his arm.

Their table was beside an impressive ice sculpture, one as beautiful as it was large. Two bulls locking horns in a dramatic clash, Knox was not happy.

"Please move us to somewhere over there." Knox pointed to a table that was a bit cosier and closed in by its decorations, which made for a more private setting.

. . .

"Is there a problem, Sir?" The maitre d' asked.

"Yes, my beautiful wife will catch her death of cold," Knox said sternly at being questioned, leaving all traces of his easy-going nature behind. Then he rubbed his hands on the tops of Dani's arms as she felt the chill of the massive piece of ice. Dani was frozen in her movements, not at the cold, but from the statement Knox just made. As false as it was, she liked the sound of him calling her *his wife*, almost as much as she enjoyed the feel of his hands caressing her bare skin.

As they both sat, Knox tried to decipher not only the wispy scroll of gold lettering which covered the double folio menu but the whole menu that was all in French. As Knox beckoned to the waiter he turned to Dani.

"Have you decided… on a cocktail?" Knox asked Dani.

"I would love a Green Ghost, please," she said simply, and went back to her study of the menu.

"A bottle of red, cold," requested Knox, to which the waiter looked at him oddly and Dani raised an eyebrow. After their drinks arrived Knox held up his glass and Dani did the same.

. . .

"I can't drink to you and your beauty without knowing your Christian name," Knox said as he had always known that 'Dani' was short for her surname Daniels. She looked to Knox with a little embarrassment and disbelief.

"And how do you know Dani isn't my first name?" she said shocked that Knox knew it wasn't. Knox gave her a look of enquiry.

"It's my job, I know a lot of things about you." Knox smiled over the rim of his glass as he thought about all the erotic depictions on canvas stored in his lockup. Now they gave Knox his biggest insight to the mind of the stunning woman who sat before him, one he couldn't keep his eyes off.

"Well, it is also my job to hide and keep secrets. So, you're out of luck there Lucas, but don't worry, I may tell you one day. Here's too handsome dates in tuxedos." Dani smiled as she clinked her glass to Knox's, not realising that by that statement it was like waving a red flag to a bull. 'Game on' Knox thought with a hidden smirk.

"Have you decided what you would like to have for dinner?" Dani asked as she tried to change the subject, beating him to saying something that would no doubt take her to an uncomfortable place. A place Knox sadistically wanted to take her, loving that blush of hers. But instead of the sexual come back he had really wanted to say, which included something like 'Torturing that name from her screaming lips', Knox smiled and silently thought to himself 'I will get it out of you one day.'

"No, I haven't and if I am totally honest, I am not sure what everything is, my French isn't the best." Dani's eyes lit up, and she jumped at her chance.

"Please, let me help you, it would be my pleasure," she said with clear excitement as this was Dani's other passion in life. Fine food and drink. A passion she didn't get to indulge in as often as she would like, due to the cost, but she read every book and watched every cookery show going. She even made notes and had a full wall dedicated to them in her kitchen.

So, like a child at Christmas, she sat and explained in great detail the menu, origins of certain dishes, how the flavours worked together. Knox loved to listen to her speak so passionately.

"Let's go all out, pick whatever you like," Knox added as he sensed Dani's hesitation in ordering something too expensive.

"I mean it, Dani, pick the most expensive thing on there if you like," Knox told her and before she could speak, as it looked as if she was going to protest again, he took her hand and said,

"When you look a million dollars, sweetheart, it's time to eat like you own a million dollars. Plus, getting to behave like millionaires occasionally is a wonderful treat and if you know what you want, then go for it." Knox finished, kissed her hand and looked up to enjoy that blush of hers once more.

"Well, I'm struggling between two choices, and either would have been delicious, but … well, I'd like to start with caviar and then have a plain grilled rognon de veau with pommes soufflés. And then I'd like to have fraises des bois with a lot of cream." Dani placed her order to the waiter.

"Is it shameless to be so certain and it be so expensive?" She smiled at Knox inquiringly.

"It's a virtue, and anyway I admire a woman who knows what she wants." He turned to the waiter.

"And bring plenty of toast," Knox said looking at the waiter as though he didn't want to be short changed, before turning back to the menu.

"I will have the caviar too with extra toast also, but then I would like tournedos, underdone, with sauce Béarnaise and a coeur d'artichaut and I would like to add queue de homard au beurre galique. And while you enjoy the strawberries, Dani, I will have the Canelés. Thank you." Knox delivered eloquently, to which the waiter nodded and walked away.

"Do you approve?" Knox smiled at Dani before taking a sip of his chilled red wine, which was a no, no in the wine world but he didn't care he liked his red wine cool.

. . .

"You ordered extra toast… and what was this rubbish about not understanding the menu?" Dani laughed after her mouth dropped a little in shock. His French had been flawless.

"The trouble is, not how much caviar, but how much toast they serve with it. There is never enough toast or bread," Knox said as he winked at the bemused Dani.

"And that you understood the menu and pronounced everything so well," Dani questioned again with a sceptic tone.

"You explained things so well, and it's my job to learn fast and understand orders." Knox tried his best to sound believable and hide a cheeky grin. When really, he had played dumb over the menu as he had known of Dani's love of fine food as she had her own blog on the topic, one she updated weekly. A blog he read regularly.

"Lucas Knox…with a face like yours, you could have me believing anything you say," Dani said as she cut him a playful look.

"Nice to hear my rugged looks still work," Knox said with just as cheeky a grin.

"Carte des vins, Monsieur." The waiter offered the wine list, breaking the moment between Knox and Dani.

...

"Please, can I select us something?" Dani said as she placed a hand on Knox's, and gave him a look he couldn't say no to. A look that just made him want to put his hand around her throat and kiss her.

"Go right ahead," Knox replied as he opened and closed his hand trying to shake his thoughts from his head before his face gave him away.

"Thank you, I know champagne is the drink to have. But I would prefer to drink a brut Cava with you tonight. It is the perfect wine and suits the occasion of us being here in Spain, I hope you agree," Dani said as she clapped her hands in excitement.

"Then that is what we shall have, anyway I am not the biggest fan of champagne, not that I know much about it," Knox said as he called the attention of the wine waiter.

"May we have a bottle of the 2005 Recaredo Reserva Particular," Dani said and looked so happy that Knox looked on and thought it was easy to forget why they were there. And would it be so bad if they forgot the mission and just enjoyed the evening?

...

Their food came and they enjoyed every mouthful along with the drink, but most of all they enjoyed each other. Knox was given a look at what his life could be like, and with a woman like Dani, it seemed like a beautiful dream if not a perfect one. And as he didn't know when he would have a chance like this again and as they had finished their meal, he took Dani's hand as he stood up.

"Where are we going?" Dani looked puzzled.

"Come with me," Knox said before he led her through the maze of tables and dinner guests all sat enjoying themselves.

"Lucas... No, I don't..." Dani tried to say but it was too late, Knox had her on the dance floor.

"I can't dance..." Dani whispered into Knox's ear.

"I don't know why you are whispering, Lass, the music's very loud," he teased, with his lips touching her tender skin just under her ear. He liked the breathy sound she exhaled because of it.

"Just follow my lead, Sweetheart," Knox said, taking hold of Dani in a firm grip, one she couldn't help but like as Knox led her perfectly to the Bolero dance. Taking her hand in his felt like the perfect fit but pulling her body into his even more so. His hand pressed at the small of her back, he took control of her body, leading it around the space and slowly the reasons they were there became blurred. A deck full of people surrounded them but for Knox and Dani, they lost themselves in each other and the romantic setting. Neither wanted it to end and just as Knox pulled back to look at her he knew in that moment that he was no longer falling...*he had fallen.*

So, he leant down ready to continue what they had started in the bathroom when reality stopped him, just as he reached her lips.

"Lucas?" She uttered his name in a breathy whisper and the only words he wanted to say was 'Fuck it' and take her lips... but responsibility was a bitch, so instead said,

"Time to go to work, Darlin," as he spotted who he thought was Howard. He was easily given away by the sheer number of security around him. And security was used in the loosest sense of the term, as the men looked like a motley crew of mercenaries forced into suits that were too small for their steroid fuelled upper bodies.

"Come with me." Knox leant in and whispered in Dani's ear as she took a breath, Knox then led her off the dance floor and they made their way to a corridor. They found themselves out on deck as they made their way to a door that had a guard stationed at it. Knox put his arm around Dani and acted like he was drunk.

. . .

"No access here, go back the way you came," warned the guard who came over to meet them.

"Sorry my date's a little drunk, can you help me?" Dani surprised Knox by playing along without being asked. It wasn't his plan but he would roll with it. And as the guard smiled and took pity on what he thought was Dani's trouble, Knox took the man clean out with a well-timed strike to his chin. Dani let out a surprised little shriek that thankfully for Knox wasn't loud enough to alert anyone. He ignored her reaction, Knox picked the guard up and dragged the lump of a man inside the door that Dani opened. They hid him inside a storage cupboard where Knox took a fire axe from the wall and wedged it in the door frame.

"Remind me not to piss you off," Dani joked as they walked along the hallway. Knox looked at a map on his smartphone and directed them to a small elevator. They stood and waited what felt like an age, they willed the doors to open as they hoped no one would walk past and see them. A ping sounded loudly as the doors finally opened, only to find they were greeted by a crewman. Knox and Dani smiled, and just as the crewman was about to question them, Knox leapt forward into him and he struck him across the face with his elbow. Then he repeatedly punched to his body followed with a close quarter jump and knee into his gut. Finally finishing him off with locking his fingers behind his head and pulling his face hard down into Knox's rising knee. The crewman fell in a heap on the floor of the elevator, Knox leant out took hold of Dani's hand and pulled her inside.

. . .

All the while Dani could barely catch her breath and it was nothing to do with keeping up with Knox. No, it was all down to the sight of this side of him and the killer she knew he kept a tight lid on. It was the natural violence his training had burrowed deep into the roots of his soul. Even now, his gentle hand wrapped around hers, she knew what it could actually do to a person in real life. Not just written down in some file she had obsessed over. She knew his past, everything about him in fact, something she told herself was part of the job. But memorising every factor about him, no matter how small, no matter how bad, she knew that wasn't down to the excuse of it being part of the job. It was because she was... *in love with him.*

Now on the correct floor of the yacht for the office and server room, they just needed to make their way down twenty or thirty metres of the corridor. As they reached a corner Knox stopped and took a quick look to see there were two guards at the door to the server room.

"Dani, just follow my lead okay?" he said as he walked them both closer and just in view of the two men at the end of the hall. Now if he could just make them look this way. He knew what to do, he pulled her tightly into his body, making her yelp as he took her off guard. Then he pressed her up against the wall and started kissing her neck. She let her head fall back and moaned unknowingly. Knox hated that this was all for another's benefit, feeling like a bastard but he needed the distraction...and Dani was one hell of a distraction!

He caught her ass in his large hand and pulled her flush with his growing arousal making her moan louder this time. Yes, that was it, now they had the guards' attention.

"Hey, you two, you can't be down here!" One of the men said and the other one started laughing at seeing them fooling around. Knox pretended not to hear and still kissed her neck, stepping them out of sight around the corner. Then he painfully tore himself from her body and moved her so she wouldn't get hurt.

"Stand back," he ordered, as he noted she still had a look of bewilderment on her face.

Knox crouched down and listened, waiting for the footsteps to get closer. But he could only hear one guard coming their way. The guard came around the corner ready to confront them both and Knox was ready for him. He hooked his arm up and between his legs as he lifted him in one fast move and sent the guard head first into the wall. Then in one swift move, delivered a boot to the head for good measure. Dani looked at Knox wide-eyed and with a small amount of fear and disbelief in what she was seeing.

The commotion sent the second guard running to see what was going on. He pulled a gun on Knox who instantly put his hands up at head height. Knox waited, Dani looked at Knox as if it was the end, but he just smiled and winked.

"Don't move or I will shoot," the guard said, as he pushed the gun muzzle into Knox's back. This was what Knox was waiting for. The second he felt the gun make contact he spun quickly to his left. In the blink of an eye, he had knocked the gun to the side with his left hand and hit the guard square in the throat with his right, using his extended thumb for extra pain. He grabbed the gun and struck hard into the pressure point of the guard's wrist, pulling the gun safely away then used it to knock him out. On inspection of the gun, Knox smirked as the safety switch was still on.

"Amateurs", Knox muttered down at the two as he stepped over the body in his way. Knox then walked into the server room, making sure his tech genius was following and saw that it was clear.

"Okay beautiful you are on, back in a moment." He left Dani and shut the door behind him. Dani stood there frozen, unable to move.

Knox returned with one of the two guards and dropped him in a heap on the floor making her jump.

"Hey, what's wrong?" Knox touched Dani and she flinched before taking a step back. Knox couldn't stop the hurt he felt and tried to mask the feeling before it made its way to his eyes.

"Sorry Knox, I am just not used to... I don't know, seeing you kicking the crap out of people," Dani said in a way that suggested she was only just holding it together. Knox looked sympathetically and took hold of Dani's hands after putting himself in her shoes for a moment. After all, what was second nature to Knox, wasn't second nature to the warm-hearted Dani.

"You can do this, they are bad guys working for even bigger, bad guys. And you're here to help me stop the bad guys, remember? I can't do it without you," Knox said looking intensely into Dani's eyes and hoping what she saw reflected back was the truth. Dani nodded and became focused. She took the USB device that she had stuffed in her dress. Knox looked at her as though he didn't know how she kept it there.

"I will be right back, okay?" he said as he left the room, but first he gave Dani one last reassuring look, telling her silently that she could do this. Dani looked around the server room and found what she was looking for. She plugged the USB device into the server system, then looked around for an interface but there wasn't one. Knox bust back in carrying the second guard and dropped him onto of the first.

"Okay, so how many more are you going to stack up?" Dani looked at the sorry looking men.

"As many as it takes to get the job done, Lass," Knox said with a little heavy breathing.

"Well it may take a little longer," Dani said tensely, then gave him a look of panic and said…

BLOOD RETRIBUTION

"We have a problem."

18

SPLASH & GRAB

"We have a problem," Dani said with a worried look.

"Why, what's wrong?" Knox asked as he checked over the guards.

"I need an interface to get my drive to connect and transmit," Dani said worried that she had failed them.

"What about the main computer in the office?" Knox suggested as if it wasn't a problem.

"That would do it," she said beaming at him. He took her hand and they made a move as the office was only a few doors down the corridor. Once they reached the door to the office it was locked, and the only way in was with a keycode.

"Shit think, Knox, think." Knox stared at the keycode, and Dani looked up and down the corridor, waiting for someone to see them. Knox then noticed that four of the numbers were faded more than the other six.

"Dani, the nine, four, one and three are more faded and dirtier than the rest." Knox pointed to the keypad, and Dani looked. She punched in three, four, one and nine and was quickly rewarded by a click and a buzzing sound before the door opened. Dani looked at Knox with the biggest grin, obviously proud of herself.

"You jammy minx... come on, let's get you to work," Knox said as he swung the door open, looking at Dani as though she had the luck of the Irish. Dani took a seat at the computer on the double sized carved oak partner desk. The office walls were completely covered by book shelves and there wasn't a single inch spared.

"The computer is, as I expected, encrypted, but I will just work my magic," Dani said and her fingers moved faster than Knox could make out. Dani was obviously in her element.

"I am in," she said clapping her hands before punching the air making her look cute as hell.

"What are you doing in here?" yelled a voice from the doorway. Knox turned to face a three-hundred-pound giant of a man and he groaned inwardly. The last thing he needed now was a wrestling match with a juggernaut, one that might get Dani hurt in the process. So, Knox did the only thing he could think of... he acted like an arrogant ass.

. . .

"Why shouldn't I be in here, and how dare you interrupt us?" Knox said as he stared at the brute, who for a moment looked confused and wasn't sure what to say.

"My good friend Malcolm Howard kindly offered his office so my lovely wife here could do some private banking," Knox said and he looked back to Dani, who smiled at Knox as she fixated on him making the 'wife' statement again.

"I… I am sorry, but I will have to call this in to check." The brute's body language became less aggressive and almost hangdog, as he put a finger to his ear and was about to speak.

"Yes, yes you call it in. I want your name as I will be taking it up with your boss, Mr Howard. Darling can you believe….?" Knox bold as brass said as he walked slowly over to the brute. When he was close enough and just as the brute was about to speak, Knox turned back to Dani, stopping mid flow of his rant and delivered a swift kick to the brute's wedding tackle. The big guy bent over in sheer pain no man should have to feel in his balls and Knox upper cut him sending the brute backwards into the bookshelves.

Knox turned back to Dani whose eyes peered over the monitor screen like a rabbit in headlights. Then she winced and Knox thought that's odd before he looked back over his shoulder. The brute was getting up and once upright he wiped the blood from his mouth and spat the rest down on the floor. Great, so much for not getting into a wrestling match, Knox thought rolling his eyes.

Then, with a look of a man ready to go to war, he charged at Knox. But he shifted quickly, standing to one side as the guy stopped himself just as he reached the massive desk. The brute roared in anger as he slammed his hands down on the desk, making Dani jump before she steadied the now shaking monitor screen.

"You do have a temper, Tiny," Knox said with a smile as he beckoned his sparring partner over with a simple flip of his finger and took a fighter's stance. His opponent smiled a bloodied grin and came at Knox with a big telegraphed right hook, one Knox easily read stepping to the left and then forward into him, so that he could land his own right-handed punch. A sharp crack rang out as his fist connected with the brute's jaw, sending the enraged bulk of muscle stumbling. Knox took up his stance again, waited and then beckoned him over once more.

The guy was stupid but had finally learned his lesson, this time taking a slower approach and with his guard up he got within striking distance of Knox. A right followed by another right came Knox's way, he ducked the first and blocked the second with his arm. The guard smiled and let off a second barrage of punches. Knox dodged the first two then blocked the third, and a fourth came within millimetres of Knox's face as he pulled his head back. The brute almost laughed as he gave Knox a look of 'you weren't expecting that', then he beckoned Knox to him.

. . .

Knox went to right hook his opponent, who lifted his guard up to block and without mercy Knox snap kicked the guy's knee. Then he launched an attack consisting of a flurry of punches to the half falling body, before delivering a low swinging punch to his groin. But Knox didn't stop there as he shoulder barged him to the floor before taking advantage of his adversary's new position. Knox then continued his assault, brutally punching the guy's head, one that only stopped when Knox couldn't lift his hands anymore. Knox took a second, panting like an enraged beast after the kill, before getting up and dusting himself down as if nothing had happened. He adjusted his tux after he wiped his hands on the brute's shirt.

"I am all done, and I can see that you are too," Dani said as she stood up and pushed the monitor off the desk, letting it smash on the floor. Knox looked at Dani, almost shocked at her destructiveness.

"What, you can beat a guy's head in, and I can't break something? It will slow people down from finding out what I have done," Dani said as her cheeks flushed red. Knox smiled, walked over and took her hand.

"Let's get you out of here," Knox told her taking her smaller hand in his. But then something stopped him and he raised the back of his knuckles to her face and ran them down her soft skin.

"Great job, Dani," Knox told her tenderly, making her blush before he led her out of the office, pulling out the smartphone as he went, to call it in.

"Harris, the device is in place, you are good to go," Knox said urgently as they picked up their pace making their way down the luxury yacht's corridors and passageways. He then found his exit and they slipped outside, the cool air making Dani shiver.

"I am waiting at the pickup point, good luck Captain," Harris said before hanging up.

Two guards appeared from around the next corner, making Knox and Dani stop in their tracks. Knox turned to Dani and suddenly yanked her body to his frame. He lifted her face up with a firm but gentle grip under her chin and the wide-eyed look she gave him nearly had him kissing her instead.

"Do you trust me?" Knox said seriously as he looked Dani in the eyes... eyes he wanted to lose himself in.

"Yes Lucas, I trust..." He never let her finish that sentence as he suddenly picked her up, kissed her quick and said,

"Good girl." Then he dropped her over the side.

"AHHH! Lucas! You...Crazy...Bastard! What the hell!" Dani screamed as she struggled to swim. The roar of an outboard motor fired into life and a boat rushed over to her position. Harris, at the helm of the powerboat, cut the power to the engine as he rushed to Dani's aid pulling her from the warm waters and onto the boat. Harris quickly checked her over before heading back to the helm and steered at full power for a swift getaway.

Knox turned his attention back to the two guards who were still looking over the side in disbelief. It was now time for Knox to bring Howard in.

Knox pulled his gun and as he beat the two guards on the draw, he fired off four rounds which sent the two targets back hard to the floor. Knox needed to move fast, the music in the Gala was loud and would have masked gunfire but anyone on the ship near his position would have heard. Knox picked up one of the guard's weapons and ammo clip.

Knox entered the corridor from the outside deck that led back to the elevator and opted for the stairs. This turned out to be a bad move when as soon as Knox entered the stairway he was greeted by three men. They walked up from half a flight below, all the men looked at each other before it clicked. The three men began to run up the stairs, Knox fired taking one of the three down before he backed out through the door.

As he ran at full pelt, Knox just made it around the corner of the T-junction, when gun shots landed on the wall in front of him. Knox took cover, plastering his back to the wall. The lights dimmed as emergency red lighting came on and an alarm sounded, Knox heard the heavy boots of the men as they ran down the corridor towards his position. One, two, three and Knox ducked and rolled to the other side of the T-Junction and fired at the incoming men. The closest man's kneecaps took the first shot, the second missing and the third a slug right to his chest. Knox rolled behind cover and lay flat to the ground holding his gun up aimed at the corner and waited. The second guard came around the corner, wary, not looking at the floor, but when he did, Knox shot and hit his target clean in the forehead.

The sound of a helicopter coming into land could be heard. Knox knew it could only be for one man...*His target*. Knox wasn't about to let Howard get away so, finding the closest staircase he continued up trying to reach the helipad before it was too late. As he reached the top level and as far as the staircase would take him, he soon realised he needed to get up higher and fast. Knox in his haste, surprised a guard having a smoke. The guard fumbled and Knox ran into him, his momentum sent them to the rail and Knox pushed him clean over, into to the water below.

The quickest way to the helipad was for Knox to climb up over the railings and shimmy over and up some panelling that he could use as a makeshift ladder. The only issue with that was he would be exposed to a sixty-metre drop to the water's surface.

"Look up, only up...focus," he said to himself as he almost lost his footing, the roar of rotor blades over the ship giving Knox the added motivation to get a move on. Once he reached the top, Knox cautiously looked over the edge of the deck. Howard, nor any of his personnel, had reached the open helipad, just two ground crew awaited their imminent arrival. Knox had a plan and he would need to be quick about it. He pulled up and over onto a ledge, then took out his smartphone and dialled Gregory.

"Captain, is everything okay?" answered Gregory.

"Gregory, I need you to get your ass up to the helipad, this is the plan," Knox replied with no time for pleasantries or banter. With the crewmen focused on the now landing chopper, Knox climbed up onto the platform and ran over to the nearest man who was guiding the craft down. Grabbing the scruff of his neck he held a gun to his head, then looking at the pilot he mouthed the words 'I WILL SHOOT HIM, LAND!'. Knox rounded up the second crewman by waving him over as he and the guy he still had in his grasp backed up to the edge of the helipad.

"I will make it an easy choice boys, get shot or jump. Quick now, I don't have all day," Knox said with a glint in his eyes. The two crewmen looked at each other and after one of them shrugged his shoulders, he jumped. The other looked over as his colleague plummeted down and then back up, scared and with no intention of following.

"To be honest lad I don't blame you so here, let me help you out," Knox said as he took hold of the terrified man in a tight arm and head lock, and before the crewman had a chance, Knox had him right up to the edge where he let go of his hold, kicked him in the arse and sent him over the rail. Turning instantly and without a second thought for if the crewman survived the fall or not, he aimed his gun back at the pilot who was looking at Knox like a rabbit caught in headlights.

Minutes later, Howard arrived at the helipad with two of his security staff in tow, his private helicopter's engines still running, ready and waiting. In Howard's rush to get off the yacht and to safety, neither he nor his security noticed that there wasn't any ground crew. No, Howard just ran over to the chopper and his guards followed in a crouched position, looking up as the rotors whirled overhead.

"Knox!" Howard shouted over the wind and engine noise. Rightly so, he looked on in shock as he opened the door to see him sat in the back of the helicopter alone and no sign of the pilot.

"Get in Howard, you are coming with me," Knox said with a gun pointed directly at his head. Howard's security reached for their weapons.

"I would tell them to back down if they know what's good for them," Knox yelled as his eyes stared at Howard with a look that told him he was ready to kill.

"I don't know what you are playing at Knox, but you are out manned," Howard said with a smug grin on his face, a look that made Knox want to stamp his size twelve boot on it. But Knox would take his satisfaction in what would happen next.

. . .

"Last warning Howard, tell your men to stand down," Knox snarled. And just as Howard ducked to the ground and his two men drew their weapons, shots could just be heard over the vortex roar and engine whine. The thugs that were Howard's security fell to the deck as exit wounds exploded with bursts of blood. Howard looked back at his men, then around him before finally seeing the silhouette of a man holding a gun walking with resolve towards him. Gregory had lain in wait to provide cover.

"Get in the chopper, now!" Gregory shouted over to Howard who begrudgingly did as he was ordered.

"Buckle up Howard, safety first," Knox said with his own smug expression.

"You're sure you know how to fly this bird?" Knox said to Gregory as he hurried into the pilot's seat.

"It's been awhile, and I have never flown one as posh as this. But hey it's like riding a bike, right?" Gregory said as he flicked switches and looked around as if he had no idea what the controls were.

"You know how to inspire confidence, Gregory," Knox said knowing full well Gregory had years of experience flying army helicopters before he was recruited into T.I.7, but he wasn't going to let onto Howard as he sat there with the fear of God etched across his face.

. . .

"Where do you Cowboys think you're taking me, who do you work for?" Howard said trying to hide his nervousness.

"You will find out soon enough Howard, now sit back, shut up and enjoy the ride," Knox said as he tapped Gregory on the shoulder to signal let's get out of here, to which he nodded as the helicopter effortlessly lifted from the pad and made its way out over the marina steadily as it rose, building up speed.

"Who do you work for... the Cartel, the Africans? What are they paying you? I will double it, you know I am good for it don't you Knox? Tell your friend." Howard's desperation doubled as the realisation of his situation set in. Knox smiled before swiftly leaning over to Howard and cracked an almost jaw breaking punch across his chin. Gregory looked over at Knox with a look of 'did you really just do that?'

"I warned him to shut up, it will make for a more peaceful flight," Knox said smiling as he shrugged his shoulders and cracked his knuckles. Gregory swallowed hard as he remembered what one of Knox's right hooks felt like and he muttered a quiet,

"Right," before getting back to the job at hand.

It wasn't long before they landed outside the warehouse of T.I.7's mobile headquarters. Carter and Harris could be seen waiting, sat inside one of the Jaguar F-space, parked to the side of a clear area of wasteland perfect for the chopper to land on, even if it would kick up a tonne of sand and dust.

It was time to deliver Howard to Carter and for…

Howard's interrogation.

19

TRUTH OR BULL CRAP

Howard awoke to darkness, his movement restricted to mere millimetres as gaffer tape bonds secured him to the chair he was sat upon. His breathing became quick and shallow, his eyes almost hurt as they dilated in vain to find some source of light.

"Sir, he is awake," Gregory informed Knox. Howard moved his head from side to side shocked at the sound of a voice as he tried to work out where in the room the voice came from.

"Are the instruments ready?" Knox asked which sent Howard's breathing into an even more erratic state as he desperately tried to overcome his fear and speak.

"Almost, Sir," Gregory replied as he placed metal surgical instruments down on a stainless-steel work surface. The sound unmistakable as each one tapped and scraped against each other, as the two metal surfaces met.

. . .

"What do you want from me? Who are you!?" Howard screamed uncontrollably as his fear and survival instincts took over.

"Listen we can make a deal, I can make you very wealthy," Howard said in a high-pitched panic as he became more and more desperate.

"Trust me, you can be long gone and stinking rich, before whoever you are working for knew you had let me go," Howard said as his head dropped and he listened for someone to respond.

"Take it off," snarled Knox, and Gregory pulled the blackout hood from Howard's head. Bright light blinded him as Knox focused a single spotlight inches from Howard's face.

"When is the consignment coming in!?" Knox barked out as he stood behind the light looking down at Howard.

"What... I don't know what you..." Howard shouted, but before he finished was punched hard in his side. His body tried to lurch forward as he gasped for breath but was held in place by its bonds.

"The shipment! When is it coming in? We know you are involved," Knox barked down at him.

"I am not involved, I am not. Pérez is the one, I just work for him! He's the one calling the shots," Howard said in a pitiful tone as he sat with slumped shoulders. The very picture of a man willing to give them everything they needed.

"Why would we believe that, Howard? You look and act like you are partners, if not even running the show." Knox replied as he nodded to Gregory who took his cue and hit out at him again. Howard rocked on the chair from the force of the blow, then frantically looked around trying to see the room and where his attacker was but his eyes couldn't focus fast enough. As soon as they came almost close to adjusting to the light Gregory would grab the back of his head and force him to look at the light again. The light was so bright, that even when Howard closed his eyes as tight as he could, all he could see was blinding whiteness bleeding through his eyelids.

"Because I want out! I will give you all the information to bring Pérez down, I just want protection," Howard said as he winced.

"What makes you think we care about your well-being, why would we offer protection? What's the name of the ship, Howard?" Knox said as he picked up a sharp, cold steel scalpel. He signalled to Gregory to move the light away, this allowed Howard to see what Knox was picking up before he blinded Howard again with it.

"You are a government agency! MI5, MI6? You are British SIS right?" Howard said as his voice became frantic with panic at the sight of the scalpel.

. . .

"Guess again! Now tell me, when is the shipment coming into Malaga, and what is it called?" Knox said as he took hold of Howard's first finger, pressed the tip of the scalpel blade up under the finger nail and dug it in with a twist, Howard shrieked and shook uncontrollably with the pain.

"You can't torture me! There are human rights laws, your government will be hung out to dry over this," Howard said after Knox took away the simple yet effective tool.

"Tut, tut Howard, you are not listening, yet again..." Knox leant down and tapped him twice on the cheek with the scalpel before finishing off his sentence,

"...And if you don't listen, then how are you expected to learn? So, let me make myself even clearer for you...now are you listening?" Knox asked with deadly calm before taking the cutting instrument to his ear and holding it out as if ready to cut. Then he offered some crucial advice.

"We don't answer to any government, and they will never find all the pieces of your body, let alone know what happened to you. So, once again I ask you, when is the shipment coming in?" Knox whispered into Howard's ear after he gripped hold of his head in a vice like hold.

"Do your ears need cleaning out, Howard?" Knox whispered as he placed the scalpel on Howard's ear lobe. Howard froze with the feel of the cold blade on his skin.

"Maybe you will listen harder if you only have the one ear working," Knox threatened as he tightened his grip and slowly started to move the point of the scalpel down into Howard's ear.

"I will tell you, I will tell you, stop, please stop!" cried Howard.

. . .

"Time, date and name of the ship!" Knox demanded as he took the blade away and released his grip.

"Pérez will kill me, if the Cartel doesn't kill me first, you have to protect me and I will tell you everything. I need protection," he pleaded.

"Tell us the name and time of the ship arriving and if the information is right we will do a deal," Knox said lying through his teeth.

"This evening, Malaga port, Isabella, the ship's called Isabella," Howard said as his head dropped, chin firmly against his chest.

"The bloody boat's called Isabella?" Knox asked as he laughed then turned to the CCTV and nodded, signalling to Carter and the NEST team to start checking it out, if they weren't already.

"So, you are going to protect me, right? I will give you all you need and more," Howard said and couldn't have looked more like a weasel.

"Speaking of the name Isabella, where is your wife-to-be?" Knox couldn't help but sound disgusted at the man he knew had given her up.

. . .

"How would I know, they took her," Howard said sheepishly, beads of sweat dripping down his face.

"How about I take your fingernails off one at a time until you tell me, fun for me, not so much for you," Knox said impatiently as he took hold of the finger he'd first put the scalpel blade under, the nail was now black from the blood congealing under it.

"No, no wait okay, okay. Someone has been hijacking shipments. It started with a shipment of drugs, then weapons. But the last few have hit the Cartel's money!" Howard said looking at Knox trying to see if he was buying it.

"The Cartel thinks Pérez has something to do with it, but he hasn't and now he is running out of time. The Cartel is demanding he personally pay them back or they will kill him and they want to use Isabella as blackmail." Howard hung his head in shame.

"And you delivered her to them?" Knox shouted. And Howard's silence spoke volumes. Knox hit Howard across the face and this time, it wasn't just to get him to talk, it was in anger.

"You, spineless bastard! Where is she, who did you give her to?" Knox shouted as he hit Howard over and over before a cutting voice spoke over a speaker system...*it was Carter.*

"The girl is secondary, get back on point. Inform our guest his computer system has given us all the information we need.

Unless he has other information, terminate him," Carter's emotionless voice said. Knox stopped mid hit, his fist still positioned up above his head ready to rain down on Howard. Knox knew this was a tactic by Carter, but he still couldn't help the guilty feeling of them not giving a shit about Isabella. Yes, she was a bitch and a nightmare, but she didn't deserve to be treated like this. Knox stepped back and picked up his gun that was resting next to the surgical instruments.

"Last chance Howard, they have decoded your hard drives, we have the ship's details. So, if you have anything useful, then now is the time to share before there is nothing left to stop me from blowing your fucking brains out," Knox said menacingly as he chambered a round.

"No, no wait! Just wait! I handed her over to the Cartel and they took her, where I don't know. I don't know what is going to happen but they will use her to blackmail Pérez. He owes them more than he can give them." Howard spoke so fast Knox could only just understand him.

"I can lead you to who is hijacking the shipments, the person who is turning the Cartel and Pérez against each other," Howard said as he looked at Knox, then to Gregory as if to say he had more information so don't kill him. Knox put the gun to Howard's temple.

"I can give you El Toro, El Toro! I am working with him, I can give you the Bull!" Howard screamed at the top of his lungs.

"And El Toro is?" Knox asked with a raised eyebrow. Howard took a moment as if speaking the name would sign his death sentence, and the very walls had the 'Bull's' ears.

"El Toro, The Bull. That's all I know him as! He is like a ghost, no one knows who he is or fuck, what he even looks like! Yet he has an army of mercenaries and men willing not only to work for him but die for him," Howard said with an expression that Knox couldn't fully trust.

"You talk as though you admire him. How the fuck are you going to lead us to him if you…?" Knox said as he glared into Howard's eyes and hit him over the head.

"A, don't know what he looks like!?" Knox said then hit him again.

"B, have never met him!?" Again, Knox said before he hit him.

"And C, you don't know his real name!? All three mean you don't have shit to give us!" Knox said as he went to hit him again but stopped as Howard tried to speak.

"Because I have something he wants and we…we were going to meet," Howard said, tears in his eyes and close to sobbing like a child.

"And what is it you have?" Knox stepped back putting the gun down on the side, repulsed at how weak Howard was.

"Give me protection, and I will give you El Toro," Howard mumbled through his snivelling.

"Take a break, Captain." Carter's voice sounded over the speaker.

"Bag the pathetic runt," Knox sneered as he walked out of the room, as Gregory carried out his orders and hooded Howard.

"Splendid work Captain, although I would say we have found someone to rival your interrogating, Harris," Carter said looking over to Harris who looked back not at all phased at Carter's teasing.

"Thank you, Sir, I am not sure if that is a compliment," Knox said with a worried look as you couldn't make out what Harris was thinking.

"The ship, gentlemen." Harris' deep quiet voice spoke.

"Yes, yes quite right Major. Miss Rose, if you would," Carter said after clearing his throat and beckoning an anxious looking Rose to speak.

"Er… hello, gentlemen, we have decoded the whole of Pérez's computer data, and…" Rose said a little nervous to be speaking but then was interrupted by Harris.

"You mean *you* decoded the computer data," Harris corrected with a firm but unaggressive tone, making it clear to everyone that it was all down to her skills. And then motioned an apology for interrupting her. Knox couldn't help but take note of the significance of this and if he didn't know any better, he would go as far as to say that Harris had a thing for the geeky tech.

"Well, yes…okay. Er… Howard is telling the truth to a degree, there is a ship called the Isabella and it is due this evening in Malaga. It's voyage patterns stack up with what we would expect if it had MOD shipments booked onto it. It should only be half loaded up with legit weapons, but it's got a full itinerary," Rose said with a little embarrassment that Harris spoke out for her, deep down she liked it and her confidence obviously grew the more she spoke.

"What is the rest of the cargo filling the itinerary?" Knox asked as he watched Harris and Rose look into each other's eyes a moment longer than was necessary. Harris' cool persona cracked as he gave the smallest of smiles to a slightly blushing Rose. Knox wasn't the only one that noticed it, Carter coughed.

"It says... Agricultural and farming equipment," Rose said as she flipped through her notes this time on her tablet and not her hand.

"Thank you, Miss Rose you are excused," Carter said with a smile. Knox nodded and Harris grinned making the young tech blush. Rose walked away with a slight skip in her step and Knox knew that if she could have got away with it, she would have fist bumped the air. Hell, but she most likely would when she got out of sight, Knox thought with a smirk.

"Major, I want a team put together and I want you on that ship," Carter said going into full military mode.

"We are down on numbers, we will need to pull in some resources, Sir," Harris replied to Carter as he looked over to Knox.

"I will put in an order for the 22nd who are on training manoeuvres in Gibraltar, they can offer support. Right men, get everything ready," Carter said with a positive tone to his voice. Knox gave Harris a smile at the fact his old SAS regiment would be called in as reinforcements, as they both made their way out of the tactical room.

"So, calling in the SAS over the Commandos." Knox jibed at Harris.

. . .

"Yes, they do tend to get the easy glamour missions, don't they?" Harris was quick to respond and Knox looked at him with a blank expression.

"Huh… glamour missions?" Knox asked back with a big grin.

"You know what they say, Captain…" Harris said reeling Knox in.

"No Major, what do they say?" Knox asked and he couldn't help but be intrigued.

"Stars are for Hollywood, but real actors are found on the stage," Harris said with a grin, Knox laughed.

"Come on Harris the Commandos are more like understudies." Knox winked as they both met Dani as they passed the canteen tent. Harris smirked with a 'we will finish this later' look as he nodded to Knox and then smiled at Dani tipping an invisible hat. Harris walked on but looked back at Knox when he was out of sight of Dani and gave him the thumbs up.

"Dani… look I am…" Knox began to speak but stopped when Dani pulled back her arm and punched Knox in the bicep.

. . .

"I would bloody slap you, but I like that damn handsome face of yours too much. Blast your genes!" Dani said trying to look mad but in truth, she was glad to see him. Knox took the punch and didn't even try to stop the grin that crossed his face. Dani was wearing army fatigues with her hair tied back and her glamorous makeup washed off. But God strike him down now if she wasn't sexy as hell.

"I am sorry Lass, I had to do it to keep you safe and I made sure Harris would have your back," Knox said trying not to sound cheeky and failed miserably. So, he held his arms out for a hug.

"You have got to be bloody joking! You should see the state of my dress," Dani said again trying to sound angry, but a smile was playing at the edges of her mouth and Knox could see it. He took hold of both her hands and gently pulled her to him. Dani played at pulling back but then let Knox wrap his warm, strong arms around her and she sank into his chest.

"I can't lie, Lucas, as mad as I was and looking like a drowned rat, I was worried and I was really scared," Dani said as she pulled herself into Knox, closing her eyes and taking relief in getting the chance to be close to him and hear his heartbeat. Knox held Dani tighter and took in a deep breath through his nose, losing himself for a moment in her sweet scent, and even now after a dunk in the Marina, she still smelled amazing.

"Look Dani, my job, my lifestyle, well… it has never worked

with a relationship," Knox said and Dani opened her eyes at the words she feared the most.

"But... I care for you and you know I think it's time maybe I change that," Knox said as he struggled to get the words out.

"Lucas, what are you saying... are you...?" Dani's sentence trailed off as she looked up at Knox with hope-filled eyes... eyes that just melted all two hundred and forty pounds of skin, muscle, and bone of him. Knox took Dani's face in his hands and bent down to kiss her. Dani's eyes shut as soon as his hands touched her cheeks, and she pushed herself up onto tiptoes. Their lips met and everything went silent around them.

"When all this is finished with, I want to spend some time together and..." Knox said after pulling his lips away from Dani's delightful soft embrace but kept his as close as he could when he spoke.

"And...?" Dani whispered and she swallowed hard before taking a breath.

"Talk out what this is and see how we can make it work," Knox calmly said trying to keep his desires at bay and not just take her right there and then. Dani's face lit up with a smile that could warm the coldest of souls, and Knox just had to kiss her again before asking her,

. . .

"Can you wait here for me?"

"I don't know, will I not be in the way?" Dani tentatively asked, still thinking about their last kiss and stopping herself from doing something embarrassing like touching her lips as though she could still feel his mark branded there.

"You are protected here and I want you as safe as can be when I am away. Please," Knox said as he looked Dani intensely in the eyes. Suddenly a warmth the likes she had never known ignited deep down, in the depths of her soul. She had never felt *safe*, something Knox didn't need to know about. But right then and there, just knowing that someone in the world cared that much for her well-being, was like finally finding water after spending years of drowning in sand.

"Okay, I will wait here. Olivia is lovely and she sorted me out with the…erm… uniform," Dani said blushing as she showed off the fatigues.

"Then remind me to thank her personally," Knox said with a raise of his eyebrow and a cheeky look.

"Lucas!" Dani said playfully, hitting his hard chest and nearly biting her lip at all the muscle she encountered with just that one touch.

. . .

"Captain…" called Harris.

"Major?" Knox looked up at Harris with a questioning look.

"You're needed," Harris said and then walked away to give them privacy.

"Go… do what you do best and I promise to stay safe and will wait here for you," Dani said with a smile and a feigned light-hearted tone that Knox knew was trying to hide the sadness and worry. So, Knox kissed her forehead and began to walk off.
    "Lucas?" Dani called.

"Yes, Lass?" Knox looked back with a smile.

"Stay safe and you'd better come back to me…after all, I need a lift back to the hotel," Dani replied with a smile and a wink. Knox beat his chest over his heart twice then pointed to her.

"Well then, I have to come back," Knox smirked and Dani walked into the canteen.

Knox walked into the kit room and opened his cabinet of weapons. Then with an exhale out and a clearing of his mind, he entered his meditation as he…

. . .

BLOOD RETRIBUTION

Prepared for the mission.

20

ISABELLA RAID

"Whisky one, Bourbon one, ETA on target one minute." The radio comms operator stated.

"You heard that lads, get your heads in the game, we're going in!" Harris yelled out at the squad of SAS boat troopers who all replied sternly 'Sir' over the roar of the outboard motors. The waves crashed on the side of the rigid inflatable tactical boat with the stench of diesel that overpowered the muggy sea air.

Over in the distance and coming in at speed, the dark blue N3 Dauphin helicopter operated by six five eight Squadron, dropped down from high off the coastline mountain ridge and down into the Bay of Malaga's port. Two miles out to sea, anchored down, was their target, The Isabella. The two-hundred-and-ninety-metre Panamax class vessel dominated the horizon.

"Deploy in sixty seconds, Captain." Carter sounded over the headset of the helicopter's intercom to Knox.

"Copy that," Knox replied in a locked, focused manner as he held his hand up and gave the eight-man SAS team a signal that they were about to deploy. Ropes, knots and carabiners were double and triple checked all over again as Knox opened the sliding door next to him. He positioned himself at the edge and leant forward until his rope took the strain. He readied his weapon and focused his eye down the sight and locked onto the ship's deck.

"Armed targets on deck, targets on deck," Knox said over the headset intercom.

"Permission to engage," Carter replied clinically, as the N3 circled around and then held a hovering position over an area of the deck with the best tactical position for the team to deploy.

"Go, go, go!" sounded around the chopper, as ropes spiralled down to the deck below with a whip and a snap. Two elite SAS servicemen moved to the doorway as Knox lay down covering fire and took out two mercenaries that couldn't have looked any more out of place on a ship if they tried. The ship was crawling with a hired band of what looked like a malevolent African nation's force.

"Good luck, Captain," Carter called out as the last of the SAS men had descended to the ship.

"Sir." Knox's final word as he abseiled down at a blistering pace before slowing his descent with a yank of his rope brake. Then he joined the team who had setup in a circular covering formation as they lay down fire on targets as they waited for the arrival of their team leader. Knox took a knee as he assessed before motioning in the direction they needed to go. Each member of the team worked in perfect efficiency as they steadily made their way around the deck and its many turns and corners. Knox had his hand on the shoulder of the last man, in their clearing sweep a hatch lid flung open and slammed back on itself as a mercenary jumped up firing.

"Down!" Knox and a few others of the SAS team yelled in lightning reactions, hitting the ground, the rear man and Knox fired direct and in controlled bursts of fire from their C8 carbine assault rifles, taking out the threat.

"Smoke that hole!" Knox called out as he and the rest of the team got to their feet as the body of the mercenary slumped over. His order was quickly executed as one grenade was dropped down the hatch and the blast lifted the body of the mercenary, ripping his lower half into blood soaked tatters of flesh.

"Keep moving, clear this deck," Knox ordered and they all moved in sync, a timing and fluidity that was forged in endless drill after drill on the training grounds of their Hereford base.

"Up high, eleven o'clock!" One of the lead men shouted as they spotted and passed under two mercenaries that came from behind a container above them. Knox grabbed his man in front of him and pulled him into cover as shots rang out around them. Nothing was said, it was just accepted as Knox would expect the same from any one of the team. They all had each other's backs, no matter what. They both looked at each other as they waited for their cue, click, click, click and the first of the two mercs was out and reloading. They had to time this right, they stood ready to move as they waited…click.

"Go…!" Knox shouted as he heard the first click of the second merc empty his mag. Locked in his sights, Knox shot at the first mercenary who was just pulling his gun up after reloading. The shot blew the man down, the second merc was too slow, and Knox's next shot blew the merc's jaw clean off with his third shot planted cleanly in his chest. Knox carried on moving as he trusted his man to take out the second mercenary, which he did with just as deadly accuracy. Their bodies landed with a thud behind them as their focus returned to what was in front of them, forgetting the last two kills as if they were paper targets on a training drill.

"Team split, fifty-fifty," Knox ordered as they reached an

intersection that took the teams down the port and starboard sides of the ship.

"Whisky, come in." Knox heard over his comms.

"Whisky one, receiving over," Knox replied as he fired off two clean well-aimed shots at an assailant thirty or so metres away up on a gantry.

"Bourbon has boarded and we are making inroads to your location, over," Harris informed Knox as the gantry assailant fell to his demise and his body bounced off corners of different containers.

"Grenade!" shouted the lead man as it passed him. Knox was pushed back before his partner stepped forward to kick the cheap Soviet F1 hand grenade away, sending it fifteen or twenty metres across the deck. It exploded sending a boom that echoed and reverberated around the stacks of forty-foot containers. As the air settled around the blast zone, Knox and his team setup behind available cover, as their training had taught them that an attack was imminent. Right on cue, four suicide mercenaries came from their cover and fired as they ran with as much skill and accuracy as an overweight, hungover, stag party at a paintball park, and ones in the rain blinded by steamed up face masks at that. The team picked off each of them in succession, it was almost like shooting fish in a barrel.

Knox spotted Harris as he signalled that the deck from their location had been cleared.

"All teams check in," Harris called over the comms, and the two teams members all checked in one by one.

"Bourbon one, clear inside the ship, Whisky one, find the bounty." Carter spoke over the comms from the patrolling N-3 chopper above, both Knox and Harris signed off 'copy' and gave each other a head nod as they both led their teams away.

"Take cover! Threat from above!" Carter screamed over the

comms, as the teams unquestioningly dived for cover where they could find it.

Up on the bridge castle of the ship, a group of mercenaries were setting up a tripod mounted heavy gauge machine gun, as one of them fired a shoulder mounted RPG at the team. They all watched it as the rockets downward projection came at them in what felt like slow motion. The two nearest SAS men it was directed at ran and jumped for cover. They narrowly escaped its blast as the anti-tank weapon blew a hole in the deck and nearest container, sending a hail storm of shrapnel through the air, catching one of the team across his arm.

"We need air support!" Knox called over the comms.

"Copy that, Whisky one," Carter replied as the N-3 swung around and came in on the blind side of the group of mercenaries. Knox and his men kept cover as the mounted machine gun let rip, the high calibre bullets drilling holes and bouncing all over the deck. Carter sat at the open door of the N-3 and fired his own RPG at the group of mercenaries. And with a direct hit, it blew the target and large area of the bridge to smithereens, sending one of the covered mercs in flames over the edge backwards.

To the cheers of the SAS men, Knox lay down a printout onto a make do surface, and ran his index finger down the list of container locations that had been highlighted by Rose. He established the nearest suspected container and directed the team to it over the sound of muffled gunfire and flash grenade explosions, as Harris and his team entered the ship.

"Cover me!" Knox shouted as he reached the first container. He was handed a pair of bolt cutters to break the Klicker K2 bolt seal, once cut, it allowed him to open the cam lock system to gain access inside the container.

"Stand back..." Knox said as he waited for his team to move within a safe distance, he opened the locking system with a twist and shunt and the door was free of the cam locks. He mentally counted to three, pulled the heavy steel door wide open as he took cover behind it.

"Sir, it's empty!" One of his team called out.

"What the hell, did I get the wrong number or location?" Knox said as he looked into the dark empty space, then looked at its location and back at the printout. Everything lined up, a container ship would never sail with empty containers.

"Eye in the sky, negative on the first container, moving to next target." Knox got on the comes to Carter, before leading his team again to the next suspected container.

"Whisky one, Bourbon one pinned down, repeat pinned down," Harris called over the intercom.

"Bourbon one, what is your location, over?" Knox replied to Harris.

"Two decks down near the mess hall, six or eight combatants dug in," Harris said to the sound of gunfire and shouting. Knox looked at the blueprints to the ship on the tactical tablet.

"Bourbon one, hold targets, Whisky one coming to support," Knox reassured.

"Copy, Whisky one. Out." Harris acknowledged before getting back to the firefight. Knox turned to his eight-man SAS team and split them six to two, after giving the six-man team instructions on how to find the containers. He then instructed the other two to follow him. He had a plan but he just hoped they could execute it soon enough.

Making his way over the top of Harris' position two decks above the mess hall, Knox's plan was to come at the mercenaries from the rear. As they entered a stairwell, Knox led the way and instantly heard and saw down between the rails, armed men running up the stairs from two floors below. As they made their way up, Knox did something instinctively and not in the SAS training handbook.

He knew they didn't have time to get bogged down in a stairwell gun fight. So, he pulled a pin from his flash grenade, and with perfect timing, he dropped it over between the rails. It landed in the direct path of the mercenaries and it bounced twice on the steps in front of the surprised leading merc. Then with an eardrum busting bang, the flash grenade blew before the men could have time to dive for cover. Knox had started running down the stairs as soon as he had dropped the grenade, arriving just moments after the blast, fired concentrated bursts of rapid fire at the mercenaries lay prostrate on the stairs. His two SAS back up men rushed down and surveyed the aftermath as they double checked the mercenaries were dead, then looked at Knox.

"You crazy bastard!" said the first SAS man.

"I have never seen anything like that before, and I don't want to ever see it again. I thought you had lost the plot, Sir," the second said.

"What's your names lads, and don't give me any of the nick and call names crap," Knox said to both with a slightly unnerving look in his eyes.

"I'm Conor, and he is Will, Sir." said Conor the Irishman of the two.

"Well Conor and Will, if you ever see me try to do something like that again… don't let me," Knox said as he winked at them both, then reloaded and turned to carry on down the stairwell.

When they reached the deck level of the mess hall, Conor and Will took point on the entrance and threw a flash grenade into the hallway leading off the stairwell.

"Whisky one calling Bourbon one, over." Knox radioed into Harris.

"Bourbon one, receiving.," a stressed Harris answered.

"Bourbon one we are on your level, one-hundred metres in front of you, we will engage the enemy from behind their lines. Over." Knox said over an interference laced connection, Harris could only just make out what Knox had said before his attention was drawn by one of his team taking a shot to the arm.

Conor and Will entered the smoke-filled hallway, one body moaned on the floor nullified by the shock of the flash grenade. Will put two shots in his head and carried on sweeping the hall with Conor. Knox followed as he guarded the rear. Making good ground Conor and Will flawlessly take out the oncoming enemy threat who couldn't match the skill set of the elite trained men.

Knox passed a door that was first checked by Conor and found to be to be locked when he passed it. The door smashed open as Knox passed, by the force of a 300lb beast of a man who instantly tackled Knox to the wall. Gripping Knox's assault rifle the animal ripped it out of his hands sending it flying down the hallway floor. Conor and Will couldn't get a clear shot as the asshole that tussled with Knox bounced from one wall to the next down the narrow hallway. The heavy breathing colossus punched at Knox's head, who ducked just in time to hear the knuckles break on the hand as it hit the steel wall. Knox didn't like going to ground but he had no choice when the asshole pinned Knox by the throat and leant his face into Knox and said something in Sudanese Arabic.

"Kuring bakal ngahakan haté anjeun." (I will eat your heart)

Knox snarled back before suddenly punching his arms up then with a firm grip on his hidden blade, he brought both hands down, brutally hitting the elbow joint of his attacker's arm breaking the grip of his throat. Knox then sent a flurry of strikes and punches, with the blade still in hand, that was almost too fast to see. He targeted the neck, arm pit and abdomen of the massive guy and silence fell as the Sudanese giant stood staring into Knox's eyes as a look of realisation swept over his face. Blood began to pour from the neck and torso of his giant assailant as he dropped to his knees. Knox then ran the blade of the knife in his hand across his opponent's throat in one swift and unforgiving move. He simply walked away and picked up his gun as the animal bled out.

"I didn't even see you use that blade.," Conor said in astonishment to Knox as he walked up to him, passing the Sudanese giant that was now slumped, still kneeling, with his chin on his chest and as dead as they come.

"A knife as a weapon is to be felt, not seen," Knox replied as he wiped the blood off the blade on his thigh.

"You used it to break his grip on your throat?" Will said who looked puzzled.

"Yes, I brought it down hard into the inside elbow joint. It's an effective break, do they not teach that move in Hereford now?" Knox said with a smirk as he knew they didn't, the last instructor who taught it was retired off early.

"Brutal.," Conor said in awe, as they regrouped and began moving to Harris' position again.

They had five mercenaries that were pinning Harris and his team down in their sight.

"Bourbon one, we have a clean line of sight of the enemy. Take cover, over," Knox said over the intercom.

"Copy Whisky one, ready when you are," Harris said in reply then ordered his team to hold fire and take cover. The five mercenaries continued to fire for a brief time, then visibly looked confused at one another as they didn't understand why their adversaries had stopped fighting. Knox, Conor and Will sent in a flash grenade and after the explosion stormed in and mercilessly neutralised all five men.

The room sounded off to the calls of 'Clear!' as both teams met over the fallen bodies of their enemies.

"It's good to see you, Major," Knox said to Harris who looked like his patience had been tested.

"Not as good as it is to see you, Captain. Thank you," Harris said as he shook hands with Knox.

"Captain, Captain, over." came over the intercom, it was one of the six-man SAS team Knox had ordered to find the arms, drugs and money.

"Receiving, go ahead over," Knox said as he looked at Harris and mouthed the words 'they have found them.'

"You need to get up on deck Sir, over." the team member said with a note of urgency in his tone.

"You have found the goods? Over." Knox questioned.

"Like I said Captain you need to come and see this."

Knox and Harris instructed the team to confirm that there were no more threats on board as they left for the deck. Once on deck they could see the six SAS men stood next to a container, they were holding their hands up, as if to say 'stop don't move' as they stood looking into the container.

"Sirs, look at this." they said to Knox and Harris as they made their way over.

"The weapons?" Harris asked as both he and Knox looked around the big open door. Their eyes adjusted to the darkness and then Knox pulled a small torch from his belt and shone it into the container taking in the heart-breaking sight. Twenty to twenty-five young almost skeleton-like girls, weak and barely able to stand through malnutrition, sat and lay in the stench of their own urine and excrement.

Knox had to hold his hand over his mouth and nose as it was too much for him to bear. And then irate mumbles and bangs echoed in the container. One of the girls lay near the back kicked her legs into the air and banged her feet down on the rough wood panel floor. She achieved her aim and gained Knox's attention.

There, lay before Knox, was *Isabella*.

21

CORPSE

Knox ran over to Isabella and scooped her up in his arms, taking her out of the container and into the smoky haze where he could finally take a large breath to try and rid the stench from his airways. As he set her down he drew his blood-stained knife which made Isabella's eyes almost pop out at the sight of it. He cut through her tight bonds and exposed her broken sore skin as he slowly pulled the dried blood encrusted hemp rope. Isabella winced as her eyes teared up and she wrapped her arms around Knox. Then she quietly sobbed with her body jerking as she battled to control her emotions but lost.

"You're okay, you're safe now, Isabella look at me," Knox said in a soft comforting tone as he gently held her, she gripped onto him squeezing as hard as she could but she couldn't bring herself to look at him.

"Isabella, no one is going to hurt you now, I promise," Knox said as he lifted her chin with his hand so that their eyes met.

Knox with his dark intensity and Isabella's tearful make-up blackened, with sadness.

"I thought… they were going to… *kill me.*" Isabella managed to stutter out before totally breaking down as she buried her face once more into Knox's shoulder. He held the back of her head as he looked to his men.

"Don't just stand there, help those women!" Knox demanded with a deep-felt anger, and just as the team jumped into action an echoing ringtone came from inside the container. Everyone except Isabella looked around to the direction of the sound, a sound that amplified as it rung.

One of the team ran into the container and found a basic mobile phone gaffer taped to a dark corner of the container. He quickly brought it to Knox who opened the flip phone and held it to his ear saying nothing.

"Always the hero, Lucas." An electronically disguised voice spoke but still, Knox said nothing.

"Come now Lucas, you haven't turned shy, have you? Speak." Even with the disguised voice, Knox could hear the contemptuous tone, but still, he said nothing.

"You are no fun Lucas, I was looking forward to a little repartee. Shame, I find it makes the next part a little easier." Knox listened to the disturbed voice and it sent a chill down his spine as that gut feeling screamed at him from inside.

"If you're not going to play ball then I will cut to the chase," the voice said with annoyance.

"Finally, you say something worth hearing and responding to. I was getting bored," Knox said as he gritted his teeth.

"So, the hero speaks, do you know who I am? Well, at least what those who fear me call me?"

"Can't say I really give a shit what the fuck they call you, so, get to the fucking point already!" Knox said his frustration growing.

"Lucas, you are so impatient but have it your way. I have rigged the ship to blow, enough to send it and everything on it into an inferno even Hell would struggle to match," the robotic voice taunted with an almost joyous overtone.

"There are women on board, you fucking coward! Why don't you come meet me here and I will show you Hell!" Knox said as he couldn't hold it back. Harris took the phone from Knox's hand and held it out switching it to speaker phone.

"Language Lucas, is that any way to talk to the man holding a detonator switch?" the voice said. Harris looked to Knox and Isabella's head shot up and glared at them.

"So, there is a bomb, get on with it!" Knox snapped as he held Isabella tight as she wriggled and squirmed, he put his hand firmly over Isabella's month as she was about to scream.

• • •

"You have a choice Lucas, save the girls, your men and yourself…" the voice said before it paused.

"Or stay on the ship and die with the other poor souls locked away somewhere," the voice said before erupting into laughter. Harris took hold of Isabella and handed the phone back to Knox.

"You are bluffing!?" Knox said in a questioning unsure manner, Harris shook his head in disbelief, then moved into action signalling the men to round up the girls as he rushed over to them with Isabella.

"If you think so Lucas, then be the half-assed hero and save only those you can see."

"Don't do this! Just tell me, are there more girls on this ship!?" Knox demanded.

"Tick tock Captain, you have ten minutes," said the voice as sirens sounded and red lights flashed around the ship as its warning system activated.

"Name? Tell me your fucking name?!" Knox shouted.

• • •

"The clock is ticking down Captain, do you have time for this?" mocked the voice.

"I like to know the names of the cowards I kill when looking them in the eyes as they die!" snarled Knox with a hate reserved for the men he despised with every cell in his body.

"El Toro…" he said with a deep haunting voice as the disguise had been turned off, followed by the line cutting dead.

"Eye in the sky, we need immediate evac, over!" Knox declared speaking directly into his comms.

"Copy Whisky one, ETA the highest container point two minutes, over," Carter responded instantly.

"Eye, ship rigged to blow ten-minute count down. We have female civilians on board for evac," Knox replied as Harris and the rest of the team cut free the women's bonds as they gathered the frightened women together.

"Whisky one, numbers?" Carter asked sharply, as Harris heard this he did a quick head count and signalled to Knox twenty-one.

. . .

"Twenty-one Sir, but there is reason to believe there are more hidden aboard in containers. Over." Knox stressed to Carter.

"Evac with known civilians, and pull Whisky and Bourbon teams. Over," Carter coolly said with no compassion.

"Copy," Knox said with as much disdain as he could with the four-letter word.

"Harris," Knox called over and Harris wasted no time in coming over to him.

"Captain…?" Harris looked on at Knox with a sense of urgency.

"If you were to blow this ship up and wanted to hide the explosives where would you do it?" Knox asked with just as much urgency.

"Captain, you heard the Brig's orders," Harris said as he was about to turn and get back to evacuating the civilians off the ship.

"Fuck what Carter ordered, I am going to go find and neutralise that bomb. You follow orders Sir and get these girls off the ship," Knox said as he grabbed Harris's arm stopping him from turning away.

"Bloody hell Knox, my brother was right about you, you're Goddamn crazy."

"Yeah, so I have been told…the bomb Harris?" he reminded him, hoping that what he planned wasn't as suicidal as it sounded.

"Alright, if it was me I would set and blow the charges on the outside of the hull under the water line," Harris said with a look that knew Knox was going to do what he had to do. To which Knox nodded in agreement.
"But if what he said in the call was a clue, an inferno…well then if I had to bet on it, I would say…" Harris continued but Knox finished his sentence for him.
"The fuel tanks! Don't wait for me, Major." Knox said as he ran to the stairwell like the Hounds of Hell were snapping at his heels. Harris just shook his head before turning to group of girls and instructed them all to follow him, wondering if he would see the crazy bastard after this one.

Meanwhile, Knox ran down flight after flight of the dimly lit staircase with only its demonic glow coming from the strobing red emergency lights. He skipped steps with every stride down. Once at the bottom level, he had sixty or so metres down a straight corridor. All he could hear was his running footsteps that rolled in a beat in sync with his heavy breathing. Sweat poured off his face as the humidity of the lower level and heat from the engines turned the claustrophobic tunnel of a corridor into sauna like conditions. Knox stripped off his gear slowing him down as he ran, but it didn't help much with the heat.

As Knox reached the engine room he found the door locked but on closer inspection saw it was welded shut.

"NEST come in over!" Knox said into his comms as he tried to catch his breath as he looked all around himself as he waited for a reply.

"NEST receiving, over." could just be heard through interference, the com system signal struggled to cut through the vast metal ship.

"Main entrance to the engine room blocked is there an alternative way in that is close to my location? Over." Knox asked as he waited hoping Carter wasn't listening in. After a brief wait, a familiar voice came over the comms, one less clinical.

"Knox, to the left of the doorway, three or four metres down is a vent, can you gain access?" spoke Rose.

"Yes, I have found it and pulled it off," Knox said as he located the vent pulling it off with brute force winning over screws.

. . .

"Good, crawl through and take the right at the first junction, you should then come across a vent that will allow access to the engine room," Rose said with urgency as Knox crawled reaching the junction and following her instructions.

"Access? It must be a sixteen-foot drop!" Knox yelled down the comms as he wiped away the sweat cascading down his face.

"Come on, big tough guy like you, you will be fine. NEST out." Rose said with a touch too much pleasure for Knox's liking. He kicked the vent out and watched it fall to the ground as it bounced off railings and pipework. He looked over his options and saw a way down, he had one chance to get it right or broken bones were a guarantee. He lowered himself down and hung by his fingertips before he began to swing himself back and forth, building momentum with each swing. He then let out a bellow as he launched himself forward with arms extended out, he just caught hold of a five-inch pipe that he thanked the heavens wasn't hot. Knox took a moment and geared himself up before dropping the last ten or so feet, breaking his fall with a paratrooper style landing.

Bingo! The start of the fuel tanks could just be made out at the end of the engine room, and the closer Knox ran over to them the clearer the bomb setup was. The fuel tanks had big blocks of Semtex stuck to them every ten metres. With the amount of Semtex and fuel, it was more than overkill, it was complete obliteration.

All the blocks were linked together via a harness of wiring, more wires than was needed for such a simple plastic explosive. The number of different coloured wires was a confuse and delay tactic. Where would you even start to work out which wire was live or redundant in a short space of time? The detonator was strapped in black tape with a basic mobile phone connected to it.

Shit! What was he going to do, Knox thought to himself as he stood looking at the device, then a glance at his watch informed him he had only two minutes left. Knox took his com interface and took a photo of the setup, and as he was about to send the picture back to the NEST he saw he had no signal. With a slap of his hand on the nearest solid object out of frustration he ran back the way he came, constantly checking if he had signal, but nothing.

"Come on... damn you!" Knox swore, exasperated.

He reached the bottom of the stairs that led up to the door that was welded shut, knowing that he had a signal the other side of the door. Knox ran up the steps in desperation and pushed himself against the door as much as he could.

"Yes...! Knox calling NEST, come in," he said as fast as possible.

"NEST receiving, over," replied Rose.

. . .

"I am sending you an image I need to know how to disarm, over," Knox said as he hit the send key, his whole body bounced and tapped almost like a runner running on the spot to keep warm.

"Knox, it has a mobile phone as a means of receiving a signal to set off the detonator," Rose stressed wasting no time.

"How can it get signal if my comms can't when I am near the bomb?" Knox said confused.

"I believe the cables running into the phone that don't go to the explosive but do go upwards, are a means of extending the signal, cut them!" Rose said in a way that she had no doubt, and facing facts, it wasn't as if Knox had a choice. He didn't reply, just looked at his watch as he ran back to the bomb. He had little over forty seconds. He held the wire going into the phone and drew his knife, and pinching the wire into a loop he fed the tip of the blade into it.

Knox closed his eyes and took what felt like the longest breath of his life, as he stood in front of potentially one point five million gallons of oil seconds away from detonation… *he cut the purple wire*. Knowing he wouldn't feel much if it did blow, he waited and waited then slowly opened one eye.

. . .

"Jesus…" Knox said as he slumped down on his arse, finding some oil and grease covered surface to sit on. Images of Dani at the hotel and the Gala dinner filled his mind's eye as he stared at his watch, double then triple checked the time. After five or so more minutes and still nothing, he made his way back to the vent picking up a set of ladders stowed in the engine room tool area.

Back up on deck everywhere was clear of the girls and the two teams. Knox stood at the ship's railings and looked out to the coastline where he could make out the rigid inflatable travelling at a steady slow speed as it sat low in the water, close to being overloaded.

"Calling Eye in the sky this is Whisky one, over," Knox said with a mixture of fatigue and contentment.

"Knox, you disobeyed a direct order," Carter barked down the comms which made Knox thankful it was over a comms and not in person.

"Device neutralised Sir, still live but not a threat," Knox said as he tried to deflect the bollocking that was coming his way.

"Hold tight Captain, we will soon have you airlifted out of there," Carter said in a more relaxed manner.

. . .

"Yes Sir, and the rest of the search of the ship and total deactivation of the device?" Knox cautiously asked as he spotted a Spanish coast guard's ship in the distance on an intercept course with the smoke bellowing vessel, which he was sure was attracting a lot of attention from the shoreline.

"We will inform the Spanish authorities and let them get in on the action and take the credit for taking down a people trafficking shipment," Carter said as he too knew the coast guard wasn't far away.

"I will carry on the search whilst I wait, over," Knox said as he geared himself up and got his head back in the game.

"Copy that Captain, let's hope you find nothing, over."

Knox looked out over the expanse of containers and looked for one of them to stand out to him, but the task looked impossible. Deflated, Knox kicked a red fire bucket that was filled with sand, and as the sand spread across the deck the empty bucket spun around on its own axis. Knox stared at it, and then it came to him, an idea.

He looked over at the container Isabella and the group of girls were found in. The container had Arabic markings of some kind, then he looked at the empty containers they had opened. They all had Pérez Trans Corp logos on. Knox had a theory that if they were going to load a ship full of empty containers they would have to be Trans Corp's as which other company could afford to have empty containers sailing around.

Knox found the closest container with Arabic markings and opened it up. As light flooded into the container he was not prepared for what he saw next. Knox looked away, covering his mouth with his arm trying his hardest not to vomit. He had seen horrific and blood-curdling sights on the battlefield and in war-torn cities, towns and villages. But what he saw before him, affected him deep down to the depths of what was left of his soul.

Before him, bound to a stack of wooden pallets, hung what was left of a blonde woman. Beaten black and blue, clothes torn away soaked in blood that had poured from between her legs and had dried to an almost black tar.

Used condoms littered the floor around her, along with urine stains and excrement. She had been raped, beaten and left for dead. Knox, for some unknown reason, had to look at her face, he just had too. So, with an outstretched hand, he moved closer to her. Her face was covered by filthy blonde hair that looked like damp rotting straw it was that thick with grime. Knox parted her hair to look at her battered face, he fell backwards at the sight. He stumbled and landed on the ground hard but he didn't feel it as he scrambled back until his back pushed against something solid.

Knox saw... *Dani*.

22

HURT

Harris now stood next to Knox. He had been calling him from the moment he had seen him from a distance, but Knox had zoned out. Maybe fatigue had set in or something had just snapped. Harris placed a hand on Knox's shoulder as for a moment Harris had thought maybe Knox was dead he was so still as he stared into nothing, not even a single blink.

"Captain? Knox! Are you alright?" Harris said with a forceful tone as he shook Knox's shoulder and clicked his fingers with his other hand. Knox drew his gun as he came to from his daze spooked, not realising it was Harris at first.

"Easy Knox it's me, Harris," Harris said in his normal calm manner as he took hold of Knox's hand before he had fully drawn the weapon. Harris looked over in the direction Knox was looking and saw the horrendous sight and things became clear to him.

"Major, what are you doing here? Sorry... it's...its..." Knox said as he tried to compose himself, but with the sight of Dani in his mind, he could barely find the words.

"Well, I couldn't leave you here on your own. I made sure everyone got off and I had every faith you would stop the bomb. And you don't need to explain Captain, this can affect us all in its unique way." Harris looked over again to the blonde girl.

"And the more times you see Godawful sights like that, it still doesn't make it any easier, trust me," he said as he held out an open hand. Knox looked at it and took hold as Harris helped him to his feet.

"Poor girl, she couldn't be much older than twenty, most likely from an eastern bloc country," Harris said as he looked over the blonde, his face chiselled with antipathy for the men who had done this to her.

"Eastern bloc...?" Knox said confused as he rubbed his eyes and shook his head. Harris looked at him as if he wasn't sure if Knox was fully okay.

"Yes, Captain, Eastern bloc... The Former Soviet Union, she looks Estonian or Latvian to me," Harris said as he walked past her and looked deeper into the container behind the pallets. Knox looked back up at the girl and then let out a sigh of utter relief. Thankfully, he no longer saw Dani and instead, the face of a young girl he didn't know. Seconds later he felt the guilt not only at the relief that it wasn't Dani as this poor girl had suffered something no one should have. But the biggest guilt of all was the fact Dani being in his life lay her open to this.

Knox had enemies, most of them he didn't even know. If he totalled up all the people he had killed without even knowing their names, Christ he had forgotten more than he could remember. Any one of them could have a family member or friend looking to take revenge if they could track him down. It was too big a risk to put Dani in, and seeing this girl had hammered it home to Knox in a way he wasn't ever coming back from.

Harris came back out of the girl's gruesome, metal resting place, looking sickened and breathless as he sucked in a massive inhale once he cleared the container.

"Harris to Carter, come in," Harris said right away into his comms as he caught his breath.

"Carter here, go ahead Major," replied a stern Carter.

"Captain Knox has found a second container with over thirty girls in there, Sir. There are also casualties and sadly fatalities," Harris said confirming Knox's fears of there being more dead girls.

. . .

"Copy Major, Spanish coastguard will be there to supply aid and evac, we need to get you two off that ship. Sending the chopper, so leave the Spanish authorities to it. Extract location same as drop off ETA three minutes, over," Carter instructed and Harris slapped Knox on the arm in a motion to gear Knox up and to make a move.

"Copy Sir on our way, ETA three minutes, over," Harris confirmed as they started to jog to the extract location.

Back at T.I.7 Knox and Harris walked into the NEST and Carter made a beeline for them.

"Major, Captain, report." an expectant Carter said obviously pissed off at Knox and Harris for not following orders in getting off the ship when told to.

"Sir…" Harris said but stopped as he watched Knox carry on walking and blank Carter as he headed straight to where Howard was being detained.

"Knox! I said report!" Carter shouted as both he and Harris began following Knox who still ignored Carter. He burst into the room and looked Howard in the eyes as he looked up at Knox with a smug grin. With a hard kick to the centre of Howard's chest, Knox sent him flying a few feet backwards before the chair tipped over slamming down onto the floor. Harris held Knox back as he was about to leap forward.

. . .

"You, fucking bastard! You knew those girls were on there!" Knox raged out at Howard

"Knox, stand down!" Carter bellowed as Harris let Knox pull through his grip. Harris understood how Knox felt and having witnessed what he had, he couldn't blame him. After all, he would be the same but his style wouldn't be so open and obvious. No, Harris would kill quietly in the dead of night with his victim's last sight on earth being Harris' cold dark eyes staring into theirs as he slit their throat.

Knox stood over Howard and grabbed a fist full of his boot imprinted shirt, he pulled him up off the ground, chair and all and punched him between the eyes. The crack of his nose was followed by the sound of a cough and spit as the blood flowed down the back of Howard's throat from his nose, blocking his airways.

"Who is El Toro! Give him up!" Knox roared at Howard as he lifted his fist high into the air ready to pummel Howard's head into the ground.

"Knox! Put him down! That's an order!" Carter barked and something clicked inside of Knox as he regained his control. He had picked Howard up again and was holding him twelve or so inches off the floor. He ignored the blood that streamed down Howard's face and dropped him. Howard let out a groan over the sound of splintering wood as he hit the ground hard, his face grimaced trying to hold itself up so the back of his skull didn't bounce off the concrete.

"Yes Knox, listen to your top dog. You, fucking state school mongrel," Howard said before he spat a load of blood on the floor beside Knox's boot. Carter raised an eyebrow as he walked around Howard.

"Don't just look at me, pick me up, for Christ sake," Howard said turning on the 'I am stinking rich, do as I say attitude', one that must have made him and Isabella the dream partnership, and a vivid nightmare for everyone with the misfortune of being in their company.

"But of course, please let me…" Carter said as he swung his steel toe boot into Howard's side, then leant down and patted Howard on the cheek, that were more like slaps.

"I am a state school chap myself, be a sport and keep your plum mouth shut old boy at least until spoken to. Or I could just leave the room and turn a blind eye for thirty minutes. Captain Knox seems rather upset and in need of venting some frustration, and you're tempting me to just *let him,*" Carter said in a quiet commanding way that only years of command could teach you.

"Sir, no need for thirty minutes, just ten will be enough," Knox sneered out itching to unleash his rage.

. . .

"Hold fire Captain, just stand back, I have this," Carter said turning to Knox and holding his hand up. Howard smiled with blood covered teeth, Harris put a hand on Knox's chest pushing him back a little as he looked him in the eyes, telling Knox to leave it and don't bite. In frustration Knox turned and kicked a chair to the wall, then leant with both hands on the wall, mentally counting to try and ease the adrenaline building as it flowed through his veins with a burning fire. Fucking Dani's face! He was so sure and it was messing with his head to the point he was fucking losing it!

"El Toro…you said before that you have something he wants, what and where is it?" Carter asked as he walked away and picked up the chair Knox kicked and put it in front of Howard before taking a seat.

"I need assurances before I give it up. Pérez and El Toro will both kill me," Howard said slyly, as he looked again over at Knox and smiled. Carter's patience was wearing thin, he leant forward and swung out a big right hook, one he purposely let Howard see coming. Howard could do nothing but wait for it to connect, and connect it did. The crack reverberated around the room. So much so it made Knox look up, turn around and take notice.

Carter sat back and clenched his hand and then stretched out his fingers a few times before shaking off the pain. Carter felt it and Howard sure as hell felt it as he spat out a tooth.

"I do hope that wasn't an expensive cap, old boy," Carter mocked as he looked at the tooth on the floor.

"Now let us try again, the only reassurance I will be giving you is if you don't tell me what I want to know you will be losing more teeth. And when my hands are tired these two chaps will gladly take over.

"Maybe it's all bullshit and you have nothing El Toro wants! Or there is no El Toro and you are feeding us lies to save your skin," Knox fired off over Carter's shoulder as he moved in to hit Howard again as Carter waved him in.

"Go to Pérez, you will find him with the Cartel now and what El Toro wants is there. If you have the computer data like you say, you will have enough to bring Pérez in," Howard said as he closed his eyes and braced himself for Knox's assault, but it never came. Instead, Harris hooded Howard again.

"And what is it El Toro wants?" Carter said getting tired of asking.

"He wants a file, it is in Pérez's office. The file is marked as NKM," Howard said slightly muffled by the hood and then listened as Carter stood up and signalled to Knox and Harris to join him outside.

"What do you think?" Carter asked Knox and Harris as he looked at them both.

. . .

"I think he is full of shit, Sir. He is more involved than he is making out and I wouldn't be shocked if he is playing both sides," Knox said with a tone that told them he had zero respect for Howard.

"You think he is ratting Pérez out?" Carter said as he looked at the monitor screen that displayed Howard sat on the chair with a hood on.

"I think for an operation as big and slick as Pérez's, to start going wrong like he claims, there has to be an inside man," Knox said as he looked to Carter and Harris for their view, and both men nodded in agreement.

"It is true what he said, we have more than enough evidence pulled off the yacht's computer to implicate Pérez," Harris said as Knox thought thanks to the genius that was Dani. Jesus even thinking her name right now brought him pain.

"What truth do you think is in his claims about this file?" Carter asked them both.

"There is only one way to be sure," Knox replied which made Harris stand upright as if he was ready to leave.

"Agreed Captain, you and the Major go check it out, take Gregory," Carter ordered before he walked off back to the direction of the NEST, then stopped and turned around.

. . .

"And men, don't be going in to be heroes. I want you all back alive. I don't want you taking any risks," Carter said with a cold deadpan look.

"Wouldn't dream of it, Sir," Knox said in a way you couldn't be sure if it was sarcastic or not, as he and Harris left in the opposite direction heading to the garage.

"Harris, I will meet you and Gregory at the car. I just need to sort something first," Knox said with a heavy tone as he braced himself for what he had to do, *a talk with Dani.*

Knox walked into Rose's lab, and spotted Dani, he coughed once and Dani turned around.

"Lucas, thank god..." Dani said as she got up from the computer she was sat at with Rose and ran over. She went to hug him and he felt like the biggest bastard when he stopped her by holding her arms. Dani's big smile dropped when she saw the look on his face.

"Lucas what's wrong...?" Dani said as she looked at Knox with concern.

"Dani... I want you to head back to the UK," Knox said in a quiet, cold manner.

. . .

"Well, I wasn't planning to stay in Spain forever Lucas, I can head back in a day or so," Dani said trying to joke a little and lift Knox's mood. She wasn't sure what had happened on the ship and was hoping his domineering was down to what he had just been dealing with.

"No... I want you to leave right away," Knox said sternly, so much so Rose couldn't help but take note.

"What... Now? Okay, but you will be coming to see me once you finish here... right?" Dani asked, puzzled at Knox's attitude and starting to fear the worst.

"Dani... I don't think that..." Knox began to say as he looked away, but Dani cut in.

"Look at me Lucas, if you are going to tell me what I think you are, then the least you can do is look me in the eyes when you do it," Dani said standing back, going on the defensive.

"What I said before I was getting lost, carried away," Knox said but still didn't look at Dani.

"Look at me, Lucas! I don't believe you! You said you wanted to spend time with me. You said you wanted to work out how to make *us*..." Dani said as she grabbed Knox's arm, pulling at it for him to look at her. When Knox heard 'us' he turned to Dani and looked her in the eyes.

"There is no us! There can't and never will be!" Knox said with almost hatred in his eyes. It wasn't hate aimed at Dani but at himself for saying the words. The words that caused the look of pain on Dani's face, a pain he was relying on. Dani's eyes began to well up as she tried to compose herself before she spoke.

"You don't mean that Lucas, I know you don't," Dani said fighting back her emotions that were battering down on her like raging storm waters at a flood gate. She couldn't understand it, why now?

"Dani, listen to me. I want you to go, I mean it. In fact, I have never meant anything more in my life. So please hear me when I say that I... *I don't want you and I never did!*" Knox said slowly and firmly, letting his harsh tone coat his words like venom.

Dani said nothing. Hell, she didn't have to Knox thought as the devastation in her eyes said it all. He had crushed her with the weight of his words as he knew he would and he fucking hated himself for it!

She just looked at Knox shaking, as a single tear rolled down her face. When she finally realised she was letting him see her cry, it was enough to get her to move. So, she slowly turned her face away as if he had slapped her, before barging past him and running from the room. Knox turned and before he could stop the action, he stretched out to grab her but he was too late. On instinct, he even tried to call out her name but the word just wouldn't form.

What had he done, he thought to himself, but he in reality he knew. He knew what he had done and it was mission 'afuckingcomplished'! He wasn't fooling himself, as he had fulfilled what he always knew he would do if he got too close to her...

He had hurt the woman he loved.

Rose put a hand on Knox's back as she walked up to him, he flinched before turning to see who had touched him.

"Hey, don't hit me... Listen I will go check on her," Rose said with a look of understanding and not wanting to say too much.

"I should go and..." Knox said but Rose gave him a knowing look.

"Maybe not a clever idea, she is going to be really pissed, but you already know that...I am guessing you were counting on it," Rose said thinking if Harris had said anything like that to her his bank accounts would be emptied and his information on any database would state his name as Mr Dick Head. But her and Harris were a dream and for men like them, that was all it was ever going to be. Because the simple fact remained for men like Knox and Harris, getting close to someone just wasn't an option in their line of work and the word love was more of a curse than a virtue.

"Okay, Rose could I ask a favour of you?" Knox said with sadness in his eyes that Rose couldn't say no to as she nodded and waited.

"Can you take Dani to the hotel so she can pick her stuff up and get her to the airport, please?" Knox said deflated.

"Of course, I will make sure she is okay and sort that out," Rose said with a sympathetic smile.

"Thank you, I just want her…her safe," Knox said forcing the words out as he put a hand on Rose's shoulder. Then he gave a slight smile before starting to walk off.

"I understand and Captain…" Rose called out and Knox looked back.

"Get your head straight…

Harris and Gregory need you."

23

BLOOD RETRIBUTION

Knox, Harris and Gregory headed up the same road Knox had done only a few days before when racing Isabella. It would have been nice to sit back and enjoy the views but the red mist of his anger clouded everything. Not driving for a change was a novelty for Knox as Harris had taken the wheel of his beloved 3.0-Litre Jaguar, but with too much on his mind, relaxing was the last thing he would find himself doing. For a start, what they were going to encounter at the Pérez residence was anyone's bloody guess and then, of course, there was Dani.

But he knew he had to push thoughts of Dani back to the deepest depths of his mind and keep them locked there behind a barricade of pain. Because first and foremost he had a job to do and people were counting on him. He couldn't trust the lying sack of shit that was Howard, and even if he was telling the truth, then how could he trust a man who so easily handed over the woman he was to marry. No, this whole situation had 'stitch up' written all over it. Knox wasn't sure who was pulling the strings on this one, but he wasn't going to play into their hands, so Knox was formulating a plan.

"Harris, I don't have a good feeling about this," Knox said as he looked out the window.

"Yeah, I know what you mean. I know that Howard is a spineless little shit and you were a little intimidating, but on reflection, I think he folded a little too easy," Harris said in his normally quiet and calm manner. Knox had come across only a few men like Harris, sometimes he thought the quiet and calm act was just that, an act. You always listen to someone who is quiet. Yes, it's annoying but you listen. How often do you see people switch off when they are getting shouted at or hearing someone who loves the sound of their own voice?

"It's not good going into a mission that I am second guessing," Knox said as he looked over to Harris, whose attention was drawn away when he had to overtake at speed. An old man dressed in shirt and tie that looked as if he had worn it for months, travelled at 3mph in the middle of the road, with what seemed like half his worldly possessions tied to the pillion seat with string, on a bike that looked ready for the scrap yard.

"Goddamn crazy, old Spanish," Harris muttered before he turned his focus back to Knox.

"Agreed, I have been thinking about this mission and second guessing it as well. What are your thoughts?" he asked Knox in a way that made him feel even more respect for his comrade. Harris was his senior officer, yet he wasn't telling Knox what to do. He was asking for his view with no bullshit attached to it, and to Knox, that carried a lot of weight with him.

"I just have a feeling that somehow they will be expecting us, and I don't want to give them what they are expecting," Knox said as he got frustrated at the lead weight that didn't sit easy with his gut feeling.

"Add an element of surprise, is what you are saying?" Harris said with a smile.

"Yes, just that, when I was last at the mansion there was one thing I noticed and I think it could be used to our advantage," Knox said picking up on Harris' mild smile, which for anyone else would be a full-face grin.

"I am all ears, Captain and wake up Gregory in the back, will you," Harris replied. Knox looked back at the snoring Gregory and smiled before spraying the contents of his water bottle on Gregory's face.

"Wakey, wakey sunny boy," Knox said as he and Harris laughed. Knox then discussed his plan with Harris and Gregory in detail.

Pulling up to the entrance of the Pérez driveway, something was already amiss. The green iron gate was completely open and the millionaire's fortress had been infiltrated. As Knox curiously drove forward he began to think maybe dropping Harris off wasn't such a clever idea. The CCTV cameras were both smashed and all in all, everything screamed don't go in. Which is just what Knox did as Gregory looked over at him clearly thinking the same thing.

The once busy gardens full of gardeners were now full of their abandoned tools, and the ground was soaked in water from sprinklers left on for too long. Clearly, something had gone down here, but no dead bodies yet so it wasn't a total blood massacre they were driving into. To be on the safe side, Knox and Gregory had their guns drawn and Knox's lay his on his lap ready. At least with the reinforced semi bullet proof glass fitted to the Jaguar, courtesy of Her Majesty's government, Knox felt somewhat safe. Well, that's what he was telling himself, in truth the glass would stop hand gun fire and light arms from over thirty metres away. Anything that packed more of a punch and close-up, would penetrate like a groom with his virgin bride on their wedding night.

Knox may have spoken too soon about the bloodbath, as

what looked like Juan's body lay sprawled out in a pool of his own blood. His normally perfectly white clothes now crimson. But still no sign of anyone. Was Knox too late and the Cartel had been and gone? Was Pérez dead? Only one way to find out.

Knox parked under the cover of the garage. If they had to get out fast and were under fire, the garage would offer some form of cover from hostiles. He collected his thoughts before he took a deep breath and opened the F-Space's door. Gregory followed and covered Knox as he walked, looking down the barrel of his gun as he checked every line of sight before moving from area to area as they made their way to the mansion.

As he walked up the main entrance steps, the door was wide open and blocked so it couldn't shut fully. The door swung in the wind and knocked on the body of a guard lay in its path, he was bullet ridden like holes in gun range target. Knox took note that the guard still had his weapon and ammo, so whoever came through here wasn't in need of any extra, meaning one thing, they were heavily armed.

Slowly moving through the massive mansion, its size helped them as they traversed room by room safely. Wide doors and cavernous rooms made for less fatal tunnels at least. Compromised lines of sight could lead to the enemy getting a clean shot off without them even knowing until it was too late. Each room was just like the driveway and front door, blood, bullet holes and bodies. Pérez must have stepped up his home guard, as there wasn't this many working when he was last here. He signalled to Gregory to split up, he would take the one side of the house and Knox the other. They had to find Pérez who was now sure to be dead but most important, they needed to find that file…if there fucking was one!

It was eerily quiet, the kind of quiet that made you feel as though you could hear your own heartbeat. Nature was on baited breath, no sounds of birds in song and the air was still with not even the slightest movement from a breeze as that too had deserted. Beads of sweat formed on Knox's brow as the humid heat took effect. Movement! Knox spun to the flicker of shadow and light that he only just caught in his peripheral vision, and training his eye and gun in a perfectly synchronised movement he locked onto the moving target. A deep exhale of breath escaped him as the sight of the movement was determined, a ginger cat.

Knox turned back to the direction he was originally going, ready to carry on his search, only to be met by a dark figure of a man who fell into him, arms wrapped around Knox who took his weight as the man spoke.

"They're all dead," said the man, his voice sounding as if life was draining away from him with each word. Knox helped him to the floor and lay him down as his body became heavy and limp.

"Who did this?" Knox whispered into the man's ear and the man's only response was to grab hold of Knox's clothes with a blood covered hand, his grip weak and trembling.

"Go," he said on his last breath as his eyes glazed over and his body slumped into lifelessness. Knox took a moment and closed the eyelids of the man lay before him and recognised him as one of the guards who stood watch over Pérez when they first met. Christ, how did I not hear him? Knox thought to himself, shaking his head as he stood up. As he reached the open glass bi-fold doors leading onto the terrace, he found Pérez. He was sat at the far end of the terrace, with his back to the view and looking directly in Knox's direction.

Surefooted as he scanned the open area, Knox made his way to Pérez as he walked past the inviting waters of the infinity pool. With every step closer, it became clear that Pérez was dead. His stillness and the way he was sat, made him look more like a garden statue he had commissioned of himself to fulfil his rich billionaire ego. The expression on Pérez's face, however, would not please his ego, a mix of shock and pain was a sight no one would wish to immortalise in stone. And then it was clear what had caused the pain. Carved deep into Pérez's flesh the word... 'Retribution' could be made out through the blood saturated sick artist's skin canvas.

As Knox walked around Pérez, he saw the cause of Pérez's death as the wound came into view. It spoke for itself and it screamed there is no coming back. The rear of Pérez's head was gone, the exit of a large calibre bullet had taken the back of his skull with it. Pérez had sucked on the barrel of a gun in his last moments on earth.

"Lucas Knox! Don't move!" Loud, deep, heavily accented voices called from the direction of the house. Knox turned slowly to face them. Five African mercenaries made their way towards him, AK47's and Type 85 sub machine guns aimed right at him. But the leader in the middle stood out the most, holding the unmistakable Smith & Wesson .500 Magnum revolver. He was no doubt Pérez's killer, Knox held his hands up.

"Drop your weapon, you are coming with us," the thick Sudanese man shouted as he pointed his 'I have a small dick' gun at Knox, turned on the fucking side like he was some dipshit gangster wannabe. But with no other choice, Knox tossed his gun behind a small garden wall to his side.

Then suddenly an intense buzz rasped as it cut through the air before the leader of the five men jerked backwards. A burst of blood and entrails exited out of his back and the entry hole soaked the front of his vest crimson. The crack of gun fire followed seconds later as it carried over the air from a distance. A second buzz and a second man fell, the other three looked at each other in pure shock and not knowing where to look, started firing their weapons at nothing.

Knox flung himself to the ground taking cover behind the small garden wall and picked up his gun. Three more deep shots echoed through the thick humid air, followed by stillness. Knox slowly lifted his head up as he looked down the muzzle of his gun, ready to take out any of the men left standing. Knox stood up. All five men were down on the ground, their guns still hot and smoking. One AK47 even sizzled as its owner's blood dripped through the heatshield handgrip onto the hot metal beneath.

Now, standing between the dead bodies, Knox looked out to the view as he focused on the church tower in the distance, the same one he had admired from Isabella's balcony days before. He lifted his hand in a gesture of thanks, thanks he was giving to none other than Harris, setup in the church tower as a sniper. Both Harris and Knox were right to feel as though they were walking into a trap, but a trap setup by who, that was the question that burned on Knox's mind now and he wanted it answered.

With no time to waste, Knox carried on and headed back into the house to look for Pérez's office to retrieve the file. Maybe Gregory had already found it, but where was he? If the file didn't exist, Howard was going to spill his guts or God help him there wouldn't be much left to recognise him as a man, Knox thought as he walked past more dead bodies leading down a hallway. Knox saw the boot of a man's leg twitch; the rest of his body was around a corner at the end of the hall. It was British army boot and the leg had British army fatigues, shit no. Knox sped up and rushed to the end of the hall, making sure it was clear first he then looked down, Gregory was bleeding out.

"Cap… sorry I…" Gregory tried to speak as blood pooled in his mouth.

"Don't speak…" Knox said as he looked Gregory over, he was cut up and bleeding badly from his left subclavian artery. Knox knew he wouldn't make it and he would be dead in seconds.

"It's bad… I'm… not…" Gregory said as he faded away. Knox knelt at his side holding Gregory's hand as he watched helplessly as the life drained away and the blood stopped flowing as his heart stopped. Knox shut his eyes and whispered a prayer, the same he did over Thomas and every fallen brother he served with.

"Remember, Lord, those who have died and have gone
before us marked with the sign of faith, especially those for
whom we now pray, Gregory. May he, and all who sleep
in faith, find in your presence light, happiness, and peace…"

Knox stood and tried to collect himself but he couldn't, for he had…

snapped.

He holstered his gun and drew his knife in one slow and deadly move. Then he looked at the floor and saw a few blood droplets that must have dripped off Gregory's killer's blade, and as Knox started to walk in their direction he heard sounds coming from up the hallway. They were coming from Pérez's office. Knox made a beeline for the door. His walk turned to a jog, quickly building to running at full pelt. The office door was open enough for Knox to see a man stood over a desk.

Knox kicked open the door in mid stride, the tall slender mercenary still holding the knife covered in Gregory's blood, turned in shock to the view of the mass of raging Scot coming at him. Knox launched himself, taking hold of the bastard as he took him with him clear over the desk. Knox got up and waited as he watched Gregory's killer look up at him.

"Get the fuck up!" Knox bellowed as he used his knife to motion him up, the mercenary smiled as he stood and faced Knox. The mercenary toyed as he waved his arms around as if he was in a fucking Kung Fu movie! Knox stood still as he watched with a stare that would send chills down the spine of any cold-blooded serial killer. The man came at Knox, who reacted with a rib breaking kick as he distracted the attacker with his hand movements. The mercenary buckled over as he flew back, again Knox stood looking over him and waited for him to get up. The mercenary looked up at Knox, this time the smile was wiped from his face.

"Get up!" Knox growled, once more he motioned with his knife. This time there was no Kung Fu shit as Knox's opponent now had a look in his eyes that almost matched Knox's hatred for the man stood in front of him. The man started to move around and Knox matched him as they both circled, the mercenary flinched at Knox to see if he would jump. Knox didn't flinch he just stared at his opponent, silently seething, and needing to see this guy's blood spilling from his body and soon.

The killer lunged with his knife first and Knox sidestepped into the attack and grabbed the bastard's wrist of his knife hand. Then he planted the elbow of his other arm into the face of the mercenary, splitting his lip open as the force knocked his lower teeth out and sent them down his throat. Still holding onto his wrist, Knox put his hand into a lock that made him drop the blade before pulling his arm up and around forcing him to turn his back on Knox. A swift sharp kick between his opponent's legs with his steel toe cap boot making a perfect connection to send crippling pain like no other through the mercenary.

Knox again kicked out, this time into the back of his

adversary sending him head first through the glass French double doors and out onto the terrace, a burst of glass framing his body as he went. Knox picked up the blade that killed Gregory off the floor and walked out onto the terrace. His hand gripped the handle of the blade hard enough to crack his knuckles, all the while focused on the sight of the mercenary trying to crawl away from him, terrified. He dragged himself on the broken glass as he shook his head to shake off the concussion, choking as he tried to cough up his own teeth.

But slowly, deadly, Knox walked up to him, knife in each hand so he sheathed his own…he only needed the one and it would be the one covered in his fallen teammate's blood. The mercenary now crawled leaving a smear of his own blood as the shards of glass cut up his hands and knees as he desperately moved along the floor. Knox grabbed him and flung him over onto his back and then knelt with both his knees pinning the tops of the concussed man's arms down as Knox faced him, looking down.

Taking hold of his head Knox looked him in the eyes as the mercenary pathetically wriggled and kicked his legs. Slowly Knox pushed the tip of the man's own blade into his neck, his screams became torn and gargled before silence as his vocal cords were cut. Knox's gaze never faltered from his opponent's eyes. No, he watched him as he coughed and spluttered, waiting as the mercenary's movements became less and less as the life drained away with his blood that flowed from the fuller grooves of the blade.

Knox then stood pulling the knife from the dead man's throat and swiftly plunged it into the lifeless heart of the killer lay before him without a shred of emotion. Then, with deadly calm, he simply walked back to the office as glass crushed under the soles of his boots.

Looking over Pérez's desk at a load of files that the

mercenary had dumped out from a filing cabinet, it was clear he was looking for the same file as Knox. This wasn't the Cartel's men that had killed Pérez, it was El Toro's and he wanted the file that Howard was going to give him. Knox found it, the brown card file marked 'NKM'. He opened it and what he saw made Knox's knees weak and he stumbled back and slumped into the bottle green leather Chesterfield Partner desk chair.

"You have to be shitting me!" Knox said, eyes wide open in disbelief as he tried to process everything and then it all made sense and fit together. Knox rushed out of the office and as he passed Gregory, he lifted him up and put him over his shoulder, carrying him out of the mansion. As he passed Juan he looked down to see him clutching the silver cube lighter with the bullfighter engraving. Knox rolled his eyes and made his way to the Jag and put Gregory's body on the back seat.

As Knox pulled out of the garage he stopped the car and again looked over to Juan, shook his head and gripped the steering wheel as if he was strangling the man's neck who was responsible for all of this.

Knox looked briefly in the mirror and saw his fallen comrade resting eternally on the back seat.

"I will get him pal, don't you worry," Knox said with gritted teeth and quiet rage building, before planting his foot to the floor, sending the big British car's wheels spinning down the driveway and tearing onto the main road. A mile down the road stood a dark menacing figure holding a large gun bag, it was Harris. If any locals saw him they would be feeling pity for the animals he was going to hunt, little did they know he had taken his trophies for the day. But the streets were dead and the sound of sirens could be heard coming up the valley.

"Captain," Harris said as normal in his cool calm manner as he got into the passenger side.

"We have to get back to T.I.7. Now!" Knox replied pulling

away before Harris had fully shut the door, then he looked back to see Gregory on the back-seat face down and blood pooling onto the carpets of the Jag.

"Is he...?" Harris said as Knox answered him right away before he even finished.

"Yes, and we knew it would be a fucking trap! But we have bigger problems, look at that file!" Knox shouted as he sped down the mountain road, breaking the speed limit on every sign he passed. Harris picked up the file, opened it up and looked it over and he soon looked back over to Knox.

"Is this a for Goddamn real?" Harris said, stunned at what he saw and for the first time, showing Knox that he too could lose his cool.

"I wish it wasn't, Sir... I wish it fucking wasn't!" Knox replied just as stunned as Harris.

"I am calling in, Harris to NEST come in... Harris calling NEST come in?" Harris said repeatedly trying to get through to T.I.7's mobile headquarters.

"Nothing... you don't think?" Harris asked Knox.

"Yes, I do. We need to get there asap," Knox said as he looked at the clock.

"Olivia, Knox she is..." Harris said as Rose was his first thought.

"Don't worry she was taking Dani to the airport, she shouldn't be there. But I have no doubt T.I.7...

Has been compromised"

24

BURNT NEST

As they pulled off the main road onto the old tired industrial estate, thick black smoke could be seen, as it plumed into the air from behind the building. It was T.I.7's building. Harris chambered his weapon and unbuckled his belt. The F-Space skidded to a halt as the door flung open, Knox and Harris exited the vehicle and took cover behind the doors as they scanned the main garage entrance to the makeshift command building.

The roller door was fully open, vision into the garage was hampered as it was in darkness. What they could see they didn't like the implication of, as the back end of a Toyota Hilux pickup truck could be just made out inside the garage. Not one of T.I.7's vehicles. Knox moved to the back of the Jag and opened the boot and pulled out two Black Hawk Strike tactical vests. He wasn't taking any chances as he suited up and filled his pockets with ammo. He threw a vest to Harris who was holding cover and when Knox was ready he did the same for Harris.

. . .

"Going in, cover me," Knox said before he zigzagged up to the garage door. A T.I.7 tech came into view sprawled out on the ground next to the Toyota. Bullet casings covered the floor, evidence that there had been one hell of a firefight. The shells were not T.I.7's, they were the mercenaries. Harris joined up with Knox, he switched on a flash light attached to his HK G38 assault rifle. Knox looked at him and shook his head, the last thing they needed in the dark was the enemy seeing them coming. And nothing said, 'here I am, shoot me' quite like a flashlight waving around in the dark. Knox would rather go into the dark with whatever vision his eyes could muster. It was surprising how much you could see when you gave your eyes time to adjust to the conditions.

"The circuit breakers are over here," Harris said to Knox as he made his way over to the back of the garage, jumping up onto a work bench to reach the switches on the large boxes mounted on the walls. Harris was a braver man than Knox as he wouldn't go near Spanish electrics.

Knox walked around the pickup truck, his eyes moving back and forth, monitoring the doorway that led into the main part of the building and looking inside the truck. The truck was loaded with a small arsenal of weapons and explosives in the back. Harris flipped the breakers and the lights came on. Harris looked to Knox pleased with himself before the power tripped again. Suddenly the side door into the main building kicked open and two men burst in firing shots off in all directions. Bullets sprayed all over the pickup as Knox ducked down for cover. Harris fired in the direction of the amateurish mercenaries as he dived down off the bench. Knox took five well-aimed shots as he lay down and fired under the truck taking their ankles and knees out before Harris ended their cries of pain, finishing them each with head shots.

"So far, what I have seen is they are relatively untrained, but keep sharp Captain, let's not get complacent," Harris said to him as he walked over to the dead men.

"Copy that, Major," Knox said as he stood, back to the wall, ready to go through the doorway into the vast warehouse. The same warehouse he first entered with a hood over his head and met Carter and his team for the first time.

"Three, two, one, go!" Knox counted down and entered first followed by Harris, sweeping off to the left and then right as they crossed the room. They both turned sharply in the direction of the sound of gunshots from the next unit. They focused their attention on moving to the NEST where the gunfire came from. Knox held up his fist signalling to stop as he dropped to one knee. Harris, without question, dropped down too. They waited as that gut feeling of Knox's built up in his stomach and heartburn acid festered around his throat.

"Targets!" Knox shouted as he and Harris fired off multiple rounds as four men fought their way past each other seemingly in a rush to their own deaths. Moving in a tight, compact formation and with ruthless efficiency, Harris and Knox gunned them down. Knox moved forward as Harris held station and covered him. Once Knox reached the pile of warm bodies, he took a second to make sure they were neutralised before letting his weapon fall to his waist as it was strapped around his torso. He then dragged two of the bodies out from the doorway. Harris moved up to him with total focus on the door as Knox's back was against the corrugated steel wall as he covered the area behind Harris.

"How many flash grenades do you have, Captain?" he asked in hushed tones.

"Only the three, Sir," Knox replied quietly after he checked his tactical vest.

"More than enough, Captain, when you are ready, light up the NEST," Harris said as he moved so his back was to the steel wall as he tapped Knox on the shoulder. He pulled the safety pin on the first flash grenade, geared himself up as he flicked the safety lever over which strikes the primer. Knox spun on a half-step into the doorway, threw the flash grenade and quickly half stepped again to cover on the other side of the door frame.

"Flash to the right, Sir," Knox called over to Harris and within seconds the boom of the ignited grenade sounded which set Harris into action as he entered the NEST going around to the left. Burst after burst of rapid fire prompted Knox to follow Harris in. Knox however, opted to take a few steps back and build up some speed as he rolled in through the doorway. Then, taking up a crouch position, he swept the room going right to left over the remnants of the flash grenade, the blast zone only just now beginning to clear. Two silhouetted figures could just be made out in the smoke, disorientated and holding their ears. It took Knox a split-second for him to make the call that they were hostiles and he took them down.

"Clear!" Harris called over to Knox as he checked the enemies he had taken down. The NEST was trashed, screens shot up, computers smashed and the servers had been torched. Out of the haze, an arm could be seen lifting into the air, both Knox and Harris trained their weapons onto the movement.

"Hold fire, hold fire," Knox called out to Harris as he made his way over to the man. It was Carter, alive but heavily injured.

"Brig, Sir?" Knox said as he leant down to Carter checking his wounds, shot in his legs, arm and shoulder with char marks and burns.
"What happened, Sir?" Knox asked as he pulled out a basic medical kit from his vest. Harris searched kit boxes scattered around in the area.

"We were hit from inside… first we knew was after a… explosion," Carter forced out as he winced and moaned as Knox began packing the wound that was expelling the most blood.

"Sir, we got the file it was…" Knox said but stopped when Carter passed out. Harris knelt beside Carter with a mass of medical supplies as he checked his pulse.

"Is he...?" Knox asked knowing he didn't need to finish off that question.

"He just passed out. But his pulse is weak. Go check out the rest of the areas," Harris said as he turned his attention to Carter.

"Sir, yes Sir," Knox said as he stood and made his way to the hallway entrance. Sending a flash grenade down the hallway, Knox waited for detonation down the far end before going in. Stepping over dead T.I.7 operatives, making his way past the canteen, there were no enemy threats in sight as Knox continued to sweep the area.

"Keep moving, keep moving, where are you?" Knox whispered to himself. Reaching Rose's tech lab Knox could just make out a pair of women's feet under a work bench.

"Tactical officer coming in, show your hand, friendly officer!" Knox called into the trashed lab.

"Don't shoot, please... don't shoot!" The familiar yet fraught voice of Isabella called out to Knox.

"Isabella?" Knox shouted as he entered the room making sure it was clear first. Isabella tentatively got up from under the work bench and then ran to Knox, trying to wrap her arms around him.

"Stop! Listen, it's not safe." Knox said as he put up a hand. Isabella looked at him and her fearful expression morphed into one of hurt.

"I don't understand, Lucas," Isabella said as she backed away.

"No time to explain Isabella, just trust me, why are you in here?" Knox asked her as he looked over all the computers seeing that one hadn't been smashed.

"I was in the medical tent when I heard gunfire and what sounded like an explosion. I was scared and I hid, but men came. I was so scared Lucas, they killed them…they… killed…" Isabella tried to explain but she burst into tears and Knox didn't have time for this.

"I want you to wait here, hide back under the bench. I need to make the area safe," Knox said as he pointed down to her hiding place, ignoring her emotional state.

"No… don't leave me!" Isabella cried out.

"I will come back for you, I promise when it is safe! Now get down!" Knox said forcefully and began to walk out of the lab taking note that the team members weapon's cabinets had been opened and raided.

"You promise you will come back?" Isabella said as she got down and under the bench.

"Yes, I said so, didn't I? I need to clear the area. I will be back," Knox said from the doorway with a smile he knew never reached his eyes. He felt like a bastard as he didn't want to leave her on her own but he had no choice.

Knox's nostrils flared at the stench as he entered the medical area, half of the tents had been set alight and charred black metal frames with only smouldering canvas remained. The sick sight of countless female bodies scorched to a crisp, grouped together in the centre of three of the burnt-out recovery tents. All the girls from the first container they had rescued were now *dead.*

Knox's rage hit new levels as he pulled out a face scarf and tied it around his neck as he covered his nose and mouth, trying not to gag on the smell of cooking burnt flesh. All he wanted to do now was find the one responsible and do the same damn thing to him, only being satisfied when watching his body burn!

The medical reception counter had a body slumped over it and it pained Knox to find that it was the cute medic. Knox checked for vitals and on touching her neck he pulled his hand away. Her skin was stone cold, she had been dead for a long time, she was dead before the attack on T.I.7.

The only light in the area that didn't come from fire and smouldering tents was a white light. Mac's recovery tent was illuminated from the inside and light was escaping from a gap in the entrance. Unsure of what he would find, he slowly made his way over. Knox checked his magazine was full and his weapon was at the ready.

"Mac!" Knox called out with no response, moving the canvas sheet entrance open with the barrel of his gun. But Knox soon saw that the tent was empty. Moving over to the bed where Mac once lay there was no sign of him, Mac was gone…

The Bull had escaped.

Knox wasn't surprised being that Mac was the reason for all of this, the mercenaries were his, the killing, the girls, everything from day fucking one was a setup! Mac was El Toro and everything in the file Knox recovered from the Pérez mansion pointed to it. Mac had been working with Pérez for years, he was running the private army Pérez was building to take over the drug cartels. To gain control of the Mediterranean and North African crime rings and God knows what else. Mac's joining T.I.7 was solely to use them and gain intel, staying one step ahead of everything. But it would seem Mac aka, 'El Toro' wanted it all for himself.

. . .

Looking up above the empty bed, Knox took a double take before taking in what he saw pinned to the tent wall with a knife. He stared at the photo printout, a photo that had the words 'Stay away Knox' scratched into it.

"No...*fuck!*" The photo was of Dani and Knox, taken on their way into the Gala. Dani looked stunning on Knox's arm and a rush of emotion hit him like an express train. It was a warning from Mac. He was telling Knox not to come after him or he would hurt him in the worst way possible. After all, the bastard now knew his weakness, *his only weakness...*

His beautiful Dani.

Then in the mists of his inner turmoil and building rage came a sound that made his heart drop, the sound of death to a soldier.

The click, click... of a hand gun being cocked announced someone was behind Knox.

"Mac." He muttered the name of his enemy as he closed his eyes and awaited his fate. He had lost his edge. He had let his emotions get the better of him and lost his focus. And now he would pay for that mistake with his life, by someone he once considered a brother...

Or so he thought.

. . .

"Not such a stupid spoilt brat, now Knox!" Isabella said in her smug trademark way as she held a hand gun to Knox's head and began

to squeeze the trigger…

To be continued…

Book 2 of the Lucas Knox series will be available to buy on Amazon from Decmber 2023.

Connect with me on:-
Facebook
https://www.facebook.com/Blakehudsonauthor

WORDS FROM THE AUTHOR

Thank you for spending your time reading my first novel!

If you enjoyed my book, please consider taking a moment to write a Review on Amazon or Goodreads. Reviews help other readers decide on my books and hopefully get to enjoy them as much as you have. Thank you again!

ACKNOWLEDGMENTS

I would like to thank friends and family for their massive support, words of encouragement and belief they have shown.

To my beta readers, their views and ideas have improved and helped my writing, in no order thank you.

Claire Boyle, Kathy & Tony Cini, Lisa Taylor, Andrea Kingi, Zara Duggan, Carla Mullins, Kelly Clare, Patrick & Carrie Wyman, Elizabeth Richie, Hazel Pescatore, Sarah Torpey, Margarita Lebron Vazquez, Moe Murphy, Julie Hewitt, Coryelle Kramer.

The editing team Stephanie, Claire, Sarah and Maralyn: you have been my angels.

And thank you to all the people who joined the Lucas Knox Series FaceBook group.

ALSO BY BLAKE HUDSON

Lucas Knox Series
Blood Retribution
Blood Ties
Blood Vengeance

ABOUT THE AUTHOR

Blake Hudson is an English action adventure/romance writer. He was born in Birmingham England, raised in Worcestershire, and now lives in the Costa del Sol, Spain. From a humble background, he originally aspired to be a film score composer after his studies in audio engineering. After years of working in the audio world as a technician, he then joined the TA alongside his work and served one tour in Iraq.

Returning home and having a change in life's direction, Blake found himself in the highly challenging and stressful work as a HGV driver around the City of London. After this, he was soon ready for relocation to a slower and more peaceful way of life, so he moved to Spain with his beautiful family to pursue his new dream of writing the stories he wanted to read. This was made possible with the added confidence and belief from his wife, bestselling author of the Afterlife Saga, Stephanie Hudson. She inspired him to overcome his dyslexia, as she had once done.

Blake started with his first venture into the world of action adventure novels, with Lucas Knox: Blood Retribution Book 1 of the Lucas Knox series.

OTHER AUTHORS AT HUDSON INDIE INK

Paranormal Romance/Urban Fantasy

Stephanie Hudson

Georgia Seren Mills

Harper Phoenix

Sorcha Dawn

Tatum Rayne

Crime/Action

Blake Hudson

Jack Walker

Contemporary Romance

Gemma Weir

Anna Bloom

Jax Knight

N.O One

Nicky Priest

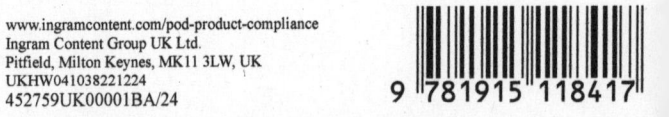